THE ARROW SHOOTER

THE ARROW SHOOTER

Jim Mather

ISBN: 0692466177
ISBN 13: 9780692466179
Library of Congress Control Number: 2015911140
Jim Mather, Carmel, CA

Chapter One

Jonathan Lusk felt naked as he jogged out the front door of Wilbur Hall, a tan, red-tile roofed dorm on Stanford University's dorm-row. The problem wasn't being dressed in nothing but running shorts and shoes. It was his lack of a weapon. Even after over a year at Stanford, the absence of one when in public still put him on edge.

Kancho Kubo remained convinced that his mock funeral had fooled those in Japan who wanted him dead. But Jonathan had never felt completely comfortable with the master general's reliance on hiding-in-plain-sight as his sole means of security. A pistol, even if kept hidden in his room, would have given him a fallback position and been a much welcomed addition. But, he reminded himself yet again, *Kancho* surely knew the threat far better than he did. And he also knew that possession of a weapon at Stanford could get him expelled, if not arrested. So Jonathan said *oos* and went about his life, while always keeping his eyes open and his fingers crossed.

At six feet two inches tall, Jonathan's long stride took him quickly up Campus Drive and down Mayfield. His intent was to take a shortcut across White Plaza, the epicenter of the sprawling campus. As soon as he rounded Dinkelspiel Auditorium, however, he knew he had made a mistake. A group of Vietnam War protestors were closing in for another assault on the administration building and he quickly found himself surrounded by an angry mob of long-haired, unbathed hippies.

"You a narc?" one of them challenged, fixing his dull eyes on Jonathan's short blond hair.

Jonathan shook his head.

"A pig?"

"Just a student."

From their signs and banners, the group was apparently protesting the university's research contracts with a variety of companies involved in the industry of war.

"Join us, brother," slurred a woman in headband, bell-bottom pants, and see-through halter top. As Jonathan shook his head, she checked out his tall, fit body. "How about a woman? You need a woman?"

A cloud of marijuana and patchouli oil drifted his way and Jonathan began running again. In less than a minute, he was passing Hoover Tower, symbol of Stanford to much of the world. Since learning a bit of little-known campus information, Jonathan hadn't been able to pass Hoover without looking up at the bars enclosing the upper viewing platform, two hundred and fifty feet above the campus floor. So many depressed and failing Stanford students had, over the years, climbed to the top and jumped that the university was finally forced to install barricades.

Jonathan's route took him around the practice field, where a group of students were playing an angry game of soccer, before finally arriving at his destination, Stanford Stadium.

The football team was running a scrimmage on the field in preparation for that weekend's game with Oregon. As Jonathan watched, a wide receiver broke free from his defender and the quarterback sent a pass his way. But the ball fell short, bounced, and rolled up to Jonathan's feet. He picked it up and threw a nearly perfect spiral that sailed over the quarterback's head. Embarrassed, he yelled "Sorry!" then hurried up the steps to the empty stands.

Built in 1921 and expanded in 1927, the giant wooden oval was one of the country's largest, seating eighty-nine thousand spectators. Staying atop its wooden bleacher seats, Jonathan sprinted up all eighty rows to the top. There, as had become his habit, he enjoyed a quick look at the panoramic view the height offered of the surrounding campus and nearby City of Palo Alto before heading back down. After completing four more trips to the top, Jonathan turned to begin his final descent and noticed someone sitting on the bottom row, watching him.

"Sorry, I didn't think anyone would mind," Jonathan offered as he neared.

The man stood up and held out his hand. "I'm Kenny York."

"The football coach?" asked Jonathan, a puzzled look on his face.

York nodded. "You play ball?"

"No but my grandfather did."

"Here?"

Jonathan nodded.

"What's his name?"

"Eli Lusk."

The coach's face lit up. "You're Danny Lusk's kid?"

Jonathan chuckled. He had never heard anyone refer to his father as anything but Daniel. There had never even been a Dan, let alone a Danny.

"Your grandfather was a gridiron legend," said York, "but, even though he didn't play ball, your father was one hell of an athlete too. I was a red-shirt freshman when he won his gold medal." York looked Jonathan over. "How about coming out tomorrow and tossing some balls around?"

The offer caught Jonathan by surprise. "Let me think about it. I'm kind of up to my gills in schoolwork. Besides," he said, his face reddening, "I'm embarrassed to admit it but I don't know anything about football. I grew up in Japan and have never even seen a game."

York reacted as if shocked. "Well, we'll just have to fix that this weekend."

An assistant ran up and stood fidgeting behind the coach, anxiously waiting to be acknowledged. "Yes, Allen?" said an exasperated York, looking around.

"Trainers think Halder broke his ankle."

"Hell's bells. It never ends. I'll be right there." York held out his hand. "What year are you?"

"Sophomore," said Jonathan, shaking the man's massive hand.

York cringed. "I was hoping freshman. Really try to make it tomorrow. But if you can't, come by and see me sometime soon. I got some things I think you'd really get a kick out of."

When his phone rang a couple of days later, Jonathan almost didn't answer it. Coach York had already called three times and had a team member drop off tickets for the rest of the season's games. Jonathan knew what York wanted but wasn't sure if he wanted to play football or not. He did, however, know he was getting tired of being pressured.

"Hello?" he said, an edge to his voice.

"*Do desu ka*?" came *Kancho* Kubo's gravelly voice on the other end.

Jonathan snapped to attention and reflexively bowed. "I am fine, *Kancho*. Is everything okay with you?"

"Aoshima *San* uncovered another traitor among the Kami seniors, Fukugawa. He taught the modern weapons courses."

"*Hai*, I remember him."

"He had accumulated large gambling debts to a bookie, who was himself heavily indebted to the Momochi Kumi. We do not know if he knew or had heard any rumors concerning your death ruse. But it would be wise to be extra vigilant until we know more."

It was clear to Jonathon from Kubo's tone that his mentor and the head master of both the Dai Kan and the even more elite Kami Kan was worried. "Also, you departed in such haste that you left behind things you might need. One of our graduates now works in our San Francisco embassy. Fortunately, business takes him to Stanford University tomorrow and he has agreed to deliver your things to you."

"Thank you, *Kancho*," said Jonathan, knowing he hadn't left anything significant behind and wondering what it was that the master general believed he might need. Whatever it was, it had to be important.

Chapter Two

Hiraku Kobayashi, the embassy official and former Dai Kan graduate (and as it turned out, also Stanford graduate), met Jonathan in a private room inside the alumni headquarters, just behind Tresidder Student Union.

Kobayashi unzipped a sports bag and held it open, revealing a *karate* uniform, rolled up and tied neatly with a black belt.

"This isn't mine," Jonathan said. "I brought my *gi* with me."

"Open it... carefully," said Kobayashi.

Jonathan untied the belt and loosened the gi just enough to see the barrel of a pistol poking out from among the folds.

Kobayashi set his briefcase on the table and popped it open. "As my area of expertise is financial matters, *Kancho* requested I investigate your inheritance," he said, removing a manila folder.

This caught Jonathan by surprise.

"You are a very wealthy young man," said Kobayashi. He laid a balance sheet on the table and pointed at the bottom figure. Jonathan stared in disbelief. "Yes," said Kobayashi, chuckling, "Being both an only child and only grandchild on both sides, you inherited all financial worth upon your parents' and grandparents' deaths. Until today, it has been held in escrow."

"That's a lot of money," was all Jonathan could say.

"I would suggest you hire a good financial counselor as soon as possible to manage your assets," Kobayashi said, setting another sheet of paper down in front of Jonathan. "Here is a list of those I consider both skilled and reputable."

"Thank you, I will do that."

"One more thing. Your net worth will increase substantially when your grandfather's and Hiroko Sama's estates are finally settled in Japan."

Jonathan hurried back toward Wilbur Hall, wanting to get the pistol hidden in a safe place as quickly as possible. Although he was always cautious, always maintained a strong defensive awareness, there hadn't been any indication that the threat he had faced in Japan had followed him to Stanford.

What to do with the money? That was the question that occupied Jonathan's mind as he hurried across White Plaza, where a different group was protesting in front of the Student Union. As he dodged bicyclists racing toward or away from distant classes, he realized there were a couple of things he needed. *I need a bike*, he told himself. *And a car*. In reality, he knew, he needed a bike but only wanted a car.

He was jogging through student housing, his mind considering which model of car he would purchase, when something caught his attention – the faint but unmistakable burning cardboard odor of a brand of cigarettes he hadn't smelled since leaving Japan.

Jonathan looked toward its source just in time to see an Asian man duck behind the corner of Casa Zapata. Maybe it was nothing, Jonathan told himself, just some guy stepping out for a smoke. But his conversation with *Kancho* Kubo had put him on edge.

Unzipping the sports bag as he ambled causally toward the man's last location, Jonathan worked the Beretta free and positioned it for quick extraction. But when he arrived, no one was there. On the ground, however, lay a smoldering cigarette butt. Near its filtered end was the small red logo of a popular Japanese brand.

This didn't necessarily mean anything. It could have been smoked by any number of Japanese living or studying in the area. But warnings often came as tiny, very subtle messages, invisible to the average person. He wasn't an average person, however. He was a highly trained Tamashii Kami and a bountied target for assassination. The price for a mistake could easily cost him his life. So he would have to be even more vigilant.

Chapter Three

A warm California wind blew in Jonathan's face as he drove down the Pacific Coast Highway in his new Porsche 356C Coupe. He had wanted to buy the convertible but knew *Kancho* wouldn't approve. Too easy to cut through a canvas top. But with the windows down, a fast car beneath him, and an open road, Jonathan had never felt so free.

Although the Japanese loved the American game of baseball, no one played football there except for GIs. So, as Jonathan had told Coach York, he had never seen a football game before. His only exposure to it had been tossing a football around with his grandfather in the back garden.

A couple of weeks later, he took York up on his invitation and attended his first game. Sitting at mid-field in the Stanford student section, engulfed by occasional wafts of marijuana smoke, he found the rules completely confusing at first. But as the game progressed, they became a little clearer, thanks partially to the coed seated beside him.

Then came the half-time show and he was lost once more. Arizona's band had marched onto the field in sharp, identical uniforms and played a variety of current hits – *He Ain't Heavy… He's my Brother*, *Spirit in the Sky*, and *Cracklin' Rosie* – while marching in precise military formation. When it was Stanford's turn, a ragtag group of what looked like hippies, each dressed unlike all others, wandered onto the field in a formless blob. What had been described as "the irreverent Stanford Band" formed into the shape of a fist. As they strolled across the field toward Arizona's side, the fist's middle finger extended briefly, then closed up once more. Jonathan looked to the young woman beside him who told him this was mild by band standards. They had just come off a year's suspension for doing something far worse.

In spite of the team's eventual loss, Jonathan enjoyed the game and could see why his grandfather had loved it. He also understood Coach York's frustration. The quarterback was not up to the job. He tripped. He failed to see unguarded receivers. He ran with little awareness of openings, seemingly overwhelmed, as if events were happening faster than he could mentally process them.

On Monday, after his morning classes were done, Jonathan climbed the stairs to the second floor of the Athletic Department and knocked on Coach York's door. "Come on in," came York's gruff voice from the other side.

When he opened the door and the coach saw who it was, his face lit up and he rushed around his desk, where he gave Jonathan's hand an energetic shake.

"You said you had something to show me?"

York led Jonathan out into the wide hallway, which was lined with tall glass display cases full of trophies and medals on one side and covered in photographs on the other. Near the far end, he pointed at one of the photos. "Know this guy?"

It took a couple of seconds for Jonathan to recognize the young blond-headed man. It was his grandfather doing one of those classic football poses, veering to one side, a football in one hand, his other thrust out in a straight-arm.

"Would it be possible to get a copy of this?" Jonathan asked.

"Sure," York said, leading Jonathan back a few feet up the hallway. "You'll probably want copies of these too." He pointed at another shot, this one of a swimmer poised on the starting blocks. It was his father as was the photograph next to it. The second one was of a young Daniel Lusk standing on stage, dressed in slacks, button-down shirt, and Stanford Block Letter Jacket. A man in a suit was handing him an award. "Athlete of the Year," said York. "The next one's him on the podium, receiving his gold medal at the LA Olympics."

The coach led Jonathan back toward his office. "Can I talk with you for a couple of minutes?"

"Sure."

Coach York led him into his office and closed the door.

"Red, right, post on 3," said the red-shirted quarterback. The team clapped once in unison then lined up in three and four-point stances. "Hut, hut, hut." The ball was snapped. Jonathan dropped back. His deepest receivers were covered. His eyes went to his secondary. Covered too. As the defense broke through his offensive line, he scrambled out of the pocket. A deep receiver separated himself for a split second and Jonathan rifled a pass far down the field and into the man's hands.

The team clapped and hooted their approval. York beamed. "Now that's pure Eli right there! I think we just found who'll replace Josh when he leaves us in June!"

Jonathan practiced with the team every afternoon that week, enjoying being part of a group that actually accepted him. Here, he wasn't the *gaijin*; he was the future quarterback, who York claimed could take them to the Rose Bowl.

The following Monday, however, they ran into a glitch. By NCAA rules, Jonathan should have passed a physical exam before he began practicing with the team. Coach York hadn't thought he needed one, not yet, since Jonathan had only come out to see if he might want to actually join the team. But the NCAA Compliance Administrator had overheard him bragging in the faculty lounge about this great new player and didn't remember seeing any paperwork on him. So he did some digging. When he discovered that Jonathan had no medical records on file because his enrollment had been expedited through some type of special deal with the State Department, he demanded Jonathan not be allowed to suit up again until he had received medical clearance.

"Just what I need, another load of bureaucratic bullshit!" said York, yanking his ball cap off his bald head and angrily throwing it down. As it dropped, however, his hat caught air and landed softly on the field, making him even angrier. York snatched his cap back up, threw it down again, then stomped it a couple of times for good measure.

In a few seconds, he picked his hat back up, popped out the crown, and straightened the bill. "I'll put in a word," he told Jonathan. "You should be back in a few days."

But he wasn't. They had managed to get copies of his medical records from Japan. When the team doctor saw that he had had two concussions within the last couple of years – one from the arrow catch and the second from the car accident – his football career was put on hold. He was out until at least spring, when they would evaluate him again. If he was deemed okay then, he could join the team for spring practice, with the starting quarterback position all but assured.

The entire thing had *Kancho* Kubo's feel to it – their getting his medical records from the Dai and Kami Kans, letters written directly to the examiners at Stanford from the doctors who had treated both of his previous concussions, one of which had almost killed him. For some reason, *Kancho* didn't want him playing football.

It was a disappointment. Being part of the football team had made him a significant cog in the most important social wheel on campus. Secretly, he had even begun fantasizing about becoming the star quarterback, taking Stanford to the Rose Bowl as his grandfather had done, and earning a letter S jacket like his father's. He had come to feel the legacy of it all, a *giri* or obligation of sorts, a family tradition demanding to be maintained. And now it had been put in limbo.

Voids always demanded to be filled, sucking in all other matters like a black hole. The void in Jonathan's mind was immediately filled with growing concerns that Nanami Yoritomo would never arrive at Stanford. She still wrote him weekly, sometimes twice, reassuring him that it was only a matter of time. But she had initially promised to arrive by second quarter. That was a year ago. He was beginning to fear that what Kiyoshi Yoritomo, Nanami's brother and Jonathan's only true friend, had said was coming to pass. "Father will never allow you to leave Japan."

Jonathan had learned that there was a traditional Japanese *karate dojo* on campus, the Stanford Karate Club, which met in Maples Pavilion three nights per week. *Karate* had always been his refuge and he turned to it again.

Knowing that different martial arts schools and organizations viewed entering black belt students differently, some welcoming them and others wanting to crush them, Jonathan decided it best to wear a white belt to his first class. He was, after all, not a black belt in their system. Plus it would make him somewhat invisible, giving him time to evaluate the quality of both the instructor and their art before deciding if he wanted to join or not.

Only one of the five local martial arts schools listed in the Yellow Pages sold equipment and supplies. Jonathan paid it a visit. What he saw was shockingly bad – strange uniforms, strange training methods and even stranger techniques, completely lacking in what the Japanese called *riai*, reality, in either attack scenario or response.

Fortunately, they sold plain white uniforms and he bought one. But to get out of the building, Jonathan had to fend off the owner, a high-pressure salesman dressed in a purple uniform and wearing a red belt. The fellow ground on him all the way to his car, pushing various deals – dismissing the usual registration fee, extending his contract for two months free, throwing in another free uniform – if he would register right then. When Jonathan told him he was looking for a traditional Japanese *dojo*, the man assured him that they were the most traditional in the area, making Jonathan fear what he would find at Stanford.

Hoping for the best, he strolled into Maples Pavilion, wearing his new *gi* and white belt. He was greeted by a hopeful sight, students in white uniforms. No black belt was present but there was a brown belt, who was going through a *kata* very similar to Pinan Godan. The rest of the thirty-or-so students ranged in rank from white belt to green.

On the brown belt's command, everyone lined up, with the highest ranking student farthest to the left and progressing downward to the lowest, Jonathan. The brown belt led them through the usual warm up drills, then *kihon* or fundamentals, and was well into the list of *kata* or forms without a black belt showing up. Jonathan began to fear the brown belt might be the instructor.

"Excuse me," Jonathan asked him, "what do we call you?"

"My name is *Sempai* Hershaw."

Your mother gave you the first name of Sempai? Jonathan thought, smiling. *Sempai* was his title, and the lowest one at that, not his name. A *sempai* was a senior student charged with ensuring those below them in rank made proper advancement in skill and knowledge and that they followed proper martial arts etiquette.

Even though Jonathan's techniques were far better than *Sempai* Hershaw's, the brown belt visited him numerous times to make corrections. But since Jonathan's techniques were technically correct already, Hershaw ended up bending his wrists out of proper alignment and moving his feet in or out, making his stances too wide or too narrow. Jonathan had never minded being corrected. In fact, he was always grateful for anyone's help. It was Hershaw's need to order people around, however, and that was starting to rub Jonathan the wrong way.

The *sempai's* head snapped around and his expression turned so quickly from arrogant to humble that Jonathan followed his gaze. A stocky Japanese had just entered and was walking gingerly across the gym floor. Encircling the man's waist was a frayed black belt that was little more than white threads accented with splotches of black. To Jonathan's disappointment, the man had the same condescending smirk and swagger he had encountered too many times over the years in Japan. The surprising part was not finding a *karateka* with such qualities, it was finding such a man on the campus of an institution like Stanford.

"Are you okay, *sensei*?" asked *Sempai* Hershaw.

"I sorry I come late. Car make crash with stupid lady," said Kichiro Ojima. Keeping his upper body rigid, he took his place in front of the class. Although the instructor was trying to hide it, Jonathan recognized the signs of broken or damaged ribs.

As planned, Jonathan hung back a bit as the class continued, using only three-quarters of his power and speed. But he had to be careful. If he tried to look too much like a white belt and his true rank was later discovered, he would be thought dishonest.

As it turned out, the instructor only glanced his way once or twice during the class and never made any comments or corrections. *Kancho* Kubo had often said that a *karateka's* rank was not what he wore around his waist; it was his level of skill. "If I put on a white belt and give my black one to a beginner," he once told them, "what has changed? Would he suddenly become able to defeat me? No. If you don a white belt and, after observing you in action, no one believes you superior in skill to a white belt, then that is your true rank regardless of what you may have been awarded. If you are truly a black belt, it matters not what belt you wear, your true rank will be visible to all."

Being ignored, Jonathan had to remind himself, was a good thing. If Ojima recognized that he was a black belt, he would become far less revealing in his demonstrations and might even call him out to prove his superiority – although, with his injuries, that was less likely, at least for that night. If he did, however, it could get ugly. It was best to remain patient.

"You train before?" asked Ojima *Sensei* at the end of class. It sounded more like a statement than a question. He must have caught more than Jonathan thought, or had hoped.

"*Hai*," Jonathan answered, "but different style." A flash of red caught Jonathan's attention, drawing his eyes down to the man's knee, where blood seeped through the white fabric. "*Sensei*," he said, pointing.

The man glanced down and reacted disgustedly. "*Che!*" he hissed. The Japanese limped over to the bleachers and sat down. The other students closed in as he hiked up his pants leg, revealing a large open gash across his knee cap.

"Would you like me to take you to the hospital, *sensei*?" asked Hershaw.

"*Iie*! One time fix, no more!"

Jonathan could see where the cut had been stitched up earlier but had reopened during the workout. Ojima angrily rummaged around in his bag, withdrew a bottle of Mercurochrome, and poured the stinging yellow liquid over the open wound as the surrounding students cringed.

"Okay," said the Japanese, standing up and beaming, "*sake* time!" As Ojima and several students strolled off, the rest quickly gathered up their things and headed out too, leaving Jonathan alone in the gym.

Taking advantage of the large empty room, Jonathan ran through the advanced *kata* he had been taught in Japan. He was surprised at how rusty he had become on the newer ones, those he had learned for promotion to *nidan*, second-degree black belt. He was still working on them when the janitor flashed the lights and yelled that it was time to close up.

Sensei Ojima also taught at U.C. Berkeley so the Stanford Karate Club only met on Monday, Wednesday, and Friday. Some nights he didn't show up at all. The next time he was absent, *Sempai* Hershaw did what he always did, spent most of his time trying to impress the other students, especially the women. But this time he made a critical mistake.

Hershaw called Jonathan out to assist him demonstrate *jiyu kumite*, free sparring, something the class had never done before, although Jonathan had at the Dai Kan. Hershaw's motivation was not hard to figure out; he thought to humiliate the newcomer in order to impress everyone with his brown-belt prowess. This presented a dilemma for Jonathan. Should he let Kershaw get away with it? Or should he reveal his true skill, blowing his cover and humiliating the man?

He decided the best course of action was to merely break even. But the longer the match went on with things not going as Hershaw had envisioned, the more frantic he became and the wilder his techniques. In a final act of desperation, Hershaw overextended himself, attempting to land a lunge punch on a target that was far beyond his reach, and fell onto his elbows and chin. The *sempai* lay there stunned for a few seconds, easy prey. But instead of following up and further humiliating the man, Jonathan allowed him time to recover and climb unsteadily to his feet.

"What I just did was an advanced technique called the Death Lunge," wheezed Hershaw, trying to catch his breath and salvage his ego. "Perhaps *sensei* will teach it to you when you get to brown belt too."

The students smiled at each other, none missing either his failure or his attempt to make his failure sound like a success.

Ojima was there for the next class. "Can I speak to you a second?" asked Hershaw, meeting his *sensei* as he walked onto the floor. He whispered something into Ojima's ear, something that made his eyes flick over and lock onto Jonathan.

"Hershaw *San* say you no cooperate with *kumite*," he said to Jonathan.

"Sorry, *Sensei*, I just tried to keep him from scoring on me. I thought that was the goal."

Ojima simply grunted. "Did you do *kumite* in your before style?"

Jonathan bowed. "*Hai.*"

"Good. Then you, me, we show everyone proper way, okay?"

It wasn't okay. It was a stupid move by the instructor, a no-win/no-win situation and could end very ugly. If he defeated Jonathan, it would be as everyone expected and he would gain nothing. But if Jonathan defeated or scored on him, or even just held his own, the *sensei* would lose face. And, being Japanese, that could ignite an all-out war. One of them would surely walk away worse than when he walked in.

With his face twisted into a smirk, Ojima gestured for Jonathan to take up a starting position across from him. Jonathan ran into place and bowed, getting little more than a dip of his *sensei's* head in return, the barest version of a bow.

Both took up fighting stances. Obviously expecting Jonathan to run, Ojima charged straight into Jonathan's front-leg heel-thrust kick, what *Kancho* called a stopping kick. But the Japanese had come in so fast and with so much power, the recoil catapulted Jonathan backward, out of range for a follow-up.

The instructor, his eyes like burning coals, closed on him. *This is going to be for real*, Jonathan warned himself.

The instant he was in range, Ojima launched a powerful cutting kick, like a low roundhouse kick only striking with his shin. The sharp-ridged bone made contact with the outside of Jonathan's calf. Normally, sweeps weren't allowed higher than four inches above the floor, to prevent knee damage. But Ojima caught Jonathan midway up his calf, sending his legs flying, then moved in on his downed opponent, blood-lust in his eyes.

As he had been trained in Japan, Jonathan rolled onto his back and pulled up his knees. Using his hands, he swiveled himself around, always keeping the soles of his feet positioned between his head and Ojima. His *sensei* darted left and right, trying unsuccessfully to create an opening in which to attack without getting stomped on the way. After almost a full minute, his movements slowed and his anger drained. Finally, the Japanese chuckled, held out his hand, and helped Jonathan to his feet.

"*Ii desu*. Very good you *kumite*," said Ojima.

Throughout the class, Jonathan felt Ojima's eyes on him, studying every move he made.

"How's your leg?" one of the students asked Jonathan when class was dismissed.

"Fine. He's very good."

"He was twice All-Japan Champion."

That got Jonathan's attention. "Really?"

"Yeah, Ferdie looked it up," he said as a nearby purple belt nodded.

Winning the All-Japan Karate Championships once was a huge accomplishment. Winning it twice, if true, would mean Ojima was incredibly good, someone who could teach him a tremendous amount.

Jonathan approached the instructor and bowed. "*Domo arigato go-ziamasu, sensei.* Thank you for taking the time to educate me."

Ojima grunted as he studied the tall American. "You *yudansha?*"

Jonathan bowed. "*Hai, sensei,* but in Shorin Ryu."

The instructor nodded knowingly. "You keep training. I make strong."

Jonathan bowed.

"Next class," said Ojima, "wear *kuro obi,* black belt. If no have, I give."

Students were surprised to see Jonathan wearing a black belt at their next class. "You're not a black belt," said Hershaw, moving around him and lining up in the lead position.

"You, go there," said Ojima, flicking his finger to Jonathan's left.

"But he's not *yudansha* with us, *sensei,*" pleaded Hershaw as he moved grudgingly to the second position.

Ojima laughed. "Maybe, like Japan, you fight for position, *neh?*" Hershaw shook his head, making Ojima laugh even harder.

The class was taken through all nine of the *kata* required for promotion to first-degree black belt in their system, Shotokan, starting with Heian Shodan and ending with Jion. Only two people, Jonathan and Hershaw, needed the forms above Heian Yondan, leaving the other students to struggle through them as best they could. When he saw that Jonathan was familiar with them all, although slightly different versions, Ojima continued through the next four, those required for promotion to Nidan, second-degree black belt.

Jonathan assumed Ojima was doing this for three reasons. First, he probably wanted to find out how much Jonathan knew. Second, he wanted everyone to see that Jonathan knew more than everyone else in the class. And third, he probably wanted to supply Jonathan with the information he would need to move upward in rank. This last possibility laid a new burden on Jonathan's shoulders but one he welcomed.

It was said that *karate* was where one learned to say *oos*, to undertake whatever was asked of him to the best of his ability and see it through to its successful completion. So Jonathan silently vowed to say *oos* and do everything within his power to achieve his *sensei's* expectations.

"See you Friday, *sensei*," said Jonathan, bowing.

"You come *sake*?" asked Ojima.

"Sorry, *sensei*. I can't. I have a big test tomorrow."

As Jonathan jogged back toward Wilbur Hall to study, Ojima headed into the men's locker room. He kicked off his flip-flops, untied his belt, and stripped off his *gi* top. His scarred upper body was a canvas of colorful tattoos of dragons, *geisha*, and *samurai*, leaving bare only his neck, lower arms, and a vertical line running down the center of his chest.

Chapter Four

Since the university's inception in 1891, Stanford had had a policy that prevented women from comprising more than fifteen percent of the student body. But the rule had been legally challenged and eliminated in the 60s, just a few years before Jonathan's arrival.

Stanford men had traditionally visited local colleges and junior colleges to find attractive, intelligent dates. If attractive was enough and willing even better, then those types of women could be found in a number of other places.

Even after the rule had been changed and students admitted on merit alone, most men still traveled off-campus to find girlfriends, claiming the selection was still far better elsewhere. It didn't help the women's situation that an ABC TV sports producer, when asked why he hadn't included any Stanford coed shots during the broadcast of a recent football game, described Stanford women as "early War of 1812."

Jonathan found it increasingly more difficult to avoid getting dragged into some of this. Every Friday night he was pressured to accompany a group of dormmates on their weekly "Babe Runs." Thinking he would one day become the starting quarterback, they believed his presence would increase the quality of "babes" they would have access to. Then there were the exclusive parties hosted by a group of football-supporting zealots, open only to alumni, team members, and potential recruits. These were extravagant events, where no expense was spared and the women said to be top San Francisco models. Although Jonathan never accepted invitations for any of these, he remained at the top of everyone's invite list, much to his chagrin. There was only one woman who interested him and she was in Japan, still in Japan.

As a new quarter began, Jonathan was surprised to learn that the pretty mini-skirted woman sitting on the desk as he filed in for their first class was not a teaching assistant, there to take roll and distribute handouts before the teacher arrived; she was the teacher – Dr. Linda Worthington, a world-renowned poet. Not surprisingly, the class was full, all twenty-two seats, with men.

Dr. Worthington, who insisted she be called Linda, went around the room asking everyone to introduce himself. When Jonathan's turn came, he said "I'm Jonathan Lusk, I…" Before he could add where he had come from, as the others had done, she stopped him. "You have an accent I can't quite put my finger on, Mr. Lusk."

"I was born in Boston but moved to Japan when I was six. I lived there until a few months ago."

"How interesting! I will have to tap your store of experiences when we study the Japanese poets."

She continued around the room, with each student giving his name and hometown. They had barely finished their introductions when the bell rang. "I would like each of you to bring your favorite poem to our next class and be prepared to read it for us and to explain how it speaks to you." She turned her attention to Jonathan. "Mr. Lusk, may I speak with you for a moment?"

Dr. Worthington waited for the last student to leave. "I'm having a small dinner party tomorrow night," she said. "My guests will be visiting professors, all of whom have a common interest in things Japanese. I'm sure you could add an interesting perspective to our discussions. Would you be interested in joining us?"

"Sorry but I have a class."

"Well, I host these little soirees on a fairly regular basis. Perhaps we can coordinate the next one to better fit your schedule."

Jonathan thanked her and hurried out to his next class.

In letter after letter, Nanami assured Jonathan that she would be joining him soon. She always sounded positive. She always sounded eager.

But she never gave him an arrival date. "I will be there soon" was all he ever heard. Soon was one of those words the Japanese loved, one that seemed to give an answer when, in fact, it didn't.

Part of him, the logical part, understood. She was a princess. Not "my princess," but an actual princess. And her family was fighting her over her desire to study in America. No other member of the Imperial family had ever sought to earn a college degree abroad. So coming to Stanford wasn't something even someone as strong as Nanami could easily accomplish.

He took all the delays patiently, at least on the outside. Inside, skepticism was steadily building. It took a quantum leap, however, when a Kami friend in Japan wrote Jonathan something he had heard from another Kami, one assigned to Nanami's security detail. He claimed that she was being heavily wooed by a young man named Akemi Nakatomi, a fellow student at Todai, Tokyo University, and heir to the powerful Nakatomi family fortune.

"I heard that you have a new friend, someone named Akemi," he had added casually near the end of his last letter to Nanami. She shot him back a quick reply. "I have heard that you too have a new friend, an attractive poetry professor who has wagered a substantial sum on being the first at Stanford to bed you. And she is not alone. Others are wagering on their own chances as well!"

Jonathan was shocked. He had always thought women were just being kind or trying to mother him, never dreaming there could be anything further to it. And perhaps there wasn't. He had known that Nanami had friends at Stanford, former classmates at Gakushⓧjo, the Peers School, friends she had never identified. Clearly, they knew far more about what was happening on campus than he did, or at least they thought they did.

What was significant, however, was the fact that she hadn't responded to his comment about her reputed suitor. Instead, she had gone on the offensive, possibly to misdirect him. That was not a good sign. He obviously needed to learn more about Akemi Nakatomi.

The unanimous opinion of Japanese journalists, from Jonathan's microfiche search, seemed to be that Akemi was little more than a wealthy *asobinin*, a playboy or carouser. News photos invariably showed him in the company of some well-known actress or top model. *Japan Today* magazine had recently published a feature article on Akemi. The cover showed him opening the door of his Ferrari for a scantily clad Chiyo Hara, the famous actress. Reading the article, Jonathan couldn't imagine Nanami being interested in a person like him… until he saw a shot of Akemi and Nanami walking together on the Tokyo University campus.

Because of a suspicious college roommate, who Nanami feared was reporting her activities to her father, she generally only wrote on weekends, when she was home and alone in her room. Then she would secretly drop her letters into a public mailbox on the Todai campus when she returned to school on Mondays. Her letters always arrived at Stanford on a Wednesday, Thursday, or Friday, depending on variances in headwinds and the efficiency of the U.S. Postal Service.

When Wednesday rolled around, Jonathan opened his post office box to find it empty. There was nothing there on Thursday either. When it was also empty on Friday, panic swept through him. It was an ominous sign. She had never missed an entire week before. Apparently there was more to her relationship with Akemi than she had indicated. But then, she hadn't denied it either.

Jonathan was afraid to check his mailbox on Saturday, knowing that if he found it empty again, she was gone. His hand shook as he tried to line up the tiny key with the slit of an opening. He hesitated, summoning his courage, before twisting the key and pulling the small door open. Empty.

Chapter Five

Jonathan needed something to keep his mind occupied. He hadn't heard anything from Nanami in two weeks and both of the letters he had sent her had been returned, making him even more sure their relationship had ended. So he focused as best he could on his schoolwork and his *karate* training, struggling to keep his mind off the pain and the constant replaying of the million things he should have said or not said.

Dr. Cey was lecturing on Immanuel Kant's notion of a "thing in itself" but little of it was sticking, forcing Jonathan to scold himself. He had to pay closer attention; there would be a test on it the following Monday. But keeping his mind focused on anything but Nanami for more than a few seconds had become all but impossible. It was Friday and he hadn't received a letter in three weeks.

"Is this seat taken?" whispered a petite woman.

"No," he said, without looking up.

Something about the woman's perfume, a combination of citrus, rosemary, and spice, pulled Jonathan's eyes up to see Nanami's beautiful, delicate face, her eyes filled with tears but a smile on her lips. He sprang to his feet and, resisting the powerful urge to hug her, bowed formally. She wrapped her arms around him and kissed him passionately on the lips, getting hoots from other students and a smile from the professor.

"Sorry," offered Jonathan as he took Nanami's hand and rushed her outside.

Seeing his eyes make a quick sweep of the Quad, Nanami laughed. "We are quite alone," she said, kissing him lightly on the lips again. "I told Father that if I saw even one of his spies, or heard any existed, I would never speak to him again."

Jonathan smiled. She believed no one was watching but there was no way Prince Yoritomo wouldn't assign at least one person to keep an eye on his rebellious daughter.

You can never allow yourself to relax when with her in public, he told himself. The Prince might conceivably accept a little innocent flirtation between them, even though that was highly unlikely. But he would never accept anything more serious, not with a *gaijin*, a foreigner or non-Japanese.

No one, including Jonathan, could completely control what the young princess did or said. And her father surely knew that better than anyone. But if anything did occur between them, she would be forgiven. He would not. If he were ever suspected of doing anything even remotely out of line, regardless of who initiated it, the Prince would make life extremely difficult for Jonathan, perhaps even preventing him from ever returning to Japan.

To get out of easy view, Jonathan took Nanami to the Stanford Coffee House, where the dim lights and single entrance allowed him to monitor anyone coming or going. The two sat in one of the back booths, facing each other across a rough-hewn wood table. Underneath, they held hands while drinking tall glasses of iced chocolate mint and telling each other all those things they couldn't risk putting into their letters.

As they strolled to Florence Moore Hall, her new dorm, Jonathan and Nanami chatted like old friends, never touching. Her father had bought her a house in the exclusive Los Altos Hills, where he intended her to live, along with a maid, a cook, a driver, and security guards. But the university required all new students to live on campus their freshman and sophomore years, even princesses. So she would live at Flo Mo, as the students called it.

Nanami laughed as she told him how red her father's face had grown when she informed him.

"I thought you were into your second year at Todai?" Jonathan asked.

"*Hai.*"

"Then you would be a sophomore here too, same as me."

"Yes but I registered as a freshman," she said, smiling slyly.

A bolt of fear shot up Jonathan's spine as it dawned on him what she had in mind. Next summer, she would transfer in a bunch of units from University of Tokyo and get Stanford's administrators to change her status from freshman to junior. Then the two of them could rent a house or apartment and live together, something that would make her father hate him even more when he discovered it, as he surely would.

Chapter Six

"**W**ant to go to a play tomorrow night?" Nanami wrote on the top of her notebook, then showed it to Jonathan, who sat next to her in their General Biology class.

The play turned out to be *The Mikado*, performed by an untalented group of fraternity brothers. With taped eyes and caricatured accents, men played both male and female parts. It was so bad Jonathan and Nanami couldn't stop laughing.

Whenever he was with her, Jonathan felt simultaneously at complete ease and on sharp pointed edge. Of the less than a handful of people who remained in his life, she had known him the longest, meeting him even before *Kancho* Kubo had.

"Now I adore that girl with passion tender," sang the character, Ko Ko, on stage. "And would not yield her with a ready will or her allot, if I did not adore myself with passion tenderer still."

To anyone who might be watching, Jonathan was engrossed in the musical. No reaction had registered outwardly when she slipped her hand under the coat on her lap and grasped his. But her touch, as it always did, had sent a tingle through him, all the way to his *kokoro*, a Japanese term for which there was no good English equivalent. It was usually translated as heart, but that was not completely accurate. *Kokoro* meant something more, something akin to a combination of heart and mind. Her touch anchored him both to the world and to her, as if they were two halves of a whole, a feeling he hadn't experienced since he was a child in Boston.

When the curtain closed for Intermission, Jonathan stood up. "I'll get us some punch."

"I will go to *otearai*," she said, standing too.

While he picked up two cups of some kind of red punch in the lobby, she tracked down the women's restroom. When Jonathan returned to their seats a few minutes later, she still wasn't back.

Soon the lights flashed, signally intermission was almost over, and Nanami had yet to return. Only after the lights had dimmed did she finally slide across the row of knees to sit down beside him.

"Are you okay?" he asked, seeing a troubled look on her face.

"I will explain later."

The play continued but her mood was chilly. She didn't laugh. She didn't hold his hand. Something had happened.

During their stroll back to Flo Mo, Jonathan tried to get her to open up, to reveal what was bothering her. But she remained silent until they reached the dorm entrance. "Maybe this was a mistake," she said out of the blue, turning to confront him.

"It was just a spoof," he answered. "It's always played by non-Japanese."

"Not the play, coming to Stanford."

He was baffled. From the look on her face, he knew he was somehow to blame for whatever she was talking about.

"Do you not like me?" she pressed.

"Of course," Jonathan said, blushing, his eyes going to his feet.

"You treat me as if I were your sister in truth, not just in pretense."

"It's just that...your father. We decided...

"So you fear my father more than you love me!" she hissed.

"Of course not. I..." He awkwardly leaned forward to kiss her. Nanami's hand lashed out and slapped him across the cheek. "How dare you!" she shouted, causing people walking by to stop and stare. Nanami spun on her heels and stormed inside, slamming the door behind her.

Jonathan had been hit with far more power before but no blow had ever hurt as badly, stunning him both mentally and physically. What had he done wrong? He had only tried to do what she seemed to be asking of him.

It took a minute before he regained enough composure to trudge back toward his dorm, feeling as completely alone as he had his first birthday at the Dai Kan, when he turned seven and the students had been especially cruel to him. Now at Stanford, twelve years later, nothing had changed. He felt as if every person on the planet had vanished and taken Earth's atmosphere with them, exposing them to the cold solitude of space.

Not wanting to be alone, Jonathan headed toward the lights of Meyer, Stanford's main library, and joined the steady stream of students filing into the multi-storied intellectual and physical beacon.

Struggling to put order back into his life, he wandered the science racks until he found a copy of *The Behavior of Organisms* by B. F. Skinner, which he needed for a coming psychology paper. Jonathan tried to read but his mind kept wandering back to Nanami. After ten or fifteen minutes, he gave up and strode out into the crisp fall air. His only escape, he knew, would be found in a run, a hard run, a run so hard and so long his heart would explode.

Jonathan bounded up the Wilbur steps to the second floor, eager to change clothes and find relief from pain with pain. He jogged down the hallway, opened his door, and reached in to flip on the light.

"No light," came Nanami's voice from out of the darkness. She almost flowed across the floor to him, then waited motionlessly. He wrapped his arms around her tiny, delicate body and held her as if finding a long lost friend. The clean, sweet smell of her hair blended with the fragrance of her perfume, flooding his nostrils, soothing both mind and spirit.

He realized she was crying. "What's wrong?"

"I am so sorry I struck you. I did not know what else to do."

"I'm confused," Jonathan confessed, putting it mildly.

"When I went to the restroom, I noticed a Japanese man in the audience. He was closely watching you. He saw me and looked quickly away. But I have seen him before, at home, as part of my father's security."

"Are you sure it's the same person?"

"I have no doubt. He has a large black mole right here," she said pointing to a spot above her right eyebrow. "I wanted to ensure tonight was possible. So I made him believe there is nothing between us." She stood on her tiptoes and kissed Jonathan on the cheek where she had slapped him. "Please forgive me."

Jonathan pointed to his lip. "You also kind of hit me here too... just a little."

She kissed him gently on the lips. "Better?"

They spent the night lying side by side on the bed, talking and holding hands, his arm around her neck. He chuckled. "What?" she asked. "Nothing," he answered, "I'm just happy." That was, of course, true. But it was not the reason he had laughed. This was the Age of Aquarius, of hippies, drugs, and free love. They were probably the only couple in the San Francisco Bay Area, the epicenter of that uninhibited era, who were not surrendering to the ultimate limits of their most basic drives.

He had kept the thought to himself partially out of fear and partially out of selfishness. He suspected he could do more, if he chose to. He even suspected she wanted him to do more. She had certainly given him enough hints.

But that was the part that scared him. He had never been with a woman before. In fact, until that night, he had never even kissed one except for when Nanami kissed him beside the river at the Dai Kan when they were seven or eight and again when she had first arrived at Stanford.

Besides, when he found such great pleasure in simply holding hands, in stroking her cheek with the soft back sides of his fingers, in feeling her body pressed against his, why would he want to lose all of that in a headlong rush toward what should be the final step, the end of the journey?

As the night progressed, Jonathan discovered that Nanami had their entire life mapped out for them, from graduation until death. They would return to Hiroko's family home, where Jonathan had started his life in Japan, where they had met, and where Nanami had so many happy memories. The only details she hadn't yet worked out were the number of children they would have and what would become his profession. He was majoring in International Relations so he could follow his grandfather into the Foreign Service, if he so chose. But it would also prepare him to teach at the Dai Kan or to serve as liaison between the Kami Kan and similar agencies in other governments.

What she wasn't taking into consideration was that he had plans of his own – to hunt down and bring to justice those responsible for both his father's and his grandfather's deaths. Only then would his obligations be fulfilled and he be free to settle down and enjoy a normal life. But bringing it up then would not only be a waste of breath but ruin a perfect evening. Plus, their days were likely numbered. Her father would surely soon find out about their relationship and bring it to an end. So Jonathan decided to let her think and plan to her heart's content. He would focus on but one thing, savoring whatever time he was gifted with her.

"Wish we could lie here forever," she whispered, "but I must return before the sun rises and they discover me missing" She kissed him, then quietly slipped out the door.

He and Nanami went to basketball games, to the Oasis for burgers, the city for plays and the zoo, but always accompanied by other people to make it appear to be a group outing. Since it wasn't something they could do together, Jonathan had cut out *karate*. But when Nanami was required to take an early-evening English for Foreign Students class, he was free to return.

Ojima was late his first night back. At least that part hadn't changed. The instructor ambled in about ten minutes later, wearing his *gi* pants and a sweatshirt. He spotted Jonathan and strode over. "You return," he grunted. "Good."

"Sorry, *sensei*, too much homework."

Jonathan could smell alcohol on his breath, which wasn't unusual for a Japanese. Alcohol was an integral part of their social system. Many didn't trust anyone who didn't drink, thinking they must have something to hide.

The *sensei* stripped off his sweatshirt to don his *gi* top, for the first time revealing his tattoos to Jonathan. The sight shocked him. Ojima was *yakuza*.

Jonathan's mind raced. *Does he know my name?* he asked himself. Had he ever asked or seen it written down? He didn't think so. But perhaps Ojima was just pretending not to know that there was a huge bounty on his head.

Kancho Kubo couldn't be reached when Jonathan called. The Master General was "occupied," according to his senior aide, Aoshima San, who took the call. This usually meant the Emperor or other high-ranking member of the Imperial Family was traveling and needed special protection. So Jonathan put the matter to the Dai Kami.

"If you do not attend class," Aoshima advised, "he may search you out and learn your identity. I would recommend you proceed as if nothing has changed but remain in a high state of vigilance, prepared to react to all possibilities."

"*Hai*, Aoshima *San*," Jonathan responded, understanding completely. He was telling him to always have his pistol within reach.

With his Beretta fully loaded and positioned for quick extraction in his equipment bag, Jonathan took the floor for the Wednesday night class. Fortunately, it passed without incident, as did most of the class on Friday. After dismissing everyone else, Ojima asked Jonathan to stick around so they could train together, immediately putting Jonathan on edge. They would be alone in the gym.

As they performed *ippon kumite*, where one side attacked with a set technique and the other countered it, Jonathan kept expecting one of his *sensei's* punches or kicks to land. Although Ojima's techniques were extremely fast and powerful, they were thankfully always well controlled. But, Jonathan reminded himself, his *sensei* didn't have to actually do anything himself; all it would take was a phone call and Ojima would be two million yen richer.

Kancho Kubo finally returned and Jonathan was able to speak with him.

"Yes," *Kancho* said, "Kichiro Ojima was All-Japan Champion on two occasions. It was long rumored that he was affiliated with the *yakuza* but never confirmed. And with no criminal charges against him, there was never a reason to investigate the matter."

"What about his tattoos? Doesn't that mean anything?"

"Yokohama, especially the poor sector where he was raised, has long been very violent. Many gangsters. It was not unusual for young people there to tattoo themselves, usually in hopes of gaining an invitation to join one of the gangs. But I will look further into the matter and call again."

He called the next day.

"The news is worrisome," said *Kancho*. "He was adopted but chose to use his birth name, which is why his history remained hidden. His adopted father drank to extreme and beat both his mother and young Kichiro until he became strong enough to prevent it. Because his step-father was a *shateigashira* in the Momochi Gumi, Kichiro was recruited and soon rose to *kodai*."

"It never ends."

"It will one day but the future is less assured for Ojima. After his ad-opted father beat his mother into a coma, Kichiro went to the bar where he and other Momochi soldiers drank. He attacked his stepfather so viciously that other *yakuza* came to his aid. Kichiro beat them with equal severity. As a result, he was banned from the *gumi* and given the option to either relocate or die, which is how he came to be in America. But you must consider his alliances uncertain. He could possibly decide to use you to gain the right to return to Japan and live a comfortable life."

"Aoshima San suggested I remain in class."

"I would agree. It is often best to keep potential enemies within sight but always, as I am sure he also advised you, with sufficient re-sources to respond to any level of potential attack."

So Jonathan kept training, which seemed to please Ojima so much that he began openly sharing all he knew, including what most martial artists would consider personal combat secrets. Every word, every technique he offered was noted by Jonathan, not just because it came from one of the world's best but also because he might have to use it to his advantage someday, maybe to keep his *sensei* from killing him.

Jonathan's concerns about his *karate sensei* eased over time, as a friendship seemed to build between them. But when Ojima invited him for a beer at the Oasis, the campus hangout a half-mile north on El Camino Real, his suspicions reappeared full-blown. They would be off-campus, where it would be easier for an attack or abduction to occur. But to reject the offer would be an insult. So with his 9mm in his equipment bag, Jonathan joined him.

Rather than sit at the bar where Ojima had gestured, Jonathan picked a table at the rear of the small room, where he could keep his back to the wall and his eyes on the entrances.

"What would you gents like?" asked the young waitress.

"Pitcher of *biru*, two glass," said Ojima.

"Better bring me an iced tea," said Jonathan. The Japanese's eyes narrowed. "I'm not old enough to drink yet. One more year."

Ojima grunted in acknowledgement and, when the pitcher arrived, had no problem finishing it by himself. He was into his second pitcher when he began opening up about his past.

"You live Japan. So know I *yakuza* before," he said, catching Jonathan by surprise. "Big mistake. My true father die so mother marry *yakuza* big shot. He have money. Car. People not just respect, fear. To me, when small boy, he like god. Then god become man, bad man. I leave *yakuza* but my body stained by their mark."

He sounded sincere and the story he revealed coincided with what *Kancho* Kubo had told him. "It is what is inside a person, not outside, that is important," offered Jonathan.

"That true here. No true Japan."

Jonathan nodded. "*Wakarimasu*. I understand perfectly. I was a *gaijin* in Japan and an outcast too."

"*Kampai*," said Ojima, clinking his glass against Jonathan's. "Outcast to outcast. *Tomodachi* to *tomodachi*."

Jonathan bowed. "I am honored that you would call me your friend."

Regardless of all the backslaps and words of friendship, Jonathan never went to *karate* without his Beretta in his bag. And a couple of weeks later, he was glad he did.

The class was nearing the end when he noticed a Japanese catch a quick peek around the front lobby door. He didn't think much of it. Things like that happened often, students fascinated by their workouts. But when the man took a longer look, Jonathan saw that his hair was greased back and his face wore the same cruel smirk he had often seen when dealing with *yakuza*.

Suddenly clutching the back of his leg, Jonathan limped across the floor to the side wall as if he had pulled a muscle. He sat down on the floor beside his bag and slipped his pistol inside the front flap of his *gi* top. Jonathan's eyes swung briefly over to check the rear door, his designated exit point, and saw another Japanese.

Tucking his right leg underneath him and extending his left out in front, Jonathan bent tentatively forward. As he pretended to delicately stretch a damaged hamstring, Jonathan readied himself to spring to his feet, pistol in hand.

Ojima, for his part, pretended to be oblivious to it all, playing his role masterfully, Jonathan thought. Not wanting to be forced to fight his way through Ojima, the man in the lobby, and whoever else waited outside the main entrance, he decided he would shoot whoever was nearest the back exit first, then make a dash for the door.

The *yakuza* stepped through both front and rear doors almost simultaneously, then stood waiting. The man in back had picked up a partner; the one in front, two. Glancing over, Ojima finally acknowledged their presence. "Class end early," he announced. "Everyone leave, now!"

Seeing the five drunken, tattooed thugs, no one had to be told twice. As soon as the last student had rushed out, the *yakuza* ambled toward where Ojima stood in the center of the gym floor. The *sensei* turned to face Jonathan, who got to his feet and strode toward the rear exit, his hand locked around his hidden pistol's waffled handle. Before he got far, however, he saw that the two men between him and the exit were focusing all of their attention on his *sensei*. They weren't there for him.

"Leave and you will not be injured," Ojima told them in Japanese.

Jonathan knew all he had to do was keep walking and he would stay out of something that had nothing to do with him, a gambling debt or drunken insult. If campus security showed up, how would he ever explain the pistol? There was much to lose and little to gain by getting involved. But among the little he had to gain was his honor. If he left his *sensei* to face a five-to-one assault alone, he could neither justify it nor live with himself. So he stopped and turned.

Ojima's head snapped around. "You leave," he told Jonathan. "This no you fight."

"Yeah, beat it, *gaijin*," slurred one of the men in Japanese.

Jonathan headed straight toward them.

"He said beat it," added the apparent leader in broken English. "This has nothing to do with you."

"It has everything to do with me," Jonathan shot back in Japanese. "You're in my country, in my house!"

A crooked smile curled the man's lips. The two nearest *yakuza* headed Jonathan's way. When they got within range, Jonathan snapped out a front kick that landed full on the man's chin, faster than he could get his hands up. The man's body went rigid and he fell straight backward, his head banging sickeningly against the hardwood floor. His partner tried a kick of his own but Jonathan easily caught his leg and upended him. He too landed hard on the back of his head.

Ojima launched himself at the three remaining *yakuza*. Feet, knees, head butts, even biting one's nose, he was like a chainsaw run rampant. Jonathan had never seen anyone attack with such fury.

The leader reached into his coat for something. Jonathan didn't wait to see what came out. He drew his 9mm and had the man in his sights by the time the *yakuza's* .45 emerged. "Set it on the floor and back away," ordered Jonathan.

With a pistol trained on him and stalked by the former All-Japan Champion, the man did as he was told. "Next time, you die," growled Ojima, snatching up the .45, removing the clip and round from the chamber, then tossing the gun back, hitting the man in the chest.

The *yakuza* gathered up their downed colleagues and staggered out of the gym.

"What was all that about?" asked Jonathan as soon as the men were gone.

"They drink too much and want impress *oyabun* in Japan. You make beautiful *mae keri*. Pop! Goodnight, *yakuza* san." Ojima was giddy, laughing and bubbly as Jonathan had never seen him before, or even imagined the man capable of being.

Then a thought occurred to him. What if this was all just a ruse to kidnap or hurt Nanami? He snatched up his bag. "Sorry. I have to go," he said, jogging toward the entrance. Ojima grabbed his things and ran to catch up.

Jonathan froze at the entrance. He was leading a former *yakuza* to a Japanese princess. Even if he had no intention of doing anything to her, Ojima might put two and two together and realize who he was. "I'll be okay," Jonathan said. "I just forgot I was supposed to meet someone after class."

"You worry for Princess Yoritomo," said Ojima, matter-of-factly. Jonathan looked at him in surprise. "Everyone know. This same like small village."

"*Hai,*" said Jonathan, nodding in apology.

"But only I know who you are truly," added his *sensei*.

Jonathan didn't stop to discover if Ojima knew as much as he intimated. He was too concerned about Nanami. They reached the Quad just as she strolled out with a fellow student for a break. Her eyes locked onto the front of Ojima's chest, his tattoos partially exposed under his *gi* top, and took a quick step back.

The *sensei* bowed almost to his knees and kept his head down. "Forgive me not dress proper."

"This is my *karate sensei*, Ojima *San*," Jonathan added quickly to relieve some of her concern. "We need to leave. Please get your things."

She looked at Jonathan questioningly but an explanation would have to wait until he was sure she was safe. As she went back into the building to get her backpack, Jonathan bowed to Ojima. "*Domo*, we will be safe now."

The *sensei* nodded. "I understand. She with Kami." Clearly, he knew who Jonathan was. He bowed low to Jonathan. "You my *tomadachi*. Risk life. I now have debt."

"Thank you. But no debt is owed. I am honored to be your friend and student."

Nanami returned and they left with Ojima bowing in the dimly lit walkway.

"Your *sensei*," she asked as Jonathan hurried her back toward Flo Mo, "is *yakuza*, no?"

"Former."

"He is a farmer? I do not think so."

Jonathan laughed, getting an angry glare in return. "Former, with an 'o'… meaning previous member of the *yakuza*. He left them. Some of his former… previous gangster brothers came after him tonight at the gym."

"Are they aware of your identity?"

He shrugged. "I don't think so. They walked right past me. Only Ojima *Sensei* seems to know for sure."

"Why would you inform him?"

"I didn't."

"Then how would he discover such a thing?"

Chapter Seven

Jonathan knocked on Coach York's door. "Come on in," came the Coach's gravelly voice. "Thanks for coming."

"What's going on?" Jonathan asked upon seeing York loading his things into cardboard boxes. The coach hadn't said anything about going anywhere when he called.

"Got my pink slip this morning and didn't want to leave without saying goodbye."

Jonathan couldn't hide his puzzlement.

"It's my own fault. Didn't win enough games," said York. "Guess I'm too old school for these new school boys. Every day it was the same. 'Sorry, coach, I have too much homework.' Hell's bells, we all carried the same load, maybe worse, when I was here and we never missed practice. And the drugs! You have no idea how many key guys showed up stoned. It's no excuse but hard to win when you're fighting all that on a daily basis."

Jonathan was clearly disappointed. "I don't know if I would have made the team or not but I was looking forward to giving it a try."

"Well hell, don't let my departure stop you. I'm sure the new coach will be thrilled to have you."

"I'll have to give that some thought. I was mainly excited by the prospect of playing for you, who knew both my dad and grandfather."

York came around the desk and gave him a warm hug. "If you ever need some fatherly advice, I'll give you the name of someone wise to call," York said, laughing. "Just kidding, if you ever need someone to talk to, day or night, call me. I'm nowhere near as great as those two men were but I'm here for you."

"God," Jonathan thought as he walked toward the Student Union to have lunch with Nanami. What would he tell her?

He had actually had mixed emotions about playing football. Joining the team would have forced him to give up *karate*, to spend large amounts of time away from Nanami for practices and games, and probably taken a hit on his grade-point average. She had been the one who wanted him to play.

Stanford was figuratively and literally a small town, with its own zip code and post office. And like most small towns, everyone knew everyone else's business. Her dormmates kept her regularly updated as to who was dating which of the top athletes, whether on or off campus, and how their relationships were going. At the pinnacle of everyone's watch list was the quarterback. Nanami, of course, wasn't immune to any of this and had, he suspected, been basking in the envied position of her boyfriend becoming the next one.

But she took the news far better than he had feared, thanks indirectly, he later learned, to the current quarterback's girlfriend, Lisa Kloss, one of Nanami's Flo Mo dormmates. Lisa was not only extremely intelligent, she had been the reigning Miss Twin Cities while a high school senior. At Stanford, she had become one of the small number of women dating star athletes. She was also the only one there who hadn't been envious of Nanami. Just that morning, she had shared the negative side to dating a star football player. What likely delivered the fatal cut, however, was Lisa's description of the number of women who regularly threw themselves at her boyfriend. Apparently, Jonathan thought, the guy was a far more successful receiver than quarterback.

At seven-fifty the next morning, the usual weekday rush of bicycles converged on the narrow entrance to Stanford's graveled inner quad. With hundreds of students fighting to make it through the bottleneck and reach their first classes before the bell rang, an ever expanding clot of bikes quickly formed, bringing almost all movement to a standstill.

Jonathan hadn't had any first-period classes on the near side of The Quad since his first quarter at Stanford. That experience had made him avoid the area altogether during the early hours. But a class he needed as prerequisite to several others only met first period. So he found himself once again facing the morning squeeze.

Instead of riding his bike, Jonathan found it faster and less stressful to simply walk to class. His first morning, an old Japanese gentleman rode past him and cheerfully navigated the entrance on an old solid-framed, balloon-tired bicycle. Had Jonathan not known that his old friend had died several years earlier, he would have thought it was Caretaker. When he saw Jonathan, the old bikerider did something odd; he stopped and gave him a formal bow before continuing on.

The next day, the old man rode by again and again did the same. Jonathan studied him more closely this time, watching to see if he bowed to anyone else. He didn't.

Since arriving in California, Jonathan had done as *Kancho* had instructed him; he had closely scrutinized every Japanese he encountered. He had never met or seen this one before.

By the third morning, his pistol was stowed in his backpack, just in case. The old man again passed, again bowed, and again rode on, repeating what was becoming his regular routine. *Broken rhythm*, Jonathan reminded himself. Establish a pattern that makes an opponent think he knows what will occur. Then, when he feels comfortable and relaxes, change the pattern and attack. But after bowing this time, the old man rode another ten feet before stopping again. Jonathan reached into his backpack and grabbed the handle of his 9mm. As he waited, the old man bowed formally to a Japanese student, then continued on to wherever he was heading. Now, Jonathan was even more curious.

During his next few trips, he began to see a pattern in the old man's behavior. He smiled at everyone but bowed only to the Japanese he encountered. It made no sense. I'm not Japanese, Jonathan thought. Why would he bow to me?

He wanted to know who the old man was and what he was doing on campus. But he only saw him at the same time each morning, when he was on his way to class. So his identity remained a mystery.

White Plaza was packed. Jonathan had hoped to make a quick run to the bookstore and pick up a workbook he needed for his Advanced Arabic class. But that wasn't going to happen. He had forgotten it was the weekend when every student club on campus set up information booths and performed demonstrations.

As he worked his way through the crowd, he heard the plunking sound of a Japanese *koto*. Ten people dressed in traditional *kyudo* attire, *hakama* and woven tops, and carrying Japanese long bows had formed into a line. All but two were Japanese. On command, the group bowed in unison to a little man who emerged from a group of spectators. With a *hachimaki* tied tight around his forehead, the man beamed as he danced, clearly having a great time, his body bobbing and weaving in synch with the tune.

As he danced, the old man waved for bystanders to join him and many did, his joy infectious. As the song continued, he snaked his way around the plaza. "Come! Dance!" he said, gesturing to Jonathan. It was only then that he recognized him as the old Japanese who bowed to him each morning.

"I'm not much of a dancer," said Jonathan, begging off.

"Do not know the old saying, 'He who dances is a fool. But he who does not dance is a bigger fool?'"

Jonathan shook his head, again wondering how the old man knew of his Japanese upbringing. Before he could ask, though, he winked and danced on, forcing Jonathan to speak with one of the *kyudoka* to finally learn his name and position on campus.

He was Professor Kaemon Shimizu, head of the Asian Studies Department and a *kyudo* master. Every weekday evening, he could be found teaching the Japanese art of archery at the Stanford range.

Since ancient times, archery had played a significant part in both Eastern and Western military arts. But in the East, they had also played a role in their religious practices as well. Confucius was reportedly a highly accomplished archer. The Indian warrior prince, Siddhartha, who later became known as Buddha, was considered an amazing bowman. In Japan, Shinto priests snapped their bowstrings and shot arrows as elements in their ceremonies.

For over four hundred years, *kyudo* had been part of every student's instruction at the Dai Kan, where Jonathan was educated. His training in the bow art had begun within weeks of his arrival, when he was only six. *Kancho* Kubo, the Dai Kan's headmaster, saw training in *kyudo* as integral to instilling in his young charges the skills necessary to one day calmly face any adversity in their lives, even death.

The Stanford Kyudo Club had its own practice range, located in a vacant field behind the Stanford Golf Course. As Jonathan ambled up, one of the two *gaijin*, non-Japanese, students was taking aim at a round straw target ninety-two feet away. Jonathan could see that the student's arms were trembling. He had waited too long. When he finally released his shot, the arrow arced out of the *yumi*, the long asymmetrical Japanese bow, fell short of its target, and skittered across the hard packed earth.

Professor Shimizu saw Jonathan and smiled. "Have you ever played *kyudo* before?" he asked in only slightly accented English.

"Some, *sensei*."

Shimizu held out a bow and quill of arrows. Jonathan tried to wave him off. He hadn't shot in over two years and had arrived late intentionally, not wanting to be put on the spot. But the professor insisted.

Jonathan nocked his first arrow, took aim, and sent it on its way. The shaft buried its tip inside the bull's-eye.

"Very good," laughed Shimizu, clapping his hands.

Jonathan groaned. He had aimed at the center and, for some reason, pulled it an inch to the left. "I haven't shot in a long time," he offered in apology.

"Nonsense, you shoot very well." The professor looked over at the student whose shot had fallen short. "See, Jones San, it is not just a Japanese thing."

Jonathan shot five more arrows. Each was inside the bull's-eye but still slightly off center, further frustrating him. He was still trying to improve his placement when everyone began gathering up their gear to leave.

"Would it be possible to borrow a bow so I can practice more tonight?" he asked the professor. "I'm happy to give you something for security."

"No need," said Shimizu. He pulled a collection of plastic tubes from his equipment bag. The old man smiled slyly as he handed them to Jonathan.

"What's this, *sensei*?"

"It is what you requested," said the professor, taking it back and looking at him quizzically. "Did you not request a bow?"

Jonathan was at a loss.

"Dr. Sasaki is one of our fellow *kyudoka*," Shimizu said, smiling at his little joke. Seeing only confusion on Jonathan's face, he quickly added "You are not an Engineering major I surmise."

Jonathan shook his head.

"Well, Sasaki San heads the Engineering Department. As he must travel frequently, he sought a way to practice his *kyudo* while abroad. Due to its length, airlines would not allow him to take a standard *yumi* with him. So he applied his brilliant mind to the construction of the bow I hold in my hand. As you can see and yourself feel, it is both light and collapsible, easily fitting into his luggage. But equally important, it lacks the flaws normally found in wooden bows, making it extremely accurate."

The Japanese snapped the pieces together, creating a bow that was about three feet long, half the length of a standard *kyudo yumi*, or bow. It was also much more tightly curved, appearing like a large letter C. Dr. Shimizu hooked a string over one end, then bent the bow completely backwards. "They call this style a recurve. It was first developed by Genghis Khan and used to conquer the known world. Accurate. Great power. Small size."

Shimizu held up what looked like a smooth, sharpened piece of thin ceramic doweling. "This is an example of even greater brilliance!"

"What is it?"

"A *ya*! Can you believe it?"

"It has no feathers. It can't possibly fly true."

Shimizu nocked one of the arrows and, without even looking at the target, released it. The flare of amazement on the American's face made him chuckle. It had hit dead center. The professor held up one of the arrows. "See the tiny slits near the end?"

Jonathan studied it and saw them.

"I do not understand the mechanics behind its design. But the arrow's acceleration causes stabilizing fins, constructed of some type of special fiber, to flip up, then retract after impact."

"Why not just attach feathers like other arrows?"

"Space and protection. Pack a dozen arrows in your suitcase and they will be unshootable when you arrive, their feathers crushed. Without a traditional arrowhead, they are also very compact."

Professor Shimizu handed the bow to Jonathan and a fistful of arrows. "You may keep these, if you wish. I have a virtually unlimited supply." He winked. "I am a very good friend of the inventor."

Jonathan examined the bow as if it were damaged goods. The pieces didn't fit smoothly together. The ends of each section were out of alignment with the next, giving it a serrated appearance, like an alligator's tail. It was ugly.

"I can see you have your doubts," said Dr. Shimizu. "Do an old man a favor, test this bow for me and report your findings tomorrow."

Jonathan bowed. "I will, *sensei*."

Shimizu ambled away, heading toward a nearby eucalyptus grove, where his bicycle leaned against one of the tall trees. With a great deal of skepticism, Jonathan readied and shot his first arrow. It hit the target with a hard thrump, much more solidly than any he had ever shot before. Perhaps it was the sound but without even looking back, the professor seemed to know where it had hit and laughed. "See, my young doubting friend!"

As the professor pedaled off, Jonathan nocked and released another arrow. It flew fast and relatively true. But it too hit slightly off-center, although closer than had his previous shots. He wasn't sure if the problem was him or the bow but, in hopes of improving things, Jonathan shot arrow after arrow until his fingers were blistered and it got so dark he couldn't see the target anymore.

"What is your conclusion?" Shimizu asked as Jonathan strode up the next day, the bow in his hand and his fingers ringed in white tape.

"I'm sorry, *sensei*, but I didn't find it as accurate as I wished I could report."

"You witnessed me shoot, did you not?"

"*Hai*. But you are a true master. You could likely hit center with a broom handle and length of clothes line."

The old man laughed. "And you would still miss even with a Kanjuro Shibata *yumi* because the problem lies not with the bow; the problem lies within you. Let me see you shoot."

Jonathan shot five arrows into the straw *mato* target. Each shot arrayed itself within the two-inch bull's-eye but none at its exact center. "Why do I keep missing?" Jonathan asked.

"Buddhism, principally Zen Buddhism, has always been integral to the art of *kyudo*," said the professor, as if giving a lecture. "Do you know Zen?"

Jonathan filled him in on some of his past training in Zen and *kyudo*, but without revealing anything about his association with the Dai and Kami Kans.

"As you surely know *samurai* were required to be Buddhists. It was the national religion. But they did not have to truly become Buddhists. In fact, it was better they did not."

"Because of its prohibition against killing?"

"Yes, its greatest prohibition, in fact. Being practical men, *samurai* were what I call 'utilitarian Buddhists.' Most borrowed from Zen only those qualities that better enabled them to confront an enemy in deadly combat and emerge victorious – calmness in the face of possible death, dying gracefully, or preferably forcing their opponents to die gracefully."

"What about this concept of unifying with your enemy so he, in essence, is trying to kill himself? That never made much sense to me."

"You probably began as a Christian, am I correct?"

Jonathan nodded.

"Well, unlike Christians, we Easterners take a more cosmic view, in which everything is connected. So we are not attempting to hit a target or person that is something apart from us. Rather, we are merely transferring one part of ourselves to another. If you are attempting to shoot an enemy in battle, one who is moving, evading, attacking, he sees what you are about and employs defensive measures. But by clearing your mind, using what we call a Zen mind, you are able to connect with him, his thoughts becoming your thoughts, and he cannot escape."

Jonathan gestured toward the straw circle across the field. "But a target has no thoughts."

"That is correct. It does, however, have matter, of which you are also composed."

Jonathan chuckled. "Well, that makes sense in theory," he said, "but..." He shrugged.

"It is nothing more than returning from whence you came. Calm your breathing, relax your body, and quiet your mind. Then the veil will be pulled back, revealing the infinite array of connections. Use your mind to will your *ya* to wherever you wish it to go and it will arrive."

Jonathan nocked another arrow, relaxed his body, slowed his breathing, and cleared his mind. He imagined the center of the target and waited. Seemingly on its own, the arrow sprang from the bow... and missed the bull's-eye by several inches.

"Well, Kyoto was not built in a day," said Professor Shimizu.

"No," replied Jonathan, half-jokingly. "It was built over several hundred years. Are you telling me that I'm so bad it will take me as long?"

The old man clapped his hands, his eyes twinkling. "Far, far less I would wager, my impatient friend. Besides, you did not consider and adjust for the headwind."

Jonathan decided to try a different approach. What were the essential elements in the instructions he had been given, apart from the stuff about becoming one with the cosmos? Relax. Breathe as in *zazen*. Clear his mind of interfering thoughts. It sounded exactly like what he had done when catching arrows. Perhaps it could be applied to shooting them as well.

He readied another arrow, then went down the same checklist he had used during the Final Test, the arrow catch, at the Dai Kan's *batjitsu* field. He separated his thumb and forefinger, sending it on its way. When he looked, the arrow quivered almost dead center.

"Very good! I see, however, that you did not merge with your target," Dr. Shimizu said. Jonathan had no idea how he knew that. "You discovered what the *samurai* did – take that which is useful and ignore the rest. And that is quite all right. I sincerely hope I will see you tomorrow." The professor waved as he climbed on his bike and rode off. "*Konbanwa*," he heard Shimizu say a few seconds later.

Jonathan nocked another arrow and shot it. Dead center. As he drew back his next shot, something occurred to him. Why had the professor said *konbanwa*, hello, rather than *sayonara*, goodbye? He looked around to see if anyone else was there but saw no one.

He redrew, pulling the bamboo shaft back almost its entire length. A sensation of being watched swept through him. Jonathan snapped the bow around just in time to catch a brief glimpse of what looked from a distance like someone ducking out of sight behind one of the eucalyptus trees.

Jonathan dropped the bow, snatched up his equipment bag containing his Beretta, and strode the twenty yards or so to the tree where he had seen movement. Shoe prints in the soft earth were all that remained, except for a cigarette butt. He picked it up and examined the tiny brand mark. It was the same Japanese brand he had found at Casa Zapata.

Chapter Eight

When summer break rolled around, Nanami's heart was set on going camping at Yosemite National Park. Everyone had told her it was America's most beautiful. So Jonathan had begun drafting a list of others to accompany them. Since spotting her father's spy at the *Mikado*, Nanami had become a more willing participant in his efforts to ensure that everything they did in public appeared to be a group activity. But this time, she insisted it just be the two of them.

When they arrived, Jonathan was worried she would want to camp on the valley floor, surrounded by the dramatic sheer granite cliffs, the soothing sounds of the river, and the gentle sight of deer bringing their spotted fawns to drink and feed in the lush green open meadows. There was also Camp Curry, where they could sleep in tent cabins and watch the nightly firefall. Or, at the other end of the comfort scale, there was The Ahwahnee Hotel, with its first-class accommodations.

"Do you mind if we stay in the mountains?" Nanami asked, pleasantly surprising Jonathan. "Kathy San said there is a secluded and most peaceful campsite beside the river above Vernal Falls."

"Sounds perfect."

They loaded everything into their backpacks and headed up the twisting Vernal Falls Trail. With each of its countless switch-backs, the steep path opened to a new and more spectacular vista of the valley below. It didn't turn out to be a particularly long hike, only around three miles, but it was a challenging one, at least for Nanami, worsened by the hotness of the day, well into the eighties.

The two stopped at the base of the falls and soaked their feet in the cold ice-melt runoff that pooled there, as if the water too needed a rest or a moment to gather its courage before making its final plunge down the mountain side.

After a drink and a kiss and a joke about going skinny-dipping as they had at the Dai Kan when children, Jonathan and Nanami undertook the final stretch to the top. This last section was especially difficult. Not only was it steep but its granite steps slippery, dampened by the constant spray from the powerful Merced River, which had seemed so placid down below.

Once at the top of the falls, Nanami led Jonathan upstream, following the directions given her by one of her dorm sisters. Soon they reached a serene grassy clearing with a view of the entire valley floor and made their camp.

"Come on!" Nanami yelled as soon as they were finished. "We must hurry."

"For what?"

She grabbed his hand and half-dragged him back to the main trail, where they headed west. An hour later, they came to the twenty-foot chasm that separated Half Dome, Yosemite's famous thumb-shaped granite peak, from the mountainside. Spanning the gap was a weathered rope bridge. A faded sign warned hikers that it was no longer safe. Ignoring the sign, Nanami started across.

"Wait!" said Jonathan. "This doesn't look too sturdy."

"Are you chicken?"

"I'm not chicken, just not foolhardy."

"Then follow me."

"Hold on a second," he said, knowing it was useless to argue with her once her mind was made up. "I'll go first."

"After you, Sir Garadad," she said, stepping out of his way. "Is that correct?"

"Galahad," he muttered.

Shifting his weight forward almost in slow motion, Jonathan crept across the series of bowed slats, as he had learned to do in the silent walk at the Dai Kan. "It's not great, but it should hold," he called back.

"Just be…" Before he could add the word *careful*, she ran across the bridge, making the wood clap under her soles. Without slowing, she grabbed his hand and pulled him to the lip of the sheer cliff, its base almost five thousand feet straight below. She sat, dangled her feet over the edge, and patted the stone beside her.

The setting sun cast a brilliant salmon hue across the world as far as Jonathan could see. The wind fluttered their hair and whistled warmly past their ears, carrying with it the echoed shriek of an eagle or hawk rising from somewhere below them. It was a perfect setting, one as delicate in beauty and as powerful in spirit as his young princess.

"Have you ever seen a more wonderful sight?" she asked.

Jonathan glanced over at her and smiled. "Yes, I have."

Nanami turned her head in surprise. When she saw him smiling so lovingly, her eyes misted. "But you are wrong. It is I who have seen something far more beautiful and truly wondrous, what Auntie must have seen in Uncle Eli." She leaned over and kissed him on the lips.

"I worry that…"

Before he could finish, she silenced him with another kiss. "Worries are not allowed today. Just know that I will never allow anyone to separate us again. You need never doubt me, Jonason. That is my most solemn oath."

It was dark by the time they got back to camp. And it had gotten cold. "What do you want to eat?" he asked as he got a fire going.

"It is too cold to eat," she said, circling her hands over the fire. "All I want to do is go to bed and get warm."

They lay in their sleeping bags, side by side, holding hands as they looked up at the black sky with its glittering patterns of bright dots of light. While he named off all the constellations he could identify from his astronomy class, she gave each its Japanese name.

"Forgive me but I cannot take more cold," said Nanami, pulling her arms into her sleeping bag. Soon all he heard was the slow, heavy sound of her breathing. Jonathan tucked the top of his bag tightly around his neck and allowed himself to drift off.

He didn't know how long he had slept before being awakened by a thrashing sound. A bear was searching their campsite for food. It would come up empty, he knew. Everything edible had been hoisted up a tree and tied out of reach as the rangers had recommended. The bear, however, needed to be convinced.

"*Nan desu ka?*" yelled Nanami so loudly she scared the animal off.

"Just a bear," he said, laughing. "It's okay. It's gone. Go back to sleep."

She tucked into a tight ball and lay motionless, but not for long. "I cannot sleep," she said. "I am freezing."

"You want my jacket?"

"No, just let me to join you for one minute," she said, scooting out of her sleeping bag.

"I don't think that's a very good idea," he insisted as she squirmed down beside him, pressing her cold body tightly against his.

"See, is this not nice?" she said, burying her face under his chin, her nose like an ice cube against his neck.

It was nice, he had to admit, too nice.

Chapter Nine

Not long after their return from Yosemite, the same day the school year officially ended, Nanami did as Jonathan had predicted – she strode into Stanford's Admin Building and informed the Registrar that she was now a junior, not a sophomore, and had the right to move off-campus. Her transcript had arrived that morning from Todai, University of Tokyo. With everything verified and documented, her status was upgraded and she was free to live wherever she desired.

Nanami came straight to Jonathan's dorm from the Registrar. After loading his books and few personal items into the boot of his Porsche, she directed him to a beautiful home inside a gated community high in nearby Los Altos Hills. To his surprise, it was completely furnished. She had obviously begun setting this up weeks, if not months, earlier.

"Where should I put my things?" he asked. He thought it a simple and logical question. There were two other bedrooms after all. Nanami shot him an exasperated look, rose up onto her tiptoes, and kissed him. Curling a finger, she led him to their bedroom and showed him which sides of the dresser and closet were his.

As soon as he had stowed his things away, she clasped his hand and dragged him gleefully out onto the wraparound deck.

The sun floated above the scalloped ridges of the Santa Cruz Mountains behind them, bathing everything in a warm golden glow. Far below, the south end of San Francisco Bay reflected the unblemished robin's-egg-blue sky overhead. The many channels and branches of the sprawling bay were embraced on both sides by the fertile basin of Santa Clara Valley, where a handful of semiconductor plants had already replaced several of the valley's world-renowned cherry, apricot, prune, and walnut orchards. It was not destined to remain "The Apricot Capital of the World" much longer.

Nanami's eyes turned almost childlike up to Jonathan, obviously hoping to see that he shared her excitement. He smiled, wanting to make her happy, but couldn't keep his growing concern out of his eyes. "I'm surprised your father agreed to this," he said.

"Agreed would not be the proper word. Relented would be more accurate."

"It has to be his worst nightmare. He hated Hiroko Sama her entire life for marrying my grandfather, and she was his sister."

"Which is why I gave him no choice."

"So he knows I'll be living here?"

"Oh, no!" she exclaimed. "He believes we merely attend school together. Even that sends him into a rage."

After moving in together, Nanami changed in ways that surprised Jonathan. She eagerly embraced the role of homemaker, taking on all of the cooking and domestic chores, refusing to allow him to help with anything, except taking out the trash.

Their first night, however, things didn't go so well. As he sat studying in the living room, he thought he smelled something burning. Since it was coming from the kitchen, he didn't give it much thought until he saw smoke curling along the ceiling above his head.

Jonathan rushed into the kitchen. Nanami, his strong beautiful princess, stood helpless, engulfed in a wonderful-smelling cloud of white smoke as pork chops sizzled in the frying pan. Jonathan grabbed the handle and slid it off the burner.

"They warned me to be most careful in cooking pork to kill some disease," she offered defensively.

"Well, you couldn't have done a better job," he said, giving her a reassuring hug. "They smell delicious!" He drove a fork into one and put it on his plate. She tried to knock it to the floor but he turned away, keeping it out of reach. He bit off a piece and chewed. "Umm," he hummed. "That is the best pork chop I've ever eaten!"

"Please do not mock me," she cried, tears running down her cheeks.

"I'm serious. It is wonderful!" he said, taking another bite. "But what makes it extra special is your secret ingredient, the love you put into it."

But instead of making her smile, the tears ran faster and she buried her face in his shirt.

Princess Nanami Yoritomo of the Japanese Imperial Family had been attended by servants her entire life, which was why he had been so surprised at her transformation. It didn't take long, however, before he realized the reason for the change – to prove to him that she would make a good wife. If so, it was unnecessary. He didn't love her because she could dust, iron, vacuum, and cook. He had not loved her any less when he thought her incapable of doing any of those things. But as was often the case with Nanami, once she set her mind on something, she attacked it with a fervor.

Against his advice, and repeated objections, she began neglecting her schoolwork, focusing all of her time on cleaning their home, washing and ironing every item of clothing he wore – handkerchiefs, shirts, pants, running shorts, even socks and underwear. She bought new furniture and artwork and seemingly took every cooking class she could find in the San Francisco Bay Area. Home cooked gourmet meals awaited him each night. He ate so well, in fact, that he put on ten pounds within the first couple of weeks.

"What are your feelings about getting married?" she asked one afternoon as he walked in from school.

"As a general proposition, I'm for it. Otherwise man would cease to exist as a species."

"I am serious, Jonason."

"Why are you asking me that now?"

"My mother. She is driving me crazy. You must return and meet this fine, fine gentleman, she just wrote me. He is from one of Japan's most powerful families and very, very much in love in you. I have never even met him! In her previous letter, she listed the many attributes of another, one of Japan's wealthiest. Missing from her list, of course, was the fact that he is well into his fifties. And these were just her latest. If we were married, she would have to stop tormenting me."

Jonathan sat down on the sofa and patted the cushion for her to join him. "I thought we decided we would wait until we graduated, then see if we both still thought it a good idea?"

"But you do not know my mother. You fear my father but he is mere clay in her hands. She is behind every move he makes."

Jonathan said nothing for several seconds, debating if he really wanted to risk posing the question or not. From what he could tell, she had never even considered it. So how she might react was a huge unknown. Would she try to prove her sincerity? Would it make her angry? Or, and this was his greatest fear, would it cause her to realize the truth and leave him.

"I don't know if you remember this or not," Jonathan started, "but the day you and Hiroko Sama came to visit us at the Dai Kan, Kiyoshi said something about you wanting to do everything your aunt did. Have you ever given any thought to that being true? If you are interested in me because it is what she did?"

Nanami studied him for a few seconds. "You are asking if I truly love you," she said, an edge to her voice, "or merely copying Auntie by collecting a *gaijin* husband?"

She sprang to her feet as if to walk away. But, instead, she moved over and sat on his lap, straddling his legs and facing him. "It is who we are when the lights are out that is the true test, not eye shape, skin tone, the bed we were fortunate or unfortunate enough to be born in." She kissed him passionately, full on the lips. Then, she spoke to him with her lips so close, they lightly brushed his. "If you were blind, would you love me any less?"

He shook his head.

"I love you because of who you are inside," she said, "not who you are outside. There is no power on this earth that can ever change that."

Chapter Ten

"**W**onderful news!" Nanami exclaimed a month later. "His Majesty is coming! He will make a three-day visit to San Francisco."

Jonathan's reaction was very different from hers. An imperial visit so close to Stanford might not be a coincidence. Nanami, of course, would be required to pay her respects, while he would be required to stay well away. However, if the Emperor was traveling abroad, *Kancho* Kubo would surely precede him to set up and oversee security, giving Jonathan a chance to see him again for the first time in over two years.

The day before the Emperor's arrival, Jonathan drove to the Japanese Embassy. "*Do desu ka?*" asked Kubo as he stepped out of the elevator.

"Fine, *Kancho*," said Jonathan, bowing, "I hoped you would be here. Do you have a minute? Can I buy you lunch or something?"

"Unfortunately, my time is very short. We can, however, talk briefly."

Kancho led Jonathan to a *tatami*-covered meeting room. Without being called, a pretty *kimono*-clad young woman shuffled in with green tea.

"Have you encountered any more *yakuza*?" asked Kubo.

"Not since the incident at the gym and the two others I mentioned, where I had possibly been watched." He decided to leave out Nanami seeing Prince Yoritomo's spy.

"You should know that Zuma has moved up. He is now the Chairman of the Grand Council of *Oyabun*, giving him more power to reach far outside Japan."

Jonathan bowed.

"What of the Arab? How goes your quest?"

"I've been so occupied with my studies that I'm embarrassed to say I haven't gotten very far."

Kubo stood up. "Please forgive me but I must go. I have much to do. Allow me, however, to offer a bit of advice, unrelated to Arabs or *yakuza*. News you would prefer not to hear but surely knew would one day come will arrive shortly. You must say *oos* and do your duty, as painful as it may be."

Jonathan bowed, remaining calm on the outside. Inside, his guts had just tied themselves into a knot.

He drove home, pushing the speed limit the entire way. But it wasn't fast enough. Nanami had already left to join her family at a private residence in San Francisco. It would be three days before he would see her again and he dreaded the waiting. But even more, he dreaded what she might tell him when she got home.

As it turned out, Jonathan only had to wait one night. The doorbell chimed as he sat on the sofa trying to study but having to reread everything two or three times. He opened the door to find a surprise – Kiyoshi Yoritomo, Nanami's brother. Jonathan's face lit up. He gave his best friend a bearhug, but got a lukewarm squeeze in return. "You should have told me you were coming," Jonathan said, trying to sound cheerful.

"I tried to tell you guys," started Kiyoshi, "do not get your hopes up. It would never be allowed."

"What?"

"Our uncle ordered Nana to marry some asshole," said Yoritomo, his lips curling. "Rich, supposedly direct lineage to some old tyrant but still an asshole and I told him so."

"Where is she?"

"With our family in San Francisco but we will all fly back to Japan in the morning. I was sent to pick up her things and to give you the bad news... and this," he said, handing Jonathan an envelope.

"Can I see her... to say goodbye?"

Kiyoshi shook his head.

Chapter Eleven

While Nanami's perfume still hung faintly in the air, Jonathan packed his clothes, books, photos, and remaining handful of other items. Her letter had said she hoped he would stay there but he couldn't. It had been their home but now it was just a house.

Jonathan had kept his room at Wilbur, assuming he might occasionally need a place to stay should a member of her family pay her a visit or her father send someone to check things out. So he simply resettled there.

It took a great deal of effort to force himself to get up and go to class the next day, with his mind still struggling to come to terms with what was apparently his new reality. It felt as if the universe had been knocked off its axis. But after a third classmate asked where Nanami was, he went back to his room, changed into his running gear, and headed out.

His mind had always worked best when his body was active. He hadn't realized he had ADHD, hadn't even known there was a term for what he had, until he and Nanami took a class in Abnormal Psychology together. As the professor talked about the symptoms of hyperactivity and attention deficient disorder, Nanami had glanced over and smiled. "Any of this sound familiar?" she had whispered.

By the time his run was over, Jonathan had convinced himself that Nanami would find a way to escape what amounted to an arranged marriage and return to Stanford. Perhaps that was why she had wanted him to stay in their home, because she would be coming back there. Maybe he shouldn't have been so quick to abandon it.

Every day he thought he saw her in the Quad, at the Student Union, walking to or from class, only to have it turn out to be someone with similar hair, build, dress, or gestures. Each day, he checked his post office box, expecting to see a letter from her. And each day, his box was empty, making it increasingly hard to continue to think positively. She had, after all, promised that no one would ever separate them again.

It wasn't her fault, he tried to tell himself. But no one had ever prevented Nanami from doing whatever she wanted before and what she was now doing was remaining in Japan.

Stanford's student store was tucked in behind Tresidder Student Union. Although small, it carried all of the standard food, drinks, and supplies carried in most 7-11s. It was where students lacking their own transportation bought their Sugar Frosted Flakes and Fruit Loops for breakfast, ramen and cans of Chef Boyardee Spaghetti for lunch and dinner, late-night snacks, shampoo, toothpaste, washing machine powder, and the hundred other things struggling students needed, all at an affordable price. Because Stanford students literally came from around the world, the student store also carried a variety of newspapers and magazines from all of the major countries.

Jonathan stopped by the store to purchase a mid-afternoon Coke, needing the sugar and caffeine rush to boost his sagging energy level and wake him up for his next class. He hadn't slept well in days. As he waited in line to pay, the latest copy of *Japan Today* caught his eye. On its cover was Nanami's smiling face.

He bought a copy and read it just outside the door, giving him a more recent look at the man whom the article described as her "dashing young knight." He didn't look dashing to Jonathan. In fact, Akemi hadn't aged well since he had done his microfiche search a year earlier. There was a dark puffiness around his eyes that hadn't been there before, likely from heavy drug or alcohol abuse. Kiyoshi had been right, he looked like a jerk. As he jogged toward his next class, Jonathan couldn't help but believe once more that she would be coming back to him.

Soon, Jonathan couldn't go into the student store, the library, campus bookstore, or any of the local Japanese markets without seeing her face... and that of Akemi Nakatomi. The Japanese people were apparently smitten with the story and thrilled by the prospect of an impending royal wedding. The country's magazines and newspapers featured her or them almost daily on their covers, while attempting to outdo each other with the most gushing headlines. *The World's Sweetest Couple!*, *The Betrothal of the Century!*, *World's Most Beautiful Face!* She had to be as sick of it by now as he was.

After another three weeks of no word, no appetite, and no sleep, Jonathan found himself getting teary-eyed for no apparent reason. A simple scene in a movie, a story in a newspaper or magazine, or an animal lying dead beside the road would cause his eyes to mist.

It took him a couple of days before he recognized the symptoms. He was depressed. Since the affliction was so pervasive on campus, where most students not only burned the candle at both ends but along several spots in the middle as well, the subject of depression had been covered in great detail in his Abnormal Psych class.

But real men didn't have depression, Jonathan chided himself. They toughed it out. And that was what he tried to do. "Snap out of it!" he scolded himself as he slapped his own cheek hard enough to leave a welt.

The Japanese believed that within our minds were three compartments, one where we stored those things we shared with the world; another where we kept what we only shared with our closest family and friends; and yet another where we locked away things we shared with no one. What Jonathan felt he needed was a fourth compartment, one where things could be hidden even from himself.

He obviously had developed what Zen Buddhists called "a runaway mind," a mind that refused to do what was asked of it, like a dog that wouldn't come when called. In hopes of regaining control, Jonathan returned to the daily practice of *zazen*, seated meditation. But focus evaded him. He needed something more physical.

Jonathan assembled the Sasaki bow given him by Dr. Shimizu and nocked his first arrow. He had driven to the range in the early morning, wanting to shoot when no one else would be there. It was so early, however, that a layer of fog still clung to the ground, making visibility more difficult. Squinting to see the black circle in the center of the fifteen-inch straw target, ninety-two feet away, Jonathan drew back his arrow and aligned its tip.

He separated thumb and forefinger, releasing the bamboo shaft. When he looked to see where it had hit, he saw the arrow imbedded two rings to the left of the bull's eye. He had missed badly. Of all the bow's supposedly superior benefits – its design and stronger, longer-lasting Kevlar strings – the only one that mattered was its accuracy and it had failed him. Jonathan shot another nine arrows. None hit the bull's-eye. He had never before missed even five out of ten, let alone ten out of ten.

Jonathan gathered up his arrows, calmed himself, and readied his next shot. When it too went wide, he threw down the bow. "Piece of junk!"

"If in your *karate kumite*," came a voice from behind him spinning Jonathan around, "your foot or fist misses its target, do you chop it off?"

"That's different," spat Jonathan, angry that Dr. Shimizu had been spying on him.

"It is the same. The problem is you, not the weapon. When your mind is right, your shots will be right as well." He picked up the bow and shot the remaining nine arrows. All hit the bull's-eye. "You are not centered, my young friend," said the Japanese as he walked to the target to retrieve the arrows. When he turned back around, Jonathan was gone.

Jonathan knew that the problem was not the bow, although it took ten or fifteen minutes before he was willing to admit it. The problem was his continuing inability to focus, the very reason he had turned to *kyudo* for help. But, he decided, it had been a bad choice. Its physical demands were minimal, leaving him unable to leash his runaway mind. In *karate*, the full involvement of both body and mind were critical. Best of all, when someone was trying to hammer or score on you, it was impossible not to focus.

His matches with Ojima had always been so intense, the exchanges so blindingly fast that they demanded an almost total synthesis of mind and body, forging a direct link from eye to muscle to hand or foot. Their fights always accelerated to such a fevered pitch, with arms, legs, and bodies flying, that Jonathan entered *Kancho's* mirrorlike mind or Shimizu *Sensei's* universal connection. The euphoria of that rare and special state would sweep over him and Ojima and they would start laughing, causing the students to look on mystified.

But he couldn't return to *karate* class, at least not yet. There would be too many questions and he didn't trust himself emotionally to train among other people, especially Ojima. He might start crying or unleash his building anger on others.

Although he couldn't practice *kumite* or sparring alone, he could practice his *kata* or forms. In fact, solitary practice had always been one of *kata's* major benefits. While performing each of the precisely defined movements, Jonathan had been trained to fill his entire body with consciousness as if it were air filling a balloon, making him simultaneously aware of the placement of every joint, the tension within every muscle, the sensations along every square inch of skin. Such a level of mental involvement left no room for thoughts of anything additional, including lost loves. So that is what he turned to.

Every day Jonathan practiced each of the four *kata* he needed for advancement in rank to *nidan*, second-degree black belt. He ran through each ten times per day, five in the morning and five at night – one rep at regular speed, two reps performed one move at a time, another at regular speed, and the fifth with as much power and speed as he could muster.

But in spite of all the workouts, depression and sleeplessness continued to hound him. His response was to double his number of daily reps. Although he had never voiced it, Jonathan had always secretly believed he could not only work his way out of most illnesses but his lifetime of hard, regular workouts had made him impervious. His worsening downward spiral in the face of it all had shattered that theory. If he could just get a good night's rest, he thought, everything would be okay again.

The Stanford Student Health Center was open around the clock for walk-ins. During the day, students and faculty could also make appointments to be seen by a specialist from the hospital. Not wanting to run into anyone he might know, Jonathan waited until just before eleven that night and paid them a visit. But instead of simply giving him some pills to help him sleep, as he expected, a nurse showed him into an examination room, where he was soon joined by a doctor. Jonathan recognized him immediately. He was a low-ranking *karate* student and psychiatry resident. *Good*, thought Jonathan. *This should make it easier.*

But if the doctor knew who he was, he didn't show it. "What brings you in tonight?"

"I'm having trouble sleeping."

"Why is that?"

"School. Family. School. Did I mention school?"

After checking his vital signs, the doctor sat down and studied Jonathan for several seconds. "Let me ask you a few questions."

Jonathan exhaled loudly. "I can't sleep. It has nothing to do with my relationship with my mother."

The doctor chuckled. "Then you came to the right place. We're not big on psychoanalysis here. Stanford's orientation is more behavioral in nature. We believe most problems have their basis in straight S-R issues or chemical imbalances generated by them, such as too much stress or too little sleep."

"Meaning what?"

"If your system gets so run down that you can't sleep, we help you identify the cause and recommend something – perhaps a behavioral change, perhaps medication – that will help you get things back to normal."

"Makes sense."

"But another couple of questions first. Is there a reason you haven't been to *karate* in a few weeks?"

"Too much schoolwork."

The doctor nodded. "And how's that going… your schoolwork?"

Jonathan shrugged.

"I take that to mean it's not going well or not as well as it was? How's your relationship with your family?"

"I have none. They all died when I was young."

The doctor pressed the tips of his fingers together and gave that some thought. Although Jonathan fought it, for some reason he couldn't explain, his eyes began to mist and the doctor noticed it.

"Have you ever had any thoughts of suicide?"

"No," Jonathan lied. It had occurred to him on a couple of recent occasions but had always been rejected.

"What you have is very common, here anyway. I'm going to give you some pills that will help you through it. Take one the same time each day with a meal. Never, I repeat, never take more than one in any given day."

Jonathan unlocked his door and strode straight into the bathroom, screwing the cap off the pill jar as he went. He had checked out the red capsules on the way home and was shocked to find they looked exactly like those the doctor had given his mother. Was that an omen? Was she calling him home? Between that and the doctor's strong warning not to take more than one, which had surprisingly had the exact opposite effect on him than the doctor surely intended, Jonathan wanted to flush them down the toilet before he could change his mind. Tilting the jar over the commode, the capsules began their slide. At the last instant, he swung his hand over and caught all but two in his cupped palm.

Jonathan stood lost in thought, trying to decide whether to dump or keep the handful of pills. After a minute or longer of reflection, he slid the remaining eight capsules back into the container, screwed on the top, and stowed the jar in his medicine cabinet.

Chapter Twelve

Finals began the next week and Jonathan's mind was kept occupied with finishing up three late term papers and preparing for his exams. Neither went as well as he would have liked, but both probably went far better than they could have, given the circumstances.

Just ten minutes into the last of his five finals, a long Scientific Statistics test, one of the students turned in his answer sheet and left. Jonathan was only on the third question. But even though things like that happened at Stanford, it still left him feeling a little inadequate. Regardless of how smart a person might be, or thought he was, there was always someone at Stanford, often many someones, who were smarter.

Twenty minutes later, he turned in his sheet, making him the fourth person to finish. The early genius and two women had beaten him; the first by a lot and the others only by minutes.

His mind was five thousand one hundred thirty-nine miles away, the distance between Stanford and Tokyo, as he headed down the hallway toward the men's room. The instant he opened the door, however, his mind cleared, his training kicked in, and his body catapulted backwards. There was blood on the walls, on the counter, and inside the white porcelain sinks. Cracks spiraled outward like a spiderweb from where a heel stomped the center of the mirror.

Jonathan peeked around the door jamb. The student who had finished early was lying on the floor, dark blood pooling around deep, ugly cuts in his wrists. A crescent-shaped shard of glass, identical to one missing from the mirror, lay on the counter, next to the bloody sink.

Kneeling beside the young man, Jonathan checked for a pulse and found one, although it was very faint. He now had a dilemma – should he take his time and honor what must have been a difficult decision and an even more difficult act? Or should he attempt to save him? Considering how quickly he had left the test, Jonathan decided the young man had likely made a snap decision. If given more thought, he might have made a very different one.

He ripped his handkerchief in two and tied one half around one of the student's cut wrists and the second around the other. Grabbing his arm, he started to pick him up but quickly ditched that idea when he realized how out of shape he was and how far he might have to carry him. Instead, he left the student where he had found him and ran to find a phone.

A group of students were gathered for their weekly study hall in a nearby lunchroom. In unison, they pointed toward a phone on the back wall and Jonathan called the Stanford Hospital. The dispatcher told him an ambulance would be there in ten minutes.

"He may not last that long," Jonathan said.

"I'll try my best, sir, but they're all tied up with other emergencies."

As he waited in the restroom for the ambulance crew to arrive, Jonathan was struck by the peaceful look on the young man's face. There was no sign of pain, as if he had moved beyond it. Blond and similarly built, he could have been his brother.

A campus security officer jogged up. Close on her heels was a pair of medics, pulling a gurney. "Begin CPR," said one of the two men. His partner knelt on the floor beside the student and quickly cleared his airway. Jonathan had heard of CPR but it was still being introduced into Japan when he left so he had never seen it performed before.

Just as the medic was positioning his palms over the student's chest to begin, the security officer stepped between them. "Please follow me," she said, "I need to ask you some questions." The woman led him out into the hallway, where she could take his statement.

"Can you tell me the victim's name?" she asked.

"I have no idea. I just came out of a test and found him here."

The ambulance crew maneuvered their gurney through the narrow door. "Will he be okay?" Jonathan asked as they wheeled him away. The sad shake of the medic's head confirmed what he had feared.

A maintenance crew ambled past the medics and into the men's bathroom, where they quickly replaced the mirror. As soon as they were done, a team of janitors went immediately to work, cleaning up the blood without comment or reaction, stoically going about their duties as if they had done it a million times.

By the time Jonathan was allowed to leave, the restroom looked like new. No one who wandered in to use the toilet or wash their hands would ever suspect that someone had recently taken his own life there. The final act of a very brave or very weak or very unstable young man had been completely erased. Soon, except for a handful of friends and relatives, his memory will be erased as well, as if he had never existed. *You cannot allow that to happen to you,* Jonathan told himself.

Chapter Thirteen

A fist pounded on Jonathan's door. It was so insistent that he snatched up his pistol, tucked his hand behind his back, and peeked out to see Ojima waiting impatiently in the hallway. It had been a couple of months since they had seen each other, putting Jonathan a little on edge. A lot could change in two months, as he well knew.

"Get *gi*!" ordered his *sensei*.

"Why?"

"Come! Much work."

Jonathan grabbed his bag and the two hurried down the stairs. On their way to the gym, the Japanese explained what was so important – he had just received word that *karate's* first true world championship would be held in less than a year.

Although he suspected the tournament was mainly an attempt by Ojima to get him out of his depression, Jonathan didn't care. The thought of possibly competing at such a historic and significant event, against the best in the world, excited him and he threw himself fully into his preparation.

The World Union of Karate-do Organizations (WUKO), which would host the first championship in Tokyo the following October and a second in Paris two years later, was the brainchild of an unlikely pair – top French attorney and judoka Jacques Delcourt and Japanese industrialist Ryoichi Sasakawa. The Frenchman, while still a teenager, had been an officer in the French Resistance. The Japanese had been arrested as a War Criminal at war's end, reportedly for running indoor boat races on which spectators bet money. He was eventually released without charges, although rumors continued to swirl for years that Sasakawa had had *yakuza* connections early in his life. If so, it was never proven and soon forgotten. Most people came to only know Ryoichi Sasakawa as a generous, dignified man who donated billions to world charities.

Each country was invited to enter seven competitors in sparring – five in team *kumite* and two in individual – and two competitors in *kata*, or forms. There would be no weight or belt divisions. Things would be as on the street, man against man – literally and figuratively as women were not invited to participate. With the full support of the major national and international *karate* organizations, the event was guaranteed to assemble the world's top competitors for the first time in one venue.

To make the team, Jonathan knew he would have to qualify in *kumite*, or sparring. There was no way he could make it in *kata*. Those slots would be dominated by people far shorter than him. In sparring, height was an asset, if a fighter knew how to use it. In *kata*, it was a liability. The longer one's arms, legs, and torso, the harder it became to prevent slight deviations in angle to be magnified by the longer length of a limb. So shorter people had an advantage.

Being slim, genetically gifted by a father and grandfather who were champion athletes, and standing over six feet tall, Jonathan had good reach, low body weight, and great speed from a preponderance of fast-twitch muscle fiber – a potentially winning combination if used wisely. *Kancho* had always said a person couldn't be smaller, slower, and dumber and expect to defeat anyone. "You cannot control who is larger or faster as those are determined by genetics and luck. But you can control who is smarter, tactically and strategically, in the same way that you can control the moves within a game of chess or *go*."

Smart fighters, as Sun Tzu had pointed out centuries earlier, intimately knew their own strengths and weaknesses – physical, mental, and spiritual – in minute detail. They also possessed the ability to quickly assess those of anyone they faced.

Jonathan had learned that whereas most people thought they knew themselves well, few did in fact. It was common for opponents to think themselves strong in areas where they were actually weak and weak in areas where they were actually strong. This prevented them from ever taking full advantage of their strengths or utilizing proper precautions to prevent their weaknesses from being used against them. While a student at the Kami Kan, Kubo had meticulously pointed out Jonathan's every strength and weakness repeatedly, ensuring he knew both to an often painful and sometimes embarrassing degree.

Besides the neutralization techniques Jonathan had been taught to enable him to capitalize on his knowledge of himself and that of his opponents, Ojima had added extensively to the list. So even if he didn't know every single trick in the book, he knew a fair percentage of them. But what Jonathan really lacked was tournament experience. There was a huge difference between knowing what to do and being able to do it spontaneously, especially under high-pressure conditions. And with only six months remaining before team selection began, that weakness had to be remedied quickly.

A small local tournament, hosted by one of Ojima's former Japanese teammates, gave him his first chance.

Hiding his nervousness, Jonathan crossed the San Mateo High School gym and seated himself in the far corner. As he stretched, he could see the other black belts glancing his way. Everyone seemed to know everyone else, which meant they had all likely fought each other many times before.

Jonathan hoped he would be called last so he'd have a chance to watch each of them fight before facing them himself. But that wasn't to be. It turned out they were all students of the host instructor and he had stacked the deck. Not only did he structure the matches to better insure one of his fighters won, he did it in such a way as to increase the likelihood they would make a clean sweep.

Jonathan assumed he would be paired first with their weakest competitor. If they risked their best in the first round and he lost, the championship could go to an outsider. Better to save their best to fight him, if he turned out to be any good, in the finals. And he was right. The first match was with someone slow and clumsy. Jonathan could have easily finished the man in a matter of seconds. Instead, he chose to take his time, using far less than his usual speed and employing only his most basic tactics and techniques, not wanting to give any useful information to the other competitors.

His second opponent was tougher. The stocky man came out with the intention of making quick work of him, obviously encouraged by what he had seen in Jonathan's first match. This forced Jonathan to dig a bit deeper in order to eke out a win by a *waza ari*, a half-point.

Jonathan also led the next match by a half-point as they neared the end of the regulation two-minute period. With the clock ticking and everyone in the gym screaming his opponent's name, the man recklessly hurled his body toward Jonathan. As he fell, his fingertips slid across Jonathan's shoulder. The host, who had refereed all of the black-belt matches, awarded a half-point to his fighter for the worthless technique, evening the score. Ojima howled in protest but Jonathan showed no re-action. He was used to bad calls. Almost every match he had fought in Japan had been filled with them. So he merely waited for the match to end and the sudden-death overtime period to begin.

Having already gone two minutes with his opponent, Jonathan be-lieved he could predict what he would do next. But to his credit, the man dug down to the bottom of his limited arsenal and came out with a pleasant surprise, a slow spinning back-kick. As he rotated, Jonathan slid inside the curl of his leg and scored the winning point with a punch to the back of his neck. It was so clean that even the biased referee couldn't ignore it.

With only a handful of black-belt competitors, the win put Jonathon into the finals, where he would face the school's best. Believing his fight-er could easily handle what he had seen in Jonathan thus far, the host made a magnanimous gesture – he invited Ojima to referee the finals.

Jonathan hadn't been given an opportunity to watch the man fight. Normally a competitor was only allowed one bye, which enabled him to advance to the next round without fighting, owing to an odd number of competitors. But this guy had drawn three byes. He had sat stretching throughout the preliminary matches, enabling him to closely watch each of Jonathan's fights.

"Carl and Jonathan!" called the event stager. The two men rose and headed toward the eight-meter by eight-meter square ring that had been taped onto the gym's hardwood floor. Just before entering the ring, Carl's instructor whispered something into his ear, something that made him chuckle.

It was only when they toed their starting lines that Jonathan saw how much bigger Carl was. He not only had a good seventy-five pounds on him, he was at least three inches taller. Someone in the line had earlier commented that Carl was a San Francisco cop and Jonathan believed it. He looked and moved like one, with an overriding air of confidence.

Ojima chopped his hand downward and yelled "*Hajime!*" starting the match.

Carl slid forward, cautiously closing the gap between them. But as *Kancho* had taught him, Jonathan slid back, always staying just out of range. A long-legged kick sent Jonathan to the edge of the ring. His opponent immediately launched another, obviously wanting to drive him out of bounds. By tournament rules, the first time a competitor crossed the boundary line, a warning, known as a *jogai*, was issued. The second time, his opponent received a half-point. For a third exit, his opponent received a full point and was declared the winner. Instead of going out of bounds, however, Jonathan evaded the kick by circling out, then launching a kick of his own. The big man jumped to avoid it and crossed the line himself.

The two were lined back up on their starting marks, where Carl stood fuming, hands defiantly on his hips, as Ojima stabbed his finger at the boundary line and called "*jogai*, warning!"

When the match was restarted, Carl pressed forward, having lost some of his initial wariness. But Jonathan continued to evade him, backing or circling away from every technique he initiated. After another full minute of this, Carl had lost all caution, clearly convinced that Jonathan was afraid to engage him.

He strode straight forward, closing the gap, thinking only of what he was going to do with Jonathan. The instant he hit his set-point, that split second of complete stoppage before launching an attack, Jonathan lunged forward, scoring with a perfectly timed punch to the man's face.

"*Yame*! Stop!" ordered Ojima, directing the two back onto their starting marks. His arm swung diagonally up in Jonathan's direction, giving him an *ippon*, or full point. "*No kachi*! Winner!"

A gasp went through the host, his students, and spectators alike. Jonathan's opponent was livid. "Just you and me!" Carl yelled as Jonathan bowed and backed out of the ring. The man strode across the ring to confront him but Ojima stepped into his path and chucked him in the chest with both hands, knocking him back.

"You lose!" spat Ojima. "Leave ring or we fight… just you, me!"

The host ran into the ring and pulled his fighter away. The man glared at Ojima, who only smiled and crooked his finger, inviting him to come on if he wanted a fight.

As the top three finishers in black-belt division were called up to receive their awards, Carl grabbed his bag and strode toward the exit, refusing to accept his second-place trophy. Ojima laughed at him, then at his friend, who had finally figured out that he had been outsmarted.

"You asked to be kept informed of Kami Lusk's progress," said Aoshima.

Kancho Kubo looked up from the report he was reading.

"He easily won his first three tournaments. But they were regional events. He never faced any among the country's best. So the results are not significant."

"*Domo*, Aoshima San," said Kubo." When will the selection be made?"

"Those considered will be invited to one of seven training locations around the country. His will be held north of San Francisco at the *dojo* of a *Kyokushin* instructor. After these sessions are completed, those in charge of each site will submit their recommendations."

Kubo nodded.

"Should I contact Lusk San and inform him to remove his name?" asked the senior aide.

"Not yet. It may soon become unnecessary and the training will surely enhance his skills while also refocusing his mind off his sorrow. If he is selected, then we must inform him that he cannot continue."

In the end, Jonathan had far less chance of making the team than even he, his *sensei*, and *Kancho* realized. The team had been set long before the team selection workouts even began, and perhaps rightfully so. The best fighters Jonathan trained with in the special sessions were in awe of those already selected, fighters like Frank Smith, Tonny Tulleners, James Yabe, and John Gehlsen, all extremely strong and highly experienced. Men whom Jonathan found difficult opponents at the training sessions had all lost to those on the team.

Even though he was disappointed that he hadn't been selected, Jonathan understood – he wasn't yet good enough to deserve a spot. The next world championship would be held in Paris in 1972. With two more years to prepare, he believed he had as strong a shot as anyone.

Across the Pacific, Kubo was relieved too, although he hid his true feelings when Jonathan called to give him results he already knew. But the following Monday, both men got a surprise that pleased one but not the other. WUKO announced that because of the larger number of potential competitors in the two countries, Japan would be allowed to enter five teams and the United States, four. Jonathan had been named to the USA's C-Team.

It was still dark outside when *Kancho* called to inform Jonathan that he was not to compete, period. It was too risky. He was to withdraw his name, giving too much schoolwork as an excuse. Although Jonathan was crushed to have his hopes raised so high, then dashed before the day was even out, he was a Kami and heard himself say "*Oos.*"

Kazio Zuma looked up from the sheet of WUKO stationery. On it was a list of countries and competitors' names. "Could this possibly be the same Jonason Lusk?" Zuma asked his lieutenant.

"I do not know but have requested our contact inside FAJKO supply us with a photograph and more detailed information. America is so large, many have the same name."

"If there is a chance it is him, send one of the Los Angeles *koban* to verify it."

"Ojima is reportedly the man's *sensei*. Those who last attempted to reason with him were severely beaten."

"Does his mother and grandmother still live in Yokohama?"

"*Hai.*"

Chapter Fourteen

With Nanami in Japan, perhaps out of his life forever, and his dream of competing at the world championships on hold for at least another two years, there seemed no better time to settle the issue of his father's death.

Whereas Zuma's involvement in the death of his grandfather was all but irrefutable, as he had admitted it himself, Makram's was not. Except for the day of the explosion when he had clearly been drunk and in a rage, Dr. Makram had always been a kind, soft-spoken man. His son, Saied, had been his best friend and Jonathan had come to understand just how special that relationship had been. Had Dr. Makram been an unwitting accomplice in the bombing? Had he been set up or forced to plant it? Or had he and his father simply misjudged Dr. Makram back then? Had he always been a terrorist at heart? Jonathan's first task would be to clear up the question of his guilt or innocence.

Unlike Stanford's Cecil Green Library, which closed at nine each night and reopened at eight the next morning, the university's new J. Henry Meyer Memorial Library never closed. Jonathan began spending so much time there that one of the librarians joked that he should bring a cot. Buried deep in the Arab Studies racks, he tracked down every article and book in their collection on Yusuf Makram. Most of it was in Arabic. But, thankfully, *Kancho* Kubo had anticipated Jonathan's need to one day read and speak the language and had required him to study Arabic at both the Dai and Kami Kan, and to continue his studies at Stanford.

The most helpful of the many pieces on Makram was a biography entitled *The Pure Fedai*. In it, Jonathan learned that the prosperous Makram family, or *aeleh*, went back ten generations in the low hills surrounding the small Palestinian village of Deir Yassin. There, they had grown olives and produced what was considered the best olive oil in the region.

What had put Yusuf Makram's name on the world map, however, had nothing to do with olives or terror or even Palestinian or Arab issues; it was his economics book, *Breaking the Chains of Generational Poverty*, which outlined what economists considered a brilliant solution to reducing poverty in third-world countries. Quickly becoming the definitive work on the subject, it earned Makram consideration for a Nobel Prize, although he was ultimately beaten out by high-profile Harvard economist Daniel Lusk, Jonathan's father.

Every major educational institution had wanted Makram on its faculty – including Harvard, Stanford, Yale, MIT, Berkeley, Centre d'économie de la Sorbonne, Cambridge, Oxford, and London School of Economics – and each wooed him in earnest. In the end, Makram decided on Cairo University. In Egypt, he could remain closer to home, making his wife happy, and share his knowledge with other Arabs, making his father happy.

But a surprise visitor changed his mind. The same Dr. Daniel Lusk, dean of the Harvard Department of Economics, did more than merely send an invitation and another offer of huge sums of money, a beautiful house, and important committee positions; he had crossed the ocean and endured the hot, dusty drive to his front door in hopes of convincing Yusuf Makram to join his handpicked staff of top economists.

"How could I refuse such an offer from such a man?" Makram was quoted in the book as saying. "And how did I thank this great man, who believed so much in me and my solution to this problem?" Makram reportedly asked the writer. "I was responsible for his death."

The comment caught Jonathan by surprise. His father's killer was admitting his guilt. Disappointingly, however, nothing further was said to either clarify his statement or supply any additional details about the bombing. What he did do was talk a lot about what happened afterwards. In fact, Makram was clearly very proud of himself for overcoming the many difficulties he had faced while attempting to leave the country. According to him, these challenges changed him from being just a simple college professor to a true *fedai*, willing to sacrifice himself for the Palestinian people.

During the intervening fourteen years, Yusuf Makram had worked his way up within the PLO, reaching a position of prominence before a bitter break with them to create his own organization, the Heroic Fighters for the Freedom of Palestine, HFFP. He was never able to discover the cause of the rift. But the two organizations were now violent enemies.

For Jonathan to travel to the Middle East and attempt to speak directly with him without first doing more research could be suicidal. He would return to Boston, where it all began. Then, depending on what he found, his next step would be to track Makram down and either speak with or to kill him. And, Jonathan told himself, *If God wants to take my life, He will have a great opportunity. But He will have to dirty His hands.*

Chapter Fifteen

It felt strange walking down Limewood Drive, Jonathan's old street, not knowing what he would find or how it would affect him. But his old house was exactly as he remembered it, still a spotless white, the yard immaculately groomed. It was as if nothing had changed.

Through the windows, he could see a man, woman, and young boy and girl talking and laughing at the kitchen table. He studied them with a tinge of envy. That should have been his family in there.

Jonathan steeled himself as he drove to where he remembered the Levys' house was located, where his father had died and his mother's death shoved into motion. But it wasn't where he thought. Many of the facts had shifted or grown fuzzier in his mind in the years since the explosion. Plus he had only been six.

It was deep in the *Boston Globe's* archives that Jonathan found some of the missing pieces. Since only the last five years had been put on microfiche, he had to read through a tall stack of yellowed back issues for the months of April and May, 1948.

Several articles and op-ed pieces discussed the explosion. From them, Jonathan learned times, names, addresses, and details he had forgotten or never known. But what he most wanted to know was still missing – clear facts about who was responsible. Although no one knew for sure, there was no shortage of theories. The main one, of course, was that Makram intentionally delivered the bomb with the goal of killing as many Jews as possible. Nine people had died immediately, eight of whom were Jews. Besides his father's, the only names he recognized were Dr. and Mrs. Levy, their daughter Sarah, and Dwayne Ackerman. Four others died soon thereafter from their injuries, all Jews, which meant they hadn't counted his mother among them.

The second most popular theory was that Makram had been used, the bomb planted unknowingly in his briefcase by a Palestinian operative. From there, the theories got bizarre, some a little and some a lot.

A couple tried to implicate Jonathan's father as some kind of activist. He had, after all, gone to Palestine to recruit Makram, one writer argued, which was when he had been swayed to their side, if he hadn't been there already. Another argued that he had gone outside that night to get the briefcase from Makram so he could plant it inside the Levys' house, only to die himself when it went off prematurely, giving him what the writer thought he deserved.

Using the address included in one of the articles, Jonathan located the Levys' old home in Harvard University's faculty housing section. It looked vastly different. The front of the house had been completely rebuilt and the place turned into a campus daycare center.

Dad was standing right here, Jonathan told himself as he positioned his feet over the spot where he remembered his father standing when the bomb exploded. He shivered. It felt as if bits of his father's flesh and bone still littered the surrounding earth, lawn, trees, and bushes. He knew it was impossible that anything physical could actually remain after so many years. But he could definitely feel the presence of his spirit.

Jonathan didn't know what to say to his father's *kami*. There was much he wanted to explain, much to ask. But even though his father had been in his thoughts every day since the bomb had torn his family apart, Jonathan realized that as a man he really didn't know his father very well. So he told him what had happened since leaving Boston. He told him of his grandfather, Eli, and Reiko and Nanami and Hiroko and how sorry he was for not taking better care of his mother.

Tears flowed unashamedly down his cheeks as Jonathan drove across town. He parked just across the street from the Hotel La Fleur, where he and his mother had spent their last few months, where she had died, blind and disfigured by the same bomb that had killed his father.

The area was far worse than he remembered – or maybe it had simply gotten worse since he last saw it. The streets were strewn with garbage. Plywood and wrought-iron bars covered the windows of the pawnshops, bars, liquor stores, massage parlors, and sex shops. Pimps, winos, prostitutes, hustlers, and drug addicts lined the streets. Jonathan made a wide swath around two men fighting with knives. One slashed the other across his bare chest. His dark skin pulled sharply apart, creating a wide diamond-shaped cut on his left breast that looked almost as if he were wearing a red farmer's kerchief.

Jonathan passed the war-surplus store, where he had gone the day he sneaked outside. It was still open and exactly as he remembered it – the frizzy-headed plastic bird still dipping its beak into the water glass, the false teeth still chattering.

When he reached the steamy grate where his mother had stood, blind and crying hysterically for her missing son, the image of her face popped as clear in his mind as if she were actually standing there – her bright red lipstick smeared unevenly across her lips, the pasty white makeup that she had thickly applied but was still not thick enough to cover the pink scars zig-zagging across her eyes and cheeks. Until that instant, his mother's face had always appeared to him as merely a pale oval with blonde hair resting on a pair of frail shoulders. But the setting had thrown open previously closed doors in his mind, no longer holding anything back, presenting him with the full extent of the damage the bomb had done.

Jonathan's gut clinched and nausea swept through him. It had been his fault, but not his fault. As a man, he understood it better than he had as a child. But it was no less painful. For an inquisitive romp down the street, he had made her leave the shielded safety of her room, to blindly face what he wasn't completely comfortable facing even as a sighted man and a Tamashii Kami.

The Hotel La Fleur had deteriorated from a pre-burial dumping ground for senior citizens into a flophouse. Hookers brought their customers there for cold passionless sex. Winos took rooms to sleep off their drunkenness as did addicts to shoot up.

The elevator reeked of a combination of beer, urine, and vomit, forcing Jonathan to fill his lungs and hold his breath as he stepped inside. The lift obviously hadn't been repaired, or likely even inspected, since he and his mother had stayed at the La Fleur. Other than the smell, the only difference was that it dropped two feet instead of just one before starting upward.

By the time the elevator's doors slid open at the third floor, Jonathan's face was red from lack of oxygen. He leaped into the hallway, sucking in a lungful of air only to discover that it didn't smell much better. Hurrying across the frayed carpet toward their old room, 327, Jonathan heard the sounds of drunks snoring and lusty couples rhythmically rattling beds.

His chest tightened as he slid in the key and opened the door, half expecting to see his mother still sitting in her window chair. But there was no chair. The room, in fact, was almost empty, only a cheap iron-framed bed and a white particle board dresser. The once heavy drapes that had covered the sole window, keeping the room in perpetual darkness, had been replaced by a curled mini blind that did just the opposite.

Jonathan's eyes were drawn to the corner of the room, where the old rosewood bed had stood and where he had hidden the night she slapped him, the night before she died. The sensations from that night returned – the sting of the blow, the metallic taste of blood, the lump in his throat, the screech of her voice in the darkness.

Brief flashes of memories flooded his mind like a quick-cut movie. The explosion. The hospital. Trying to shake his mother awake. The funeral. Tossing the white flower onto her muddy coffin. He couldn't stand it and ran out of the room and down the stairs.

The air outside was putrid and laden, each breath bringing with it even more vile, long-forgotten images. As Jonathan strode toward his car, he renewed his vow to find the truth and, if demanded, extract retribution.

Chapter Sixteen

"**C**an I buy you dinner and *sake*?" Jonathan asked Ojima after class ended and the last student had left. His question brought a smile to his *sensei's* hardened face.

They went to Katsuo Sushi, popular with expats for its home-style food, old-country service, and, if a local Japanese newspaper write-up could be believed, the Bay Area's best selection of *sake*.

The young Japanese waitress brought them an expensive bottle of rice wine and a pot of *cha*. Ojima was clearly smitten with the young woman, but she was clearly smitten with Jonathan, who didn't seem to notice.

"*Kampai!*" said Ojima, raising his tiny glass in a salute before downing it. He smacked his lips and stared at his cup. "*Domo, domo*, Jonason San. I never *sake* so fine."

Jonathan returned the toast with his cup of *cha*. "I'm pleased," he said, smiling as the Japanese polished off another cup, then another.

"I've never asked how much you know about me?"

Ojima's eyes narrowed to serious slits. "Everything. You brother. You *tomodachi*. No need know more."

"But what about my years in Japan? What do you know of that?"

"Ah, *wakarimasu*," he grunted. "You Kami. Before, you student at Dai Kan. You friend Yoritomo Kiyoshi and boyfriend his sister. Imperial princess grandmother adopt you. Grandfather famous man, murdered by *yakuza*."

Jonathan reacted. "Do you know that for sure?"

"*Hai*. Bad stepfather *shatei*, like *yakuza* white belt, when I small boy. One day, he come home, very drunk... like celebration. He say he and one more *shatei* throw *gaijin* judge from building roof... far high."

"Do you know who gave the order?" Jonathan asked, excited to perhaps finally get independent confirmation.

"His name Zuma. He *wakagashira*… ah…"

"First lieutenant?"

"*Hai*. He first lieutenant, like most high underboss. Now he *oyabun*."

"Are you sure it was my grandfather they threw?"

"He say same man who hang Murakami *Oyabun*… not Murakami you kill, father. Now, *yakuza* pay much *yen* you dead."

"So by 'everything', you mean everything."

The Japanese bowed.

"The money does not tempt you? It would make you a wealthy man."

"Money is for merchants. I not *samurai* but maybe *ronin*. You *tomodachi*. Treat me like brother, no matter my bad past. I die before harm come to you, *neh*?"

Jonathan sipped his tea as Ojima finished the jar of warm rice wine.

"I must leave soon to honor my *giri* to my father. I might need to ask a favor of you."

"No need ask. I come."

"*Domo* but I must do this alone. There is, however, also the matter of my grandfather's murder. It is also my *giri* to ensure that debt is settled."

"Ah…*wakarimasu*."

"If I return, I will handle it myself. But if I don't return, then I would ask you to consider becoming my *kaishaku* for this man in Japan, this Zuma."

"I most honored," he said bowing. "But Kami achieve same more better?"

Jonathan shook his head. "They can only use legal methods. For this man, that will not work. I suspect *Kancho* Kubo, my mentor and Kami head… but you probably knew that?"

Ojima smiled, making Jonathan smile too.

"*Kancho* surely knows who is responsible but has not been able to deal with him in all these years."

"For me, your grandfather, he become like *Daimyo* Asano and I like forty-seven *ronin*. I one man but fight like forty-seven, *neh*?" Ojima let out a big laugh at the ridiculousness of his comparison.

Jonathan didn't find it out of line. Ojima could fight better than anyone he had ever met, even at the Kami Kan. He bowed. "Among those I know, here and in Japan, you will be honored as such."

Ojima bowed formally. "You *gaijin* but more strong, more *tamashii* than all Japanese I ever train with. We brothers, *neh*?"

Jonathan nodded. "*Hai*, brothers and *tomodachi*."

A loud drunken laugh pulled their attention to the next table, where a middle-aged American businessman sat with a Japanese associate. The young Japanese waitress stood beside them, pen and pad in hand, to take their orders.

"How come I don't see flied lice on menu?" the man exclaimed in a fake Asian accent, then laughed.

"I am sorry, sir," answered the waitress. "That is a Chinese dish. This is a Japanese restaurant."

"No argue with guest. You number ten waitress," he said, laughing even louder, embarrassing his Japanese companion and making the other customers shoot him dirty looks.

"May I recommend the beef teriyaki, sir? It is one of our most popular dishes."

"Okay, sweetheart, I'll take your word for it. But bring us some real glasses. I'm sick of drinking from these thimbles. It'd take a real man a month to get a decent buzz on."

As the waitress left to turn in their orders, Jonathan could see that Ojima's dark eyes were locked onto the man.

"Van *San*," said the *gaijin's* Japanese dinner guest, "she does not understand that you are only joking."

"Sure she does," said Van.

The waitress hurried back with two bowls of *miso* soup. When she bent over to set Van's hot bowl in front of him, his hand reached around behind her. The young woman shot upright, spilling the soup.

"Please forgive me, sir," she pleaded. "I will get a towel and clean up."

He looked at his finger. "While you're at it, you might want to add some oil. Felt a quart low." He laughed to his buddy, who just disgustedly shook his head.

The waitress quickly returned with a towel and wiped the table dry. Van pointed to his lap. "There's a spot you missed down here." Her face reddened as she stood motionless, unsure of what to do. The man took the towel from her hand and reached out to wipe her groin area. "Then how about I do you."

A belly laugh was half out of Van's mouth when Ojima lunged across the few feet between them in a split-second. He hit the big man in the chest with the heel of his hand, then drove him backwards and down onto the floor. Dropping onto his chest, Ojima applied a powerful cross-choke. Van's eyes were bulging, his face growing puffy and bright red by the time Jonathan and the restaurant's owner reached him.

"Please release him or I must call the police," said the owner when they couldn't get the Japanese to turn loose.

"*Sensei*," whispered Jonathan. "Don't let this drunken jerk get you into trouble. He's not worth it."

Slowly, Ojima released his grip and stood up, raising his hands in surrender. As the owner helped his customer to his feet, Van swiped the back of his hand across his nose and looked at the smear of blood. "You stupid Jap," he spat.

In the blink of an eye, a pair of calloused knuckles struck his left cheekbone, cracking it. Jonathan and the owner latched back onto Ojima before he could land a second punch. As they struggled to hold him back, the *sensei's* eyes clearly saw nothing but the *gaijin* in front of him. Even after two other patrons joined forces to help restrain him, several seconds clicked by before Ojima's expression finally softened and he became human again.

Jonathan turned to Van's Japanese companion. "Get your friend out of here." The unfortunate Japanese didn't need to be told twice. He ushered his *gaijin* acquaintance toward the front door, with Van's nose pointing upward to keep it from dripping blood onto his white shirt.

"I'll sue you for every penny you have or ever will have, you and the owner of this dump," screamed Van.

"Hold it right there," said Jonathan. "How old is your waitress?" he asked the owner.

"My granddaughter is sixteen."

Jonathan strode over to the American, snatched his wallet out of his back pocket, and wrote down his name, address, and driver's license number. "If any of us ever runs into you or hears your name again, you will be arrested, charged with sexual assault of a minor, and declared a child molester." Jonathan looked to the girl, "Unless you'd like to charge him right now?"

Her head snapped back and forth. Jonathan looked to the owner. "No," her grandfather agreed. "But we hold open the option to change our minds."

As Van bolted through the door, his companion turned and bowed. "*Gomen nasai.*"

After the two were gone, everyone inside the restaurant – customers and staff alike – clapped for Ojima. The owner shuffled over and bowed almost to his knees. "I thank you for defending my granddaughter."

The *karateka* returned the bow, then bowed to the customers. "I apologize. Too much anger from seeing her bad treatment. I must strive to better control myself."

"Please," said the owner, gesturing toward their table. "Allow me to thank you properly."

As the owner rushed back into the kitchen, Jonathan and his *sensei* retook their seats. Soon, the waitress arrived with a free bottle of their best *sake* and another pot of tea. Ojima glanced sheepishly across the table. "Sometimes I do things not so good," he said.

Jonathan couldn't stop himself from smiling at the contrite look on his face. "Yeah, me too. I do stupid stuff all the time."

The two men looked across the table at each other and began laughing.

Chapter Seventeen

Leaving the country without Ojima accompanying him had not been easy. The Japanese had only relented after Jonathan swore it was merely an intelligence-gathering trip and promised to take him with him if he ever went after Makram in earnest.

It was critical he get this trip right. He would not get a second chance. If anything appeared threatening or amiss, no member of the Makram's family would speak with him and he would come home empty. Ojima was the poster boy for the term 'loose cannon' so there was no way he could take him along.

As Jonathan flew across the United States, then the Atlantic Ocean, and finally the Mediterranean Sea, he studied his notes, re-reading highlighted passages from *The Pure Fedai*, and outlining the steps he would take when he landed in Tel Aviv. His first would be to rent a car and drive the forty-five miles or so to his hotel in Jerusalem. From there, he would head west to Deir Yassin, Makram's ancestral home, and speak with any family members who remained.

But when he arrived in the small village, things didn't go as planned. No one seemed able to understand either his English or his Arabic. Regardless of what he asked, they would shrug their shoulders, shake their heads, and amble off. Since no one in other parts of Israel had any such problems, Jonathan interpreted it to mean that the Makrams were a forbidden topic, at least with outsiders.

On his drive back to Jerusalem, he passed a roadside sign that caught his attention. "Israel's Best Tours! The Old City, Wailing Wall, Dome of the Rock, Deir Yassin Massacre."

The tour guide turned out to be an English-speaking Palestinian named Ehab Deeb. "I am your man, boss. I make your dreams come true," gushed Ehab after Jonathan explained what he wanted to do and what he had experienced so far. Ehab was not only Palestinian, which could open doors clearly closed to him, but he was born and raised in a small town not far from Deir Yassin. The Makrams, according to Ehab, were among his closest friends. Jonathan hired him. If he proved capable of even half of what he claimed, he would be an asset.

Fake papers and the Red Crescent logo on a local Palestinian doctor's license plates had been required to sneak Yusuf and Saied Makram past Jewish roadblocks when they first landed in Transjordan. Jonathan's driver, Ehab, needed no papers and his battered Mercedes sped along the road unchallenged.

"These are the fields where the famous Makram family grew olives for over five hundred years," said his guide as they neared Deir Yassin. "They were good, very good in fact, but not as good as those grown by my family." Ehab pointed. "Ahead you can see the Makram *dar*, the family home built by the famous Doctor Makram's great-grandfather."

The well-maintained, two-storied plaster and stone house sat atop a low rise. Children played in the yard. Women chatted as they washed clothes and hung them on long lines. Instead of slowing to pull into the driveway, as Jonathan expected, his driver kept going.

"Aren't we going to speak with them?"

"If that is what you desire. But why would you want to speak with Jews who stole the Makram *dar* from its rightful owners?"

Makram had spoken in his biography of the outrage he had felt when he arrived in Deir Yassin to find the Israelis had taken his family home for their command center. Soldiers had guarded the entrance and a Star of David flag flown from a newly erected flagpole. Makram's family, according to the book, had relocated to the nearby residence of a cousin. For some reason, Jonathan had just assumed their property had been returned during the interim.

In *The Pure Fedai*, Makram had described the streets as deserted and strewn with rubble. Vultures, crows, and green clumps of flies had taken flight as his car had passed, only to quickly reaffix themselves onto the scattered carcasses of dogs and chickens and goats that spotted the roadside. The small store, where Yusuf had gone as a boy for candy and a cold soda on hot days, had been leveled. Only the sandstone front of the barbershop had remained.

Even though it had been almost twenty years since the war, Jonathan could still see remnants of the heavy fighting that had occurred there. They passed houses, walls, stores, and buildings along the way that were still missing major sections. Huge divots pocked the earth here and there. But the streets and roadways were clean and people walked and rode their bikes and motorcycles freely to and from town.

"Were you able to locate the cousin's house?" Jonathan asked his driver.

"Yes. It is not far."

"And they'll speak with me?"

"Oh, most assuredly."

The guide's black Mercedes pulled onto a rutted dirt driveway that ended in front of a two-storied plaster rectangle. Although the house was larger than most of the others in the area, its residents were equally hard-pressed. His driver could barely get out of the car before an angry man stormed out the front door.

He and Ehab spoke in heated rapid Arabic, so fast that Jonathon missed some of it. But he caught enough – the man said he had told Ehab over the phone that he would not speak with him.

Jonathan tried not to be too concerned. The convention in that part of the world seemed diametrically opposite that in Japan, where conversations even between two worst enemies were always calm and civil. Here best friends seemed to scream at each other.

As the men argued, Jonathan's eyes drifted around the yard, noting the small detached guest quarters, recognizing it from an old photo included in the book.

Ehab pulled out his wallet and offered money, which the Makram cousin pushed indignantly away, then allowed himself to be persuaded to accept.

His name was Amir Makram. His father had been Yusuf's brother. And, thankfully, he spoke good English, having driven a cab in New York for two years. He made it clear right from the start, however, that he neither supported his uncle's politics (but understood them) nor had any contact with him.

"I understand he came here after leaving the United States," Jonathan began. "Do you know anything about what he did here and where he went after he left?"

"He came too late. Had he arrived but one day sooner, he may have been able to do something to save her." Amir shrugged, "Or he may have died too and history changed. I am leaning to the latter."

"You're referring to his wife?"

Amir nodded. "'Where is my Hannah?' These were the first words he uttered when he stepped out of the car. No one wanted to be the one to tell him. But his father…"

"Jorges?"

"Yes, Jorges, his father, pointed at the old servant's quarters, now my son's home," said Amir, himself pointing at the nearby cottage. "'You will find her there,' his father said."

Jonathan had read the story in *The Pure Fedai*. A plain lidless coffin had rested on a low table in the center of the living room. Fearing he would find his wife inside, the crude box, according to Makram, had both pulled him to it and made him want to run. What he hadn't expected was to also find the body of his unborn son. On seeing the two of them, Makram had bolted for the door. His father, however, had slid up behind him and forced him to stay.

"Jorges told him that they had come the preceding night," said Amir, repeating what had been relayed to him through the years by his own father. "A Jew, one of the Irgunist pigs, had passed as she was attempting to reach safety inside the house. Seeing her beauty, he attempted to drag her off for his evil intent. She fought him like a true *fedai*, biting him and scratching at his eyes. The coward shot her in the face and she fell, her life's blood draining into the dirt just over there," he said, pointing toward the front door. "When he saw that she was with child, he ripped open her stomach with his knife. The cut went deep and killed the son she would have borne."

Amir led Jonathan into the small house and showed him where everything had been the day Yusuf Makram arrived. "Incense, many, many sticks, burned everywhere," he said sweeping his arms around the small room. "But the weather was hot and sandalwood, no matter how strong, could not mask the decaying flesh or cloud the image of his beloved wife's body, faceless beneath her thin veil, or the naked purple child in her arms." Amir pointed at the door. "He stumbled outside, away from the horrors of this room, and ran. But he did not get thirty meters before nausea overtook him and sent him to his knees, retching."

Ehab had also lined up a meeting with another member of the Makram family, this one an outcast. Khalid Makram looked so much like his Uncle Yusuf the last time Jonathan had seen him that he thought at first that it was him. It quickly became apparent that Khalid had inherited more than just his uncle's looks; he had also inherited his predisposition for *arak*, the potent Palestinian national drink. It was his addiction, in fact, that had cut Khalid off from the rest of his family and had indirectly prompted him to speak.

Before Jonathan was allowed to ask him any questions, Ehab had to hand over the "contribution" he had promised, a case of *arak*. Khalid ripped open the cardboard box and "tested" one of them. Obviously passing muster, a longer swallow greased his lips and put them into motion, answering whatever Jonathan asked. The longer he spoke and the more he tested, however, the more his words slurred and his eyelids sagged, making him appear exactly as Dr. Makram had when Jonathan saw him at the Levys' party.

"He remained here in Deir Yassin for two more months while his father, his son, and two brothers traveled to Lebanon to join the *fedayeen*," said Khalid.

"Do you know why he didn't go with them? I mean the Israelis were in his house, his wife had been murdered, and he let his son leave? That wasn't like him."

The Palestinian looked away.

"He was drunk," volunteered his guide. "His father refused to allow him to accompany them until he was free of his thirst."

"For good reason!" interjected Khalid defensively. "As you mention, his wife was mutilated. His unborn son also. Any sane man would seek escape from such horror!" Khalid gathered up the box of bottles to leave. "You are a soft American. You know nothing of pain!"

The guide grabbed hold of the box, afraid Khalid hadn't yet fulfilled his end of the deal. The two wrestled for it until Khalid kicked at Ehab's legs. When the guide turned loose, Makram ran unevenly away. "Let him go," said Jonathan. "He can't help us. Hopefully we'll have better luck in Tyre."

Chapter Eighteen

His guide followed what he assured Jonathan were the same roads Yusuf Makram had traveled when he left Deir Yassin to rejoin his family at his Uncle Ahmal's house in the ancient Lebanese coastal city of Tyre. Makram's hot, dusty three-day ride in a mule cart, however, was completed by Jonathan in just over three hours in the air-conditioned comfort of fifteen-year-old German engineering.

His destination, it turned out, was inside what had become the Rashidyeh Refugee Camp. This could have presented a problem had Jonathan come alone. But with his Palestinian guide at the wheel, they were allowed to pass through camp security with little more than a word and a wave.

"That is their residence," said Ehab, pointing toward a walled castle-like structure near the barbed-wire fence that surrounded the camp.

Jonathan's reception by Muhib Makram, Ahmal's son, was very warm. He was eager to share what he knew about his famous uncle and the events that had occurred at what was now his house.

"One by one, the men had all gone south to join the fight," Muhib explained, "including Ghalib and Layth, Uncle Jorges's two other sons. Only the young ones like Saied and myself and the old ones, like Uncle Jorges and my father, who had a bad heart, had remained. All failed to return. The loss of those he considered his good sons tormented Uncle Jorges until he could no longer contain it. Then he too crossed the border. And he too was captured. He had only been back two days when Yusuf arrived."

"How long did they hold him?" asked Jonathan, the timeline not adding up.

"One week. 'Why would they release him so soon?' my cousin asked but knew the answer. His father had told them what they wanted to know – where our safe houses were located, who else had crossed with him." Muhib motioned for Jonathan to follow him. "Let me show you something that will help you better understand why my cousin has done some of the things for which the world condemns him."

The men strolled down the dusty road until they reached a small hut fashioned out of flattened oil drums. "Come," said Muhib. He pulled open the makeshift door, fashioned from an orange crate and hung with strips of belt leather, and they went inside. "No one will live here since that day."

Heat poured through the metal to be trapped inside the windowless hut. It felt as if Jonathan had climbed into an oven.

"Uncle Jorges sat there," said Muhib, pointing at a stiff black stain on a faded prayer rug. "Rania, my sister, sat beside him, feeding him *leban*. When Yusuf arrived and saw what the Jews had done to his father, how sadistically he had been beaten, he cried like a small child," said the Palestinian, his eyes misting as he spoke. "But the greatest damage was inside his mind. As they were speaking, Uncle Jorges's eyes suddenly fixed on the doorway. He grabbed my father's old Mauser, which since his return never left his side. '*Yehud alainou!*' Uncle cried out. Yusuf pressed the rifle back down and talked to him in soothing words. 'No one will hurt you again, Father,' he said, removing his *kafiyyah* and wiping the yogurt from his father's chin. 'I promise you.'"

Tears flowed freely from Muhib's eyes. Jonathan heard a sound behind him and looked around to see his guide was crying too.

"As Allah so willed, Uncle Jorges's mind returned from wherever it had journeyed," continued Muhib. "He removed the chain he always wore about his neck and kissed the worn silver key that hung from it. 'This unlocks the door to our home in Deir Yassin. I am entrusting it into your care,' Uncle Jorges said, handing it to my cousin, who kissed the key and slipped the chain over his head."

According to Muhib, Jorges made his son swear he would never rest until the Jews had been driven from their lands and a Makram could again unlock the door to their *dar*, their ancestral home. "And one final request," Jorges had said. "Do not allow my body to rest for long away from our home, buried among strangers in a strange soil."

"I will see you in your own fields when you die, Father," Yusuf had responded. "But may that be many years from now."

"Thank you, my son. You must now become the *wajih* of the Makram *aeleh*. I have lost our honor and you must return it."

Jorges asked his son to excuse him; it was time for his prayers. Yusuf kissed his father, then he and Rania crawled out of the sweltering hut.

"Before they had gone ten paces, they heard '*Allahu akbar*'" said Muhib, "then the firing of the old Mauser, so loud it caused their ears to ring. My cousin opened the door to see his revered father lying on his back in the dirt, smoke still curling from the rifle in his lifeless hands."

Yusuf had run to his father's side. When he grasped his head to lift it off the dirty rug, his fingers curled into a damp warm hole, where the bullet had escaped. Yusuf had jerked his hands away, starring in horror at the blood and bits of gray matter coating his hands.

While Muhib's father arranged for Jorges's burial, which by Muslim law had to be within a day, Yusuf took refuge in a bottle of *arak*. He became so drunk that he was unable to attend his own father's funeral.

"After he awoke the next morning," said Muhib, "he swore never to drink again. And to our knowledge, never has."

Jonathan explained why it was so important he speak with Yusuf or Saied. "Is there any way, any possible way, I can speak with one of them, even if only on the telephone," he begged.

Muhib shook his head. "Our telephone is tapped. Our home watched constantly. Surely, someone has taken your photograph while we have spoken. I have no way to get word to my cousin. If I did, we would have already been arrested or abducted or murdered by Mossad or the PLO or whoever else is monitoring the moves of everyone related. Knowing nothing is best for everyone – for us, for him, and for you."

What kind of man is Yusuf Makram? Jonathan asked himself as he flew back to the United States. One of his English professors had once said that bad writers often made a common mistake; they created fictional characters who were either good or evil. No real person was ever just one or the other. It was this mixture, she said, that made us human and each unique.

Makram had many qualities that Jonathan liked, even admired. The man clearly understood his obligation to avenge the deaths of his family members better than he did. After leaving the United States, Makram had spent his life focused on it, which was more worthy of respect than what Jonathan had done, only taking action after being dumped.

In Boston, Yusuf and Hannah Makram had easily been the two nicest people Jonathan had known, especially among the group of Harvard professors who made up his father's friends. Mrs. Makram had always seemed more like his girlfriend than Dr. Makram's wife, something Jonathan's mother had pointed out repeatedly to his father. Jonathan could understand how fear for her safety could have driven Makram to do something desperate, something so out of character. What he didn't yet have a handle on was the real reason he had done what he did. What had been reported didn't seem sufficient to explain his actions. There had to be more to the story.

But even if there was more, Jonathan asked himself, should his previous kindness and the remorse he expressed in his biography have any bearing on the punishment he deserved? Good people sometimes did bad things after all, even horrible things.

It was a question he could imagine one of his philosophy professors posing: how many good acts did it take to excuse a bad act or vice versa? If a person had done a lifetime of great works and committed only one bad act of this magnitude, should he be let off the hook? Society's answer had always been no. But if the person's thinking had been altered by something like drugs, bipolar disease, or alcohol (as Makram's had been), society was mixed, executing some for acts of murder while declaring others mentally impaired or insane and sending them to long stays in mental hospitals.

Had Jonathan never met Yusuf Makram, things would have been far easier... and quicker. He could have simply hunted him down and put him – or himself – into the ground. But he had known him, and known him well. And the man he had known seemed incapable of doing what people claimed. Clearly, the only person who could settle the matter was Makram himself.

Chapter Nineteen

How would he find Yusuf Makram? That was Jonathan's next obstacle, and a huge one. No one, not even Makram's own relatives, knew. But someone had to know where to find him. He ran a moderately sized organization after all. He would need frequent intelligence updates. He would need to regularly refill his stores of depleted ammunition, gasoline and parts for his vehicles, medical supplies, and a thousand other things. Someone had to get those to him.

In hopes of finding an answer, Jonathan flew to Washington D.C. to meet with Akijumi Mochizuki, a former Dai Kan graduate and Assistant Director of Japanese Intelligence.

"Difficult to say," said Mochizuki. "The Israelis want him dead. The PLO wants him dead. So he has very good reason to remain beneath everyone's radar."

"I'd heard the PLO had an issue with him but never heard why."

"For carrying out an unauthorized operation. Makram requested permission to bomb an Israeli daycare center in revenge for the death of his youngest son. Arafat said no."

"Why? It would seem right up his alley."

"Arafat is attempting to reposition the PLO as a strictly political organization. An operation at this time that targeted children would work against his goals. So he refused permission. Makram not only carried out the bombing but informed Arafat that he intended to do more, thereby earning himself a spot high on their hit list."

"So how do I locate him?"

"He reportedly changes living quarters daily, never sleeping twice in the same place. He could be in Paris, Cairo, Beirut, Tokyo, even in the United States, although he has sworn never to return here, as there is still a warrant out for his arrest for your father's death and those of the others who died that night."

"If you were me, where would you begin?"

Mochizuki gave that some thought. "You tried the front door; you went to the Middle East and attempted to find someone who knew him," he said after several seconds. "The only point of entrance remaining might be the back door."

"Which is?"

"Make yourself one of them."

"But how would I do that?"

"No one would find fault if you refused. But since you asked, I will tell you."

Chapter Twenty

The La Garde Hotel in Paris was known as a place where foreigners – intellectuals, writers, artists, activists – could stay cheaply, often for years, without having to explain anything to anyone. Although few volunteered much about their past lives or present activities, almost everyone talked freely about their views on politics and world affairs. The effect of the Vietnamese War on the class struggle and the question of whether or not America really had a working class seemed the most popular topics at the time.

As Mochizuki had advised, Jonathan immediately made contact with the La Garde's resident Marxist group, who invited him to their nightly meetings at the Bar Triomphe, just around the corner. They turned out exactly as the Japanese had described them, "barstool Marxists" – long-winded and boring, talking more and more bravely as they downed glass after glass of wine.

Uncharacteristically, luck had dealt Jonathan a trump card, even forced it into his hand against his will. He had been required to take a class in political philosophy at Stanford. The History and Writings of Karl Marx would have been at the absolute bottom of his wish list. But it was the only class available that quarter unless he had been willing to miss *karate* for a couple of months.

Although he had arrived at the La Garde knowing a fair amount about Marxism, including its many flaws, no one cared what the newcomer thought. They were too much in love with the sound of their own voices. So Jonathan bided his time, waiting until well into their second night before angrily interjecting his opinion. "It's action, not talk, I'm interested in," he told them. "You call yourself 'The Marxist

Action Committee,' but you don't engage in any action. And without action, how can you call yourselves real Marxists?"

"We are helping in our own way," shouted back the self-appointed leader of the group.

Mochizuki had recommended that Jonathan take his time, get to know them, work his way up slowly, proving himself. But after getting a good look at the group, Jonathan decided to take a different tack – become a "pain in ass." His goal was to make them want him to become someone else's problem. And it didn't take but three days before he reached that point.

"Enough!" yelled the leader, blood vessels bulging in his neck. "You THINK you want action because you are nothing but a spoiled American brat!"

"Said the spineless old man who never lifted a finger against his German conquerors and whose ass we soft Americans had to come and save!"

"A man will soon contact you," he spat. "Then, monsieur, we will see what kind of warrior you truly are."

Jonathan expected another flabby alcoholic armchair philosopher. Instead, the man who contacted him looked more like an Italian pimp – red silk shirt opened three buttons at the collar, gold chain with an Italian horn the size of Jonathan's little finger dangling from his tanned neck. He introduced himself only as Umberto, saying it as if he were so famous he needed only one name, like Elvis or Mao or Khrushchev.

Umberto even came on like a pimp, working Jonathan as if attempting to convince a young girl to join his stable. He complimented his apparent fitness, his commitment to their cause, his obvious intelligence in seeking out the very best – him. He bragged a bit about his accomplishments – including the kidnapping of Italian industrialist Antonio Bacigalupi and the bombing of the El Al ticket counter at Milano Malpensa Airport. For someone who had supposedly done so many serious crimes, he seemed unusually careless.

"I hope you've investigated the others better than you have me," Jonathan said, wanting to be the one to bring up the subject, showing he had no fear of a background check. His papers and backstory were solid – passport, driver's license, Social Security card, and Stanford ID – all under the name of Andrew Allen Robertson, a current Stanford student. In addition, Mochizuki and his staff had also created a background history for him – driving tickets, school records, and such – good enough to fool all but the absolute best.

"An extensive investigation was launched the minute Monsieur Moreau passed your name to me. This is why I did not contact you for several days. And rest easy; we did the same for the others."

"Okay. When do I begin?"

"You must undergo training before I can permit you to take part in any actions."

"By whom?" Jonathan asked. He, in fact, already knew. According to Mochuzuki, Makram's group, Heroic Fighters for the Freedom of Palestine, had recently agreed to train Umberto's recruits. This was why he had sent him to the La Garde.

"You will know soon enough, my eager friend."

Umberto's safe house was neither a house nor did it look or feel very safe. It was a small, dank, noisy room at the back of a run-down, four-storied hotel. Ragged drapes covered the two cracked, murky windows. The bedspread was dotted with suspicious white crusty deposits. And under the bed, he found a couple of used syringes and a handful of blood-stained gauze pads.

There was only one bathroom on each floor and his was at the opposite end of the hall. The toilet wouldn't flush, apparently for a long time, and had overflowed, forcing everyone who entered to walk on their tiptoes to decrease the amount of urine and excrement-tainted water that soaked into their shoes and socks.

The first time Jonathan lay on the bed, he was sure he could feel something moving – on his arms, his legs, and in his hair. When he woke up the next morning, he found himself speckled with red itchy bumps. After enduring two more nights of this, there came a knock at his door and the superintendent's gravelly voice, "Telephone!"

The phone was on the first floor. Since the management turned off the electricity in the hallways and lobby at night, Jonathan had to feel his way along the dark hallway and down two flights of stairs to the lobby.

"Hello?" he said, pressing the receiver to his ear.

"A perfect job for you has arisen," came Umberto's accented voice on the other end. "A car will pick you up tomorrow morning. Be outside at eleven o'clock."

No one was outside to pick him up at eleven. Twenty minutes later, a blue Lotus Elan, its top down, pulled up to the curb and tooted twice. Behind the wheel sat a hard-looking but pretty blonde. She impatiently waved for him to hurry up, as if it had been he who had been late.

"You Robertson?" she asked as he climbed into the passenger's side.

"I am. And you?"

"Renata," she said, flooring the gas pedal before Jonathan could even get the door closed.

The woman had obviously not spent her morning reading Marx or working to cover all bases. She couldn't even cover her own bases, literally and figuratively. She had come directly from the beach or swimming pool, smelling of coconut oil and wearing a skimpy bikini, the top of which was only a ribbon of orange fabric that failed to completely accomplish its purpose.

Renata raced in and out of the heavy lunch-hour traffic as fast as friction and the Lotus's small engine would allow. Without warning, she swerved to the curb and slammed on the brakes.

"That is your target," she said, pointing across the street at a small bar, squeezed between a butcher's shop and a Chinese restaurant. The sign over the entrance read *The Golden Bear*. "Many foreigners visit this place," she said in a thick French accent. "The one who interests us works under the name of Adam Lancaster. This is his photograph. I took it myself. Good, is it not?"

Jonathan studied the offered photo. It was a headshot of a balding middle-aged businessman. "What does he do?"

"Agent for Bulgarian DS."

The music inside The Golden Bear was loud and unmistakably American – Richie Havens, Jefferson Airplane, Jim Morrison. Jonathan took a seat at one of the back tables.

"What can I get ya?" asked the husky black bartender, his accent clearly American.

"Just a Coke."

"Where you from?"

"California."

"Well, I'll he goddamned," he said, crossing the floor and shoving a thick hand at Jonathan. "Where abouts?"

"Palo Alto."

"Oakland," the man said, thumping himself on his barrel chest. "You must be an Indian fan."

"Yeah, kind of."

"Cal man myself, as you might've guessed from the name of the place." He turned his attention to a short blonde woman behind the bar. "Marie! Bring a Coke, would you? And fry up a couple of them steaks – those T-bones I've been saving." The woman looked less than thrilled at the request.

The two men talked, mostly about the last Big Game between University of California, Berkeley, and Stanford. Jonathan had seen it. Jumbo Jerry Harris, as he introduced himself, had tried to get back for the annual cross-bay rivalry. But something had come up and he hadn't been able to go.

"I was shitting bullets," said Jumbo Jerry. "I couldn't wait for my copy of the *Trib* to get here and called my brother back home to find out the score. Cost me a goddamned fortune. Marie like to cut my balls off."

Marie carried over a pair of huge steaks covered in Jumbo Jerry's own barbeque sauce. Accompanying the steaks were baskets of thick french fries and steaming bowls of chili that, as Harris put it, "will burn the hair off your tongue." Jonathan found he wasn't far from wrong.

As they ate, Lancaster strolled through the door. "Big Jer," he called out in greeting before taking a stool at the bar. Jonathan noted that Lancaster's accent clearly sounded British, not Eastern European. But he also knew that the Soviets turned out people who could speak English with almost no detectable accent.

"Adam, my man," nodded Harris in return. "Goddamned limey spook," he muttered under his breath.

"What's with him?" asked Jonathan.

"He's friendly enough face to face but 'bloody wog' keeps popping into his conversations whenever he's speaking with his buddies and don't think I can hear. But let me show you the reason I couldn't make the Big Game."

Harris led Jonathan behind the bar and down a dark hallway that ended at an apartment.

"Is this a pisser or what?" Harris said, reaching into a lace-covered crib and picking up an infant who looked to be only a few months old. Harris delicately cradled the beige infant in his thick arms.

Jonathan heard quick, hard-heeled footsteps hammering in their direction. Harris's huge frame shuddered. "Here," he said, handing the baby to Jonathan.

"I just got him to sleep," said Marie, punching Harris in the arm. She grabbed the baby out of Jonathan's arms and put him back into his crib.

"How about another Coke?" Harris said, nodding back toward the bar.

"Sure," said Jonathan, feeling uncomfortable at being caught in the middle of the squabble.

The two men's reappearance obviously surprised Lancaster, who was huddled close to a seedy older man. Renata's supposed Bulgarian nodded and his informant left. Within a couple of minutes, Lancaster headed out too.

"He come in often?" asked Jonathan, needing to get something he could give Umberto, something innocuous to keep him happy until he could decide how far he would allow things to go.

"Whenever he's in town. Can you join us for supper tonight?"

"I'd like to but have to meet some people tonight. Maybe later this week if the offer holds?"

"Sure. Give me a call."

"How much do I owe you?" Jonathan asked, pulling out his wallet.

"Put that away, man. Your money ain't no good here."

Renata stood on the seat of her Lotus and waved. She had parked down the street, where she could see the entrance but not be easily seen herself.

"I saw Lancaster enter, then leave," she said as Jonathan climbed into the passenger's seat. "What were you able to learn?"

"Not a lot. The bartender thinks he's a spook too. Some other guy met up with him but disappeared when we took too much interest."

Renata sped away from the curb, cutting in between two delivery trucks, forcing the one behind to hit his brakes, then his horn. "He expect him to return?" she asked, seemingly oblivious to the near-miss or angry drivers.

"He didn't say."

"You are to remain in your room until Umberto calls."

Jonathan intended to do as ordered, remain in his room. But the bed bugs or fleas or whatever they were – probably both – had gotten so bad that he had to do something about it. After a quick visit to a nearby hardware store, where he bought some insect powder, he ducked into a small drugstore to pick up a tube of ointment to ease the itching. As he approached the checkout counter, the latest issue of *Vogue Paris* caught his eye. Nanami, dressed in an exquisite kimono, graced its cover.

A powerful urge to see her, to feel he was not completely alone, surged through him and Jonathan's hand lashed out. He had the magazine half out of the rack before he caught himself. How would he ever explain having a copy of *Vogue* in his room? Besides, Nanami was no longer in his life and he was, in fact, completely alone. Jonathan pushed the magazine back down and pulled out his wallet.

"Anything else?" asked the clerk.

"No."

Fortunately the bug powder did the trick and the bites stopped, allowing Jonathan to use the bed again. He was lying on it, watching television, killing time, when the show was interrupted by breaking news. "An explosion just before noon destroyed The Golden Bear Bar on Rue Perrin," came the TV newscaster's voice. "There are eight known dead." The picture went live to a street scene. Firemen and police were rummaging through the rubble of a leveled building.

Jonathan bolted upright.

"The dead include the proprietor, his wife and small child, and five customers at a Chinese restaurant next door. The Golden Bear, long rumored to be a gathering place for American and British intelligence officials, was apparently empty of customers at the time. No group has yet taken responsibility for the bombing. We will keep you informed as further details become available."

Jonathan bounded down the stairs, two and three at a time. He snapped a coin into the slot of the payphone and angrily began spinning the numbers on the rotary dial. Just before turning the final number, he hesitated.

There was nothing he could do for Jerry and his family now, Jonathan told himself. He had to stow this too inside that lockbox hidden deep – although often not deep enough – inside his head, along with the rapidly growing list of things needing to be avenged or endured. He would move forward with his plan and, when he had gotten what he needed from Umberto, he would find a way to settle this debt too.

Jonathan dialed the final digit. "I want to talk to Umberto," he said when he heard a woman's voice.

"I do not know when he will be checking in."

"Tell him I'll wait until seven o'clock, then I'm gone."

An hour later, there was a knock on his door. Jonathan had his suitcase open and was pretending to be packing when the Italian walked in.

"You wanted to see me?" he said, his eyes going immediately to the suitcase.

Jonathan took an extra beat before answering, needing to remind himself to stay calm, that there was nothing he could do to bring Harris and his family back.

"I'm leaving," he said.

"Why?"

"I got a rule – never trust anyone who doesn't trust me."

"You had been seen. We could not risk sending you in again."

"I was getting close to the owner. He even invited me to dinner. I could have helped keep this from becoming a complete fiasco and us looking like a bunch of bumbling bozos," he spat as he continued packing. "I can see now why whoever handles training for you won't give you the time of day. There's nothing here for me." He closed his suitcase and held out his hand.

"Wait. Please. What if I allowed you to become a full team member without training? We can teach you what you need to know."

Jonathan scoffed. "No disrespect but I don't think those who just botched this so badly have anything to teach me."

"Are you familiar with Yusuf Makram and the HFFP?"

"Of course. What about them?"

"We had an agreement with them to train our recruits, an agreement which they have so far been too busy to honor. But it appears they now need something from us," Umberto said, snickering sarcastically.

"So I believe I am in a strong position to arrange for you to receive training from them. Would that interest you?"

Jonathan pretended to give it some thought. In reality, he had but one other option. Mochizuki had given him the name of two groups, Umberto's and another in Spain. Both reportedly had recent agreements with the HFFP for training. But to gain entrance into the other group would mean starting all over again.

"Okay," he said, "but I won't wait forever. And I expect to have input into any coming operations."

"We meet tonight to discuss our next target," he said, writing an address down on a piece of paper. "We begin at ten o'clock. Can you find it?"

"I'll be there."

Counting Jonathon and the priest who ran the soup kitchen where the group met, there were seven at the gathering.

"Do we make another attempt on the British butcher... I mean the, ah...," Renata asked, obviously realizing halfway through that she had previously told Jonathan that Lancaster was a Bulgarian. Her blue eyes flicked to Umberto for forgiveness.

"It is okay. He is now one of us," he said, nodding toward where Jonathan sat on the front row. "But, no, it would be pointless. After such a complete disaster, we will never see him again."

"So who is next?" demanded Renata.

"A big fish."

"How big?"

"Ariel Gutfreund, a Mossad section head. He recently brought his family to Paris for what he thinks is a secret vacation."

Jonathan exhaled noisily. "Any of this sound familiar? 'Strike to create terror,'" he said, quoting as best he could remember from the *Terrorist's Manifesto*, which had been required reading for every Kami, along with the works of Che Guevara, Ho Chi Minh, and Mao Tse-tung, considered the world's leading experts on guerilla warfare. "'Force the enemies of the people to respond. Keep striking, creating chaos throughout the land, until their actions become so oppressive that they touch the lives of every common man. Then, the masses will arise and bring the government to its knees.' Ring a bell?"

Umberto nodded, impressed. "So tell us who you believe should be our next target, the catalyst for setting your landslide into motion?"

"Not an Israeli in France on vacation! That couldn't kick-start anything but our own demise! We need to do something that will set something in motion that will touch masses of people, something that will be in their faces for months or years. Hitting another Israeli will be in and out of the news in a matter of days."

"I ask again."

"Something intelligent for a change. Drop all these petty little personal attacks on people you don't like and target people who'll advance our cause. We need to start thinking like true Marxists!"

"Give us a name."

Jonathan shrugged. "The PLO."

A collective gasp went through the group. Umberto started to speak but Jonathan waved him silent. "It can be some low-level guy. We make it look as if the Israelis did it or one of the other Palestinian groups. We're not big enough to have any kind of global effect. But we're big enough to prod those who do into action. If we do it right and hit the right person, we could make Arafat look incompetent and grease the way for Makram to replace him."

Everyone looked at him in stunned silence.

"If Makram can achieve what he has with such a small group," Jonathan continued, "imagine what he could do with an organization the size of the PLO. We would be changing history!"

Umberto smiled kindly, as if at a precocious child. "Yours is a very good idea," he said. "You think big, my friend. But you do not yet grasp the financial realities we face."

"How much can a few weapons and maybe an explosive device possibly cost?" asked Jonathan.

"Weapons and devices?" Umberto shrugged, "ten, twelve thousand of your dollars. But the information necessary to find such a target? That is an entirely different matter. Perhaps the equivalent of fifty thousand American dollars, depending on who we target and which service we use."

"Which service?" Jonathan laughed. "You mean like Abdul's Rent-a-Spy?"

"Let us just say there are those who will supply anything for which there is a market," answered Umberto, dead-serious. "The good ones are very good but also very expensive."

"But if they're as dedicated as we are, they would surely find a way to see we got what we needed."

"I did not say they were dedicated, only good."

"Then how can you possibly trust them? They could sell you out just as easily to the other side."

"True. But from that day onwards, no one would trust them and they would lose all of their customers. They are capitalists. So they may only work for one side at a time. What you suggest would cost more than we can afford at present. Do you know how we fund our operations?"

Jonathan shrugged. "I assumed you did it as others do, kidnappings, bank robberies, that sort of thing."

"Fortunately, no. Because of our past successes, other organizations and wealthy sympathizers contribute to our operations. With greater fame will come greater sponsorship and the funds with which to undertake more important operations, perhaps like those you suggest. We received nothing from our last," he said, glaring at Renata. "So we must recover our losses on our next one. For that, Jewish targets have always produced the greatest contributions and we have a big one in our sights."

"Kill someone like this Israeli and we'll all be famous all right. Our faces will be plastered on the covers of newspapers around the world as they hunt us down one by one and kill us. I don't mind dying for the cause. But I won't throw my life away on a mission that's doomed from the start," said Jonathan.

Umberto glanced at the others seated around the room. "To honor our young American colleague, let us put the matter to a vote," he said. "How many think our next target should be this Jew?"

When all hands went up, Jonathan got to his feet and headed for the door.

"Come on, Andrew," said Renata. "We need you. Look at this collection of jellyfish. You think they could actually carry out such a mission without you?"

"You managed fine before I came onboard."

"Please? If you do, I will show you how much I appreciate your help," she said seductively.

"I will make you a better offer," said the Italian, "one that will not require ointments and antibiotics."

Renata shot him a dirty look.

"What?"

"I told you that the HFFP wanted something from us. Well, this is it. They informed me of the Jew's presence and requested our assistance. If we are successful, you will receive the training you desire."

Jonathan stood motionless for a few seconds, debating his next move. "Okay," he said. "I'll help, but only with the planning, not with the actual hit. I think whoever does that has to be our very best. Who bombed the bar?"

"I was not in charge of gathering intelligence," insisted Renata defensively. "I was only responsible for planting the device."

"The mission was a failure but the bombing was very professional."

"You really think so?" she said, a smile sliding across her normally sullen mouth.

"It looked like it on TV. God, you took out the whole front of the building."

"That is because I improved the device Guy supplied, adding an additional hundred pounds of chain-wrapped dynamite and fifty pounds of number-eight nails just to be sure."

"I think it's clear who should handle this one too," Jonathan said, turning toward their leader. "We just have to give her better information this time."

"I agree."

As everyone filed out, Jonathan stuck around to speak with the Italian.

"Who's Guy?" he asked.

Umberto's eyes narrowed.

"Renata mentioned his name."

The Italian relaxed. "No need to concern yourself. He is just what you Americans call a vendor of services."

"How soon do you expect we can make the hit?"

"It will depend on how quickly the device can be assembled. The average is three days. Why?"

"I hate the waiting and the bed bugs," Jonathan said, scratching his leg.

"I will attempt to speed things up."

Keeping his distance, Jonathan followed Umberto to where he had parked his canary-yellow Fiat Spider. As soon as he drove off, Jonathan hailed a cab and tailed him, which was no easy task, as he drove worse than Renata.

The Fiat eventually slid to a stop in front of a small, very busy bakery. People poured in and out, all leaving with warm baguettes tucked under their arms and white bags of pastries in their hands, carried as if they were treasures.

Umberto strolled inside but, from what Jonathan could see through the front window, bought nothing. After speaking briefly with one of the clerks, he headed outside and waited at the curb. Soon, a gray Citroën pulled up and the Italian climbed into the back.

They drove leisurely across town and into the countryside, where they parked in the graveled courtyard of a small picturesque hotel. The driver waited in the Citroën as Umberto went inside, where he staye for a little over nine minutes. Then the Italian and a heavy-set Frenchman, Jonathan assumed to be Guy, strolled back outside and shook hands.

"Where have you been?" demanded Renata as Jonathan unlocked the door to his room. She was sitting on his bed, a pistol in her hand, looking eager to use it.

"Doing your job, surveilling the target," he shot back as he removed his coat and threw it on a chair. "We can't hit the house on Wednesday. You should have known that."

"Why not?"

"It's posted. You didn't see the signs?"

"What signs?"

"The streets are swept on Wednesdays. Any cars on the street are towed. You'd have no line of access. They'd spot you in an instant." He shrugged. "But it's your life so you make the call."

"No way," said Umberto. "Everything is set. It must be Wednesday!"

Although the day couldn't be changed, Umberto agreed to implement some of Jonathan's suggested changes. Instead of driving herself, Renata would take a taxi to the apartment building where Gutfreund and his family were staying. The bomb would be in a large suitcase, which the driver would load into the trunk of his taxi when he picked her up. On their way to the airport, she would tell him that she needed to stop to pick up a friend and direct him to Gutfreund's address. When no one was waiting at the curb, she would get out, supposedly to get him. As soon as she was clear, she would transmit the signal that would trigger the explosion.

His plan would be clean. It would be safe. They would not have to steal a car, avoiding the possibility of getting stopped en route and arrested. They would not have to leave a rigged car parked close to the building, a car that could draw suspicion. They would arrive in a real cab, with a real cab driver. Umberto liked it.

There was a knock on Jonathan's door Wednesday night. He heard the strident voice of the building superintendent yelling that he had a call.

It was Umberto. "Renata is dead. They were waiting. They have already hunted down Yves and Victor. I do not know anything more. However, I must tell you, if Yves were a strong man, he would not have become a priest. He may well talk, surely so if they torture him. We are all in danger. Find a new place. I will do the same. Call Evelyn in three days."

Jonathan threw his few possessions into a bag and moved to another cheap flat several blocks away, making sure he had not been followed. He stayed only one hour before moving to another.

TV news the next morning was filled with reports of the assassination of five suspected members of a terrorist group. According to the reports, the hits were believed to have been the work of an as yet unidentified hit squad. Jonathan moved again, this time outside the city, to a country inn filled with American tourists, where he would blend in.

Not feeling comfortable being trapped inside, he spent much of the next two days accompanying other guests on sight-seeing tours organized by the hotel. As instructed, he placed his call to Evelyn but she had yet to hear from Umberto. Jonathan was to check back in two more days.

The weather turned drizzly, forcing Jonathan to remain inside his second-story room. Rain and wind peppered the outside of his windows and fogged up the insides, making it almost impossible to watch for strangers and the arrival of suspicious cars. Eventually, Jonathan gave up even trying.

It was past midnight and there wasn't much on TV, only a rerun of *Gunsmoke* with Marshall Dillon speaking in a squeaky high-pitched French voice. The steam heater hissed incessantly, filling the room with its thick, damp warmth. Before long, his eyes grew heavy, Marshall Dillon's voice faded, and the heat surrounded him like a blanket.

There was a creak in the narrow hallway, then another as two armed men crept slowly toward Jonathan's door. More men stood outside in the rain, watching the window, stubby automatic weapons in their hands.

One of the two in the hallway nodded and his partner put his booted foot to the door. The crashing sound startled Jonathan awake. He bolted upright, his hand going for the pistol on the nightstand before realizing he would never reach it in time.

Chapter Twenty-One

Two Israeli security guards, both built like football linemen, strong-armed Jonathan up the stairs to the top floor of the Israeli Embassy, where he was shoved unceremoniously into a rear office. Ariel Gutfreund sat across a cluttered desk, waiting.

Gutfreund looked as unkempt as his surroundings. Wild hair. Bloodshot eyes. Runny nose. The menthol aroma of a cough drop drifted across his desk. He flicked his fingers at a chair and Jonathan sat down.

"I want to thank you," said Gutfreund, "although I am still at a loss as to your reasons. But for myself and my family, I thank you all the same. We owe you our lives."

"My reasons are simple," said Jonathan. "I'm not a Marxist and don't believe in their methods or ideology. I came to Paris to infiltrate a group in hopes of making contact with Yusuf Makram."

He filled the Israeli in on the relevant parts of his past.

"I would like to help," said Gutfreund, "and I mean that, but unfortunately I cannot."

"You mean you won't."

"I mean I cannot. I know nothing that is certain. I also cannot help you because my country has just declared him personally off limits. Anyone else within his organization, I can give you. But Makram himself, I cannot."

Jonathan's puzzled look prompted Gutfreund to continue. "Why would my government protect him? Because the politicians, in their infinite wisdom, have declared that the past has been swept clean. Makram, according to them, is no longer a cold-blooded murderer. He is now a political figure. I must admit, I can understand their reasons, but I cannot accept them."

"What reasons could there possibly be?"

"He is attempting to take over the leadership of the PLO. If this should happen, they do not want his last memories before taking office to be that of an assassination attempt by us. That would make future negotiation impossible."

Jonathan mulled his options over for a few seconds. "I have more information to trade. It won't keep for long, two days at most."

"Concerning?"

"The leader of the group I infiltrated is still free."

"The woman was not the leader?"

"Renata? In her wildest dreams. She couldn't lead a troop of Girl Scouts to the bathroom."

"What is his name, this leader?"

"His or her name will be yours, along with where he or she can be found, when I get what I need," said Jonathan, getting up.

A slight smile slid across Gutfreund's face. "I will see what I can do."

"I'll call tomorrow. If you have something for me, we can make a swap. If not, I will move on."

Jonathan's first call the next morning went to Evelyn. She said Umberto had contacted her and wanted to meet with him. He was to call back that afternoon. Jonathan's second call went to Gutfreund. The Israeli had information and wanted to meet at a sidewalk cafe near the river.

"What do you have?" Jonathan asked, after he and Gutfreund were seated.

"I cannot give you an exact location. As I said, he wisely moves daily to stay ahead of his beloved Muslim brothers. But I can give you a place to start. If you are resourceful, as I am sure you are, it will lead you to him...or him to you. Do we have a deal?"

"I want more."

"Like what?"

"Like weapons, assistance, maybe backup."

"Of course. But if you go in appearing to work for us, you will not live long enough to depart the airport. Weapons? We can supply anything you want. But again, you would be better off with weapons that could not be traced to us. In fact, they could be watching us this very minute. That man on the telephone across the street. That couple in the Peugeot. The woman and child."

"Plus," said Jonathan, "you don't want to be traceable to me in case I get caught?"

Gutfreund smiled but said nothing. Jonathan held out his hand and the two men shook.

"Professor Abdul Moosun teaches poetry at the American University in Beirut – in addition, that is, to being an occasional courier for Makram," said Gutfreund. "They go back to their childhood. If anyone knows how to contact him, he does."

For his part, Jonathan handed over Umberto, making the call that afternoon and setting up the meeting. The Israelis took it from there.

Whatever the Israelis had in store for the Italian wouldn't bring Big Jerry, Marie, and their baby son back. But at least those responsible were no longer allowed to walk the earth either, to breathe the air, to feel the sun on their faces, or to listen to the Big Game if they so desired. Now the lead supplied him by Gutfreund would hopefully allow Jonathan to do the same to those who stole the lives from his parents.

Chapter Twenty-Two

"Wounds and death are thrown at me in great fistfuls.
I cannot escape them no matter where I run.
They kill me.
They tear the limbs from my body.
I am a mother, an olive baby glued to my breast.
I am a young man, the pink smudge of love never to touch my lips.
I am a grandfather, my hair and beard sucked white by what I have seen.
I am a grandmother, my husband and sons only photos on a wall.
I am five million dispossessed souls, screaming out for justice.
But let them know, I shall never yield.
No thief shall stop me, shall never extinguish the fire,
The fire in my heart.
The fire in my hands.
A Kalashnikov.
A grenade.
A bomb for the usurper, the thief.
I shall not rest until I am home once more."

Dr. Abdul Moosun recited the poem slowly, precisely, stabbing the air in punctuation with a burning cigarette. The young Palestinians in the open-air class watched as if he were a god, twinkles of admiration in their dark eyes.

"Professor Moosun. May I speak with you for a minute?" Jonathan asked as the professor dismissed his class and ambled toward the administration building. The baby-faced teenagers accompanying him, who Jonathan had thought were his grandchildren or a pair of admirers, turned deadly serious. In a slick, clearly well-practiced move, they positioned themselves between him and the professor, their hands grasping the pistols tucked under their shirts.

Moosun stopped and the two began patting Jonathan down for weapons.

"I have a pistol in an ankle holster," he volunteered, before they could find it.

"They will return what is yours before you leave us."

When their very thorough check was finished, the two bodyguards moved away but kept their eyes trained on the stranger.

"I'm looking to join an organization which can use a committed person who is not afraid to do whatever is needed."

"Why do you come to me? Fatah has offices everywhere."

"I heard a rumor in Paris that you might have some knowledge of the HFFP."

"A civil war rages among my countrymen. If what you say is true, such information could get me killed. Who told you this lie?"

"I worked with an Italian who called himself Umberto. The Jews killed him, and everyone else who was with us."

"Why is it you alone survived?" Moosun asked, his eyes narrowing.

"Because Umberto warned me before he was murdered. I was new to the group. Perhaps my name was last on the list, or not there at all. I also stayed on the move."

Noosun studied the young American. "I too heard a rumor but cannot attest to its veracity. It is said there is a house in the Lebaa Camp, a large white house, like a fort, that sits on top of the knoll. The only one like it. A man whose brother is said to be with Makram supposedly lives there."

Jonathan thanked him and left.

"Check him out. Find out who he really is," Moosun told one of his aides.

"Should we follow him?"

"No. We know where to find him."

Chapter Twenty-Three

From a distance, the refugee camp looked like just another Arab town, like many he had passed along the way. But as the bus drew nearer, Jonathan could see that most of the camp's whitewashed stone houses had been gutted, apparently by bombs and artillery shells, which had also uprooted trees and ripped large scoops of dirt out of the red earth. This devastation was far more recent than what he had seen in Deir Yassin.

To enter, Jonathan had to first pass the close scrutiny of five of the machine-gun-toting teenagers who served as gate guards and camp policemen. Besides flexing sinewy young muscles and the exaggerated egos that often accompanied those of such few years, the young men's obsession seemed to be rooting out Israeli operatives. Since he was clearly not an Arab, Jonathan got their immediate and full attention.

Regardless of their ages, the young *fedai* were very professional. They examined his passport and Stanford ID more thoroughly than anyone else had so far. They checked the photos, the printing, the paper, his signature, the color and material of the cover. But throughout it all, Jonathan remained relaxed. He knew his papers were good. Andrew Allen Robertson, who had no idea that his name could become well known in the wrong circles if things went south, was a currently registered Stanford student. And he and Jonathan looked enough alike that any differences could be blamed on a bad photo.

"What is your business here?"

"I'm conducting a sociological study of camp conditions for a class at Stanford University in California," Jonathan said.

The young man studied him for several seconds. "We will check to ensure you are truly from this Stanford University and will need to see your notes before you leave."

The driver of a delivery van, who had been waiting at the gate for them to finish with Jonathan, finally ran out of what little patience he had started with and lay on his horn. The teenagers forgot about the American and descended on the driver, who was now screaming at them. Assuming they were done, Jonathan strolled into the camp as casually as he could.

Plastic sheets and empty flour and rice sacks covered missing windows, doors, and roofs in the few houses that were still inhabitable. Most camp residents lived in quarters that were little more than lean-tos, tents, or huts made from corrugated aluminum and flattened oil drums. Flies rose in black clouds from piles of garbage heaped alongside the deeply pitted dirt roadway to pester any passing person or animal.

Except for the teenagers at the gate and the handful roaming the camp, Jonathan found everyone else to be friendly and hospitable. As he went from dwelling to dwelling asking questions for his supposed research study, most were eager to talk, to share their plight and their complaints with anyone who would listen and might possibly be in a position to do something about them. Each was confident that if the world knew their story, help would soon be on its way. Not a single inhabitant appeared to have even the slightest suspicion that they could in any way be responsible for even a tiny bit of their continuing sorrows.

Rather than work to better their conditions by finding ways to create new industries, as an American or Japanese would have done, they instead focused solely on further inflaming their people's hatred and instilling the same in their young. Jonathon suspected that if he were to return in a hundred years, things would likely look much the same. But even though most were barely above the survival level, all shared what little they had, insisting Jonathan have something to eat, something to drink. He found it all incredibly sad.

Their eagerness to talk, however, didn't extend to the subject of the HFFP or anyone who might be a member. Underneath, he could see that they were leery of strangers – especially light-skinned, fair-haired strangers, likely a holdover from their years under the British during the Mandate. And he understood it.

All his eggs were dropping one after another into but a single basket, the house on the knoll. This was not what he had hoped. He had wanted to ferret out additional leads before paying his inevitable visit to the structure Moosun had indicated, which could end up being a trap.

He knew the house. He had spotted it almost the instant he stepped inside the compound. Sitting alone on a barren rise at the back of the camp, it was hard to miss. But anyone who approached it would be impossible to miss too. So he had painstakingly avoided giving any indication he had any interest in the place, never even looking directly at it, wanting the route he took in canvassing camp residents to appear to lead him logically to the house late in his survey. Approaching it too soon might have aroused suspicion.

The sun had just set when Jonathan finally trudged up the hill and stopped in front of the whitewashed cinderblock structure. There was still enough light to see that the shutters were still solid, not flimsy or broken like those on other houses. The door was still in one piece and its hardware intact. Although no lights were on inside, that wasn't unusual. Few in the camp had electricity. And those who did conserved it.

Jonathan knocked on the door. He heard a rustling sound inside but got no answer. He knocked again. "*Marhaboa*. Hello," he yelled, turning the door handle and opening the door. The room was empty. "*Arjook assaireah!* I beg your pardon!" he said, stepping into the front room. A loud fluttering sound. Something went for his legs and he jumped back to see a pair of angry, bent-necked geese, apparently the house's only residents.

As Jonathan lay on the threadbare cot in the five-by-seven-foot room he had rented from the camp postmaster, he ran over in his mind the possibilities. Either Moosun had lied, something had happened in the interim, or someone, friend or foe, would soon be paying him a visit, perhaps that very night.

But there were no visitors, except for mosquitos and no shortage of them. So the next day he scratched as he revisited the house on the rise under better light with the same result. A search of the camp to find another similar house, in case he had been mistaken, came up empty. It would be his last night there, he decided. In the morning, he was going back to Beirut and pay Moosun another visit.

"How are you today, sir?" said a weathered old man who pinched a strong-smelling cigarette between his thumb and yellowed index finger. His English was broken but understandable. "May I sit?"

"Help yourself," said Jonathan, who had gone to the small combination grocery store/restaurant/bar for dinner.

"Do you need a guide? I am very good. You will not be disappointed," said the old Arab.

"Sorry but I'm leaving in the morning."

"How about having your picture taken with an old warrior? I am very famous. Ask anyone."

"Where did you see action?"

"Throughout the world. Palestine. Italy. Greece. Many places."

Almost every adult male Jonathan had spoken with while at the camp had claimed to have seen action. But all of them had reportedly fought inside Palestine, or another Middle Eastern country. This was the first who claimed to have taken part in what had to have been terrorist operations. "Would you like something to eat or drink?" he asked the bony old *fedai*.

"Perhaps just a small swallow of *arak*, to wash the dust from my throat."

"One *arak*, please," Jonathan told the waiter, then turned back to his guest. "Which group did you fight with?"

"Fatah. For me, there was only Fatah when I was still healthy, still graced by Allah to be counted among the *fedayeen*."

"What happened?"

"A shot to the leg. Here," he said, pulling up his trousers and showing a thumb-sized red oval just below his knee. "It shattered the bone and never healed, not truly."

Jonathan listened with interest as the man told about his past battles. "What do you think of all these other groups?" he asked, hoping to angle the conversation toward Makram. "It seems like there's a hundred of them now."

"I am for them, totally. They are all Palestinian, seeking the same goal."

"But you don't think they waste too many bullets and lose focus battling each other rather than your enemies?"

Before he could answer, the waiter delivered the small glass of clear liquid. The old *fedai* eagerly snatched up the glass. "To your health," he said before downing it in one swallow.

"Why don't you bring him another?" Jonathan told the waiter. "In fact, why don't you bring the bottle? And I'd like tea."

The old man's eyes hardened. "Why do you so willingly supply drink to one you do not know?" the old man scratched his *kafiyyah*-wrapped head as if puzzled. "Do you want me drunk?"

"I don't drink," said Jonathan, "and just trying to be as hospitable as your people have been to me. But I do have a motive. I'm hoping to learn more about the subject that brought me here." The waiter walked up, set a cup in front of Jonathan, and poured his tea. He started to place the bottle on the table but Jonathan stopped him. "That won't be necessary. My friend changed his mind."

The old man's eyes flared and his hand lashed out for the bottle. "I was merely making a joke, my friend. I am a funny man, ask anyone."

The two sipped their drinks as the sun neared the edge of the flat lands to the south. "I leave tomorrow very disappointed," said Jonathan.

"Why be sorry? You may leave; we must remain."

Jonathan took a minute before answering. "I came in hopes of making a contribution. What I see here is wrong," he said, sweeping his hand across the city of tents and lean-tos. "Being in the West and at one of the world's top universities, I could make a difference, sway public opinion towards the plight of your people. But no one except some Fatah PR man will even speak with me."

"Why do you not want to speak with Fatah?"

"No disrespect but I don't believe accommodation will ever get your people what you seek, what you so much deserve. Am I wrong?"

"Who am I to say? I was merely a weapon, an AK-47. Others decided on what I was to aim and when to fire."

Jonathan stood and held out his hand. "Well, thank you for speaking with me."

The old *fedai* gave his hand a shake. "If I could arrange for you to speak with someone rumored to be with the Heroic Fighters, would that be of value to you?"

"Yusuf Makram's group?" he said as if giving it some thought. "Well, if… I repeat, IF he turned out to be legitimate, I would be willing to pay you… fifty dollars?" The Arab's eyes locked onto Jonathan's hand as he pulled out his wallet and dug out a twenty dollar bill. He set the bill in front of his guest. "The rest if he is as you say."

"Are you ready to leave at this moment?" said the Arab, snatching up the bill and stuffing it into his pocket. This was a bad sign, Jonathan thought. He hadn't haggled. And although it might have been purely by chance, he had offered to put him in touch with someone in Makram's organization. As far as Jonathan could remember, he hadn't said anything about Makram or the HFFP. Was the old warrior Moosun's connection? Or was he PLO? He had, after all, fought for Fatah in the old days. But if he was now attempting to lead him into a PLO trap, would he have admitted that fact? Clearly, Jonathan needed time to think. "I'd like to clean up and change my clothes first."

"I cannot take you to the man himself, only to my friend who knows all the *fedayeen*. As he lives a distance to the North, we must leave quickly or I cannot guarantee he will still be there when we arrive."

"Okay," said Jonathan, having little choice.

"Of course, my friend should be paid something for his troubles as well. Is that agreeable?"

"Sure," said Jonathan, relaxing a little. Maybe it was on the up-and-up after all. He would likely keep a percentage or all of his friend's portion for himself. And nickel-and-diming him might actually be a good sign. If he intended to rob him, he would end up with all his money. So there would be no need to get a little here, a little there.

The Arab hired a taxi, driven by another friend and, of course, paid for by Jonathan, to drive them to a white villa that sat on the coast. There was no moon and it was almost pitch dark by the time they arrived. Although he couldn't see it, the sea couldn't be far away; he could smell the salty air and hear the lap of waves against the beach.

"Please, come," said the old Arab, disappearing inside.

Jonathan crept up to the open door. The room was dark.

"Come, come," came the Arab's voice. "My friend must be yet to return. I will make light." He struck a match and went around the room lighting candles.

Jonathan saw no one but the old Arab, who was now seated on the frayed sofa, and he moved cautiously inside. "Rest, my young friend," said the old man. "If our meeting is fruitful, we may be required to endure a long journey to find those you seek."

As Jonathan eased down onto a nearby chair, two men rushed out of a side hallway straight toward him. He sprang to his feet and kicked the first man in the groin. Spinning around, he launched a powerful spinning back kick that caught the second man in the chest, cracking ribs and knocking him back.

The old *fedai* had moved, positioning himself between Jonathan and the door. He reached into his jacket for something. Jonathan didn't wait to find out what. In a single lunge, he spanned the gap between them and landed a hard punch to the old man's face, dropping him to the floor.

His way now clear, Jonathan sprinted through the entrance, wanting to get outside and put some distance and darkness between himself and the men before they recovered. He ran, however, straight into the business ends of two AK-47s.

One of the new arrivals jerked the muzzle of his rifle toward the door and everyone moved back inside. Someone grabbed Jonathan from behind and slammed him face-first into the wall. The man kicked his legs apart and patted him down for weapons, quickly finding the pistol taped to his calf and ripping it free along with a fist full of hair.

"Why are you here?" asked the leader in almost perfect English.

"I would like to help, if I can… write press releases in the States, offer my insights into how to get the American people more on your side."

"They will never be on our side. The Jews own everything – TV, film, newspapers, magazines."

"But that can be changed. I'm a student at Stanford, majoring in Communications – TV and Journalism. If I could speak with one of your leaders, I'm sure I could come up with a better plan than you have now."

"Bullshit, as you Americans say. We know who you are not, some-one named Robertson. What we don't yet know is who you really are."

"My passport says I'm Robertson. My mother says I'm Robertson. Only you…"

The men grabbed hold of him. Jonathan reflexively snapped out a kick but they were too close for it to do much damage. He jerked one hand free and elbowed one man in the throat, then kneed another in the stomach. But there were too many of them. Even as they pinned his arms and legs, Jonathan swung his head back, butting someone in the mouth. Another's hand was on his face. He sank his teeth deep into the man's fingers, refusing to let go until a metallic, world-jarring blow to the head relaxed his jaw. The blow also took away Jonathan's ability to command his body and he fought just to remain conscious.

The men whisked him headfirst down the hallway, bumping into walls and doorways before angling Jonathan's body into a room that reeked of urine and excrement. They hoisted his feet up and shoved him down toward the toilet bowl. He felt the crown of his head dip into a cold, chunky liquid.

Jonathan strained to straighten up, to get his head out of the bowl. But they were too strong and his head dipped lower until the thick lumpy water encircled his forehead.

"Who are you and why are you here?" demanded their leader.

Jonathan didn't know what to say. If he told them his true mission, to find and possibly kill Makram, the PLO might help him. But if they were HFFP, it would get him killed.

"I told you!"

"Just a few weeks ago, the name Andrew Allen Robertson was submitted to us for training by Umberto in France. Everyone in his group, including Umberto himself, was soon killed by the Jews. Now you turn up here, claiming to be a student and offering assistance? Drown him!"

His men angled Jonathan's legs for another push.

"I want to talk with Yusuf Makram," Jonathan said.

"About what?"

"My father," he blurted out as they started him down. A neutral answer might buy him enough time to learn where their loyalties lay.

"Why?"

"He was his friend...once. He died years ago. Some say Dr. Makram killed him but he had always been kind to me and I just want to learn the truth."

The men stopped. "You came armed."

"This is a dangerous place."

"Where did he die, your father?" asked the young Arab leader.

"Boston."

The man's eyes fixed on Jonathan's face. "What was your father's name?"

"Daniel Lusk."

"When you lived in Boston, where did you go to school?" he asked.

"Ah...Jefferson, I think it was." His mind scrambled for a possible reason he would be asked such a question.

"Your second grade teacher. What was her name?"

"Miss Wormsey, Wormser, something like that."

"And what about your best friend? Do you remember him?" the young Arab said, smiling.

Jonathan looked at the man more closely. "Saied?"

"The same."

Chapter Twenty-Four

The constant motion. The blindfold. Hours of traveling – south by boat, then east by van over rough roads. The stink that he hadn't been able to wash away, even after scrubbing himself repeatedly with soap and brush, all combined to make Jonathan nauseated.

"I hope you understand why we have to be so careful," said Saied from the seat beside him. "When Arafat started licking the Jews' asses, the real Palestinians turned to my father for real leadership. They're even calling him *Abu Palestine*, Father of Palestine. But it's made him a huge target, by Arafat and his traitors even more than the Jews. So we got to stay out of the cities and lead a simple life, like in ancient times. It's some boring ass shit."

Saied laughed. "Do you remember the time you talked Dwayne Ackerman into putting on a blindfold, telling him it was for a taste-test to see if he could identify the type of sandwich you had for lunch? You gave him a big bite of your ham and cheese and he thought it was smoked turkey?"

"I'd forgotten about that," Jonathan said, laughing on the outside while hiding his sadness inside.

Saied's voice turned serious. "Do you know why someone would be tailing you?"

The question caught Jonathan by surprise. "No. What do they look like?"

"I was told he's Japanese."

If he was Japanese, it had to be *yakuza*. It couldn't be a Kami sent to find or protect him or *Kancho* Kubo would have warned him. Not wanting Saied or his father, who could soon be enemies, knowing about his enemies in Japan, Jonathan just shrugged.

"Don't worry," said Saied. "Dad's people are taking care of him. He won't be bothering you again."

Ojima sat in the back of a battered Jeep, his body jerking from side to side as the young Arab driver navigated the uneven road. "When we see friend?" he yelled.

"He is just there," said the teenager, pointing at a ravine up ahead.

The driver slid to a stop and the cloud of dust that had roiled steadily up behind them since leaving the camp engulfed the Jeep and its two passengers.

"Down here," said the driver, climbing out and heading toward the gully. When he saw that Ojima was hesitant to follow, he stopped and added, "We had to hide him from bad people, you understand? Bad people wanted to rob and kill him. We protected your friend."

The driver disappeared over the edge. Cautiously, Ojima followed.

Chapter Twenty-Five

Jonathan was relieved when the van finally stopped, his blindfold removed, and he was allowed to climb out and stretch his legs. They were parked at the edge of a dry, deserted land that extended as far as Jonathan could see.

The small group gathered their canteens and headed east on foot, following a goat-trail down into a steep, crumbly canyon and up the other side. Although it was early in the day, it was already so hot they were soon forced to make a brief respite at an aloe-lined mudhole, shaded by a single palm.

The group's trek continued across the desolate hills and valleys, rises, and depressions for another couple of hours before angling north toward a low mountain range, their apparent destination. Under the watchful eyes of two heavily-armed *fedayeen*, the small band passed through a narrow split in the cliff to end their journey inside a box canyon.

Squat goat-hair tents lined half of the encircling walls, Jeeps and supplies the other. Women with white scarves wrapped tightly around their heads cooked and sewed and washed clothes and babies. Small boys carried real rifles, real grenades. Chickens, dogs, and goats ran loose. Ducks and geese, with one leg tethered to stakes, walked in endless circles. But except for the two sentries and those in his group, Jonathan saw no men.

After speaking briefly with an old woman, Saied led Jonathan to a tent near a cave at the far end of the canyon. "My father's still gone," he said. "Until he gets back, why don't you rest here while I check in."

Jonathan lay on a threadbare Persian rug with a musty sheepskin rolled up and tucked under his head for a pillow. Between the heat and lack of sleep, he felt drained. But he knew he couldn't allow himself to drift off – he had to be awake and alert when Makram returned. Besides, the unfettered hatred he had seen in the dark eyes of the sentries, the women, even the small children, when he entered the compound, warned him against closing his eyes.

He sweltered through an intense sticky afternoon and was thankful when the sun finally neared the canyon's westernmost lip. Gunshots and a shrill eerie warbling sound pulled him to the flap of his tent. Outside, a bonfire was licking at the darkening sky. Men galloped on horseback through the entrance, firing their rifles into the air as women and girls, hands cupped around their mouths, emitted high-pitched warbling shrieks.

"You awake?" asked Saied, entering the tent through the uphill flap.

"What's going on?"

"Father's back. They're celebrating. You hungry?"

"Starved."

The smell of roasting goat drew Jonathan to the fire, the animal's fat sizzling as it dripped into the flames. Two women pulled the charred carcass off the spit, hacked it into fist-sized chunks, and piled them high on a huge silver tray. Roasted chickens and ducks were added, ringing the mutton. Chopped tomatoes, chunks of goat cheese, and beans were stuffed wherever there was room.

"Is your father going to join us?" Jonathan asked, not seeing him at the table.

"No. He's got his nightly prayers. He apologized and said he'll see you tomorrow."

"Was he surprised to learn I was here?"

"Oh, yeah," said Saied, dead serious for a change.

Chapter Twenty-Six

"*S*alaat!*"

Jonathan heard the Call to Prayer and looked out his tent flap. He hadn't risked sleeping and welcomed the beginning of a new day, a day in which he would learn the truth and either walk away, kill Makram, or die. But regardless of which it turned out to be, his waiting would soon be over.

The warm apricot glow of the rising sun brightened the sky as men, women, and children, apparently everyone in the camp, performed their pre-prayer ablutions. As they finished, they assembled in their appropriate spot – men in front, women in back – behind a white *thobed* man standing on a mound of earth, facing southeast.

"*Allahu Akbar!*" the man cried out. "Let there arise from you a band of people attractive to all that is good, urging what is right, and forbidding what is wrong. Such men shall surely triumph," he recited from the Koran, then the group bowed in unison and prostrated themselves in the dirt.

After their final supplications were completed, the worshipers disbanded and began their morning chores. Even with his scruffy, gray-streaked beard and thick horn-rimmed classes, Jonathan easily recognized Yusuf Makram – the white-*thobed imam* – heading his way. He quickly began organizing his thoughts – what he wanted to ask, how he would frame delicate questions. But without even glancing his way, Makram continued on past his tent, ambling in a kind of slow, loose-hipped swagger that gave him an elegance he had not had when Jonathan last saw him in Boston.

The sun was almost directly overhead and the heat stifling by the time Yusuf Makram finally paid Jonathan a visit. He hugged him warmly and kissed him on both cheeks. It was as if nothing had changed since the days when he and Saied had had their weekly sleepovers at their small place in Harvard University Housing, only three blocks away from where the Levys had lived. But something had changed, many some-things, and it could be seen in his eyes, although Jonathan wasn't sure what he was seeing. Was it sadness? Was it coldness? Or was it hatred?

Makram lowered himself stiffly, painfully onto an oval cushion and sat cross-legged. Except for a gold chain encircling his neck, from which dangled a worn key and a tubular steel pendant, he was dressed plainly, in clean but threadbare clothes like those of the camp residents.

"Have you eaten?" he asked, then smiled. "I cannot offer you a cheeseburger and root beer float as we used to enjoy. But I can offer fruit juice and our version of a lamb burger?"

"Nothing, thank you."

"Trust me," said Saied, "ask for something or they'll drive you nuts."

Jonathan was well aware of what some called the Muslim Law of Hospitality. His life, in fact, could hinge on it. "Some water or juice would be great."

Makram clapped his hands and a woman hurried over with a cup of some type of juice.

"In spite of all the horrible things I am sure you have heard about me, you may rest assured that you are quite safe with us," said Makram, taking the cup from her and handing it to Jonathan. "But what brings you here?"

"Answers," said Jonathan. "I was only five or six at the time so I don't remember much about that night. I tried researching it, hoping to fill in at least the major gaps in my memory, but the general consensus seemed to be that you intentionally killed my father."

Makram started to speak but Jonathan continued. "I knew that couldn't be right. One of the few clear images I have is of you stand-ing just inside the doorway, arguing with Dad. You were upset that we were there, which meant it couldn't have been intentional and made me question everything I had read." Jonathan shrugged. "Since you were the only person who could clear things up, I set out to find you, which wasn't easy."

"Your father's death was an accident," Makram said, but quickly made a face as if struggling for the right word. "An accident but not an accident. An organizer from the ALA, the Arab Liberation Army, had been sent to the United States to mobilize action committees as the Jews were doing. Because he had been sent by my family, I could not refuse him our hospitality. So he was living with us for a short time."

"His name's Saleh," added Saied. "He's one tough dude. Gave me the creeps when I first met him. Now he works for us."

"Yes, Saleh began sharing with me the horrors he had seen done to our people by the Jews – brutal rapes with different kinds of objects, the vicious murder of women in a maternity ward, setting homes ablaze with their elderly occupants still inside, blowing up a movie theater filled with children and having to remove the bodies and console the parents, things that sickened me. As the fighting approached my home-town and Hannah and my family could no longer be reached, I became extremely concerned."

"I can understand that," said Jonathan when Makram looked to him as if for an answer.

"Are you married, Jonathan?"

He shook his head.

"Me too, Bro," added Saied cheerfully.

His father shot him a silencing look. "Do you have a girlfriend?"

"I did."

"Did you love her?"

"Yes."

"Imagine you were still together and very much in love. Imagine too that she was carrying your child and had returned to her home, a very dangerous place, for a final visit. It was her fervent wish. You were against it but she had a mind of her own and would not listen to reason."

Jonathan smiled kindly. "Are they all like that?"

"Made so by Allah, Praise be unto Him in his infinite wisdom, which he has yet to reveal to man." The three men all nodded in agreement. "Do you remember Hannah? She made you and Saied those cookies with faces on them."

"Of course. She was a wonderful woman. Always had a smile on her face and a warm treat for Saied and me."

"I have been married four times and she is still the one my heart goes to in my dreams. So you will understand how frightened I was for her safety."

Jonathan nodded.

"Saleh too understood it and capitalized fully upon both my fear and my weakness for drink. After I delivered the briefcase, I intended to warn your father so he could get his family away. But I was attacked by Levy and the other Jews. See this lump?" he said, removing his glasses and running his finger over the bridge of his nose. "They broke my nose and blackened my eyes. I ran from the house, afraid they would kill me. Shamefully, it was only after I was inside the safety of my car and Saleh had pulled away that I remembered your father. As we approached the house, I reached over and honked to draw him outside but he was already standing there, my briefcase in his hand. My heart sank. I yelled for Saleh to stop but he refused. Then it was too late."

Makram looked into Jonathan's eyes, searching for a reaction. But Jonathan's mind was racing, comparing what he had just been told with what he remembered from that night. He didn't remember hearing a horn.

"I don't understand why you bombed the party or how it was connected to your wife's situation. Was it just that they were Jews?" Jonathan asked.

"No. I had many Jewish friends. Our village had lived in peace with them for centuries. It was what the Levys were doing, raising money to buy bombs and bullets to kill my people, perhaps even my own wife."

"A fundraiser for the State of Israel... I heard you read one of the checks."

"Yes. When Saleh first claimed its true purpose, my first reaction was to simply do the same, host a fundraiser for the ALA. But it was not just a matter of money, he argued. Unlike the Jews, we were a people without powerful allies. The only way we could hope to stop the slaughter was to fight them in unconventional ways. This act, he insisted, would say to the Jews, 'If you harm our people, we will harm yours. And we will do it where your armies cannot protect them.' After a few more glasses of *arak*, I agreed to go but would only leave the device if I found proof that Saleh was right, which I did. So I left it, feeling in my drunken state that it would somehow help protect my Hannah. It, of course, did not. Even worse, it caused the death of a man I idolized."

The men sat, lost in their own memories, for a minute. "How is your mother?" asked Makram, breaking the silence.

"She died not long after my father."

Makram's eyes locked onto Jonathan's. "Not as a result of the bomb, I hope? She never made any secret of her dislike of us but she was Dr. Lusk's wife and your mother."

"Not a direct result."

Makram's eyes narrowed just slightly, obviously catching his inference. "I am sorry," he offered, his voice flat.

One of Makram's aides strode up. "This just arrived," he said, handing him a manila folder. Makram opened it and glanced inside. Whatever he saw gave him reason to reflect in silence for several seconds. "Forgive me," said Makram, standing up, "but something serious has arisen. I apologize that I cannot spend as much time with you as you surely deserve, especially after going to such efforts. We must break camp. Do you need help gathering your things?"

The suddenness of it all caught Jonathan by surprise. "I didn't bring anything with me so... whenever."

Makram spoke briefly with one of his men, then he, Saied, and Jonathan walked to the narrow canyon entrance. There they were met by a surly pair of armed *fedayeen*.

"Do not be a stranger," said Makram, shaking Jonathan's hand and kissing him on the cheek. "You always have a home with us. If you would ever truly like to join us in our struggle, we would welcome you."

As Jonathan turned to leave, Saied sidled up, obviously intending to accompany him.

"I am sorry but I will need you here," Yusuf told his son. "We have preparations to make."

As the two *fedayeen* started off, a clearly disappointed Saied gave his former best friend a heartfelt hug, then waved as Jonathan jogged to catch up.

"Why did you turn him away so quickly?" asked Saied.

His father waited until the three were out of earshot. "He is our enemy. He will not be coming back."

"What do you mean?" said Saied, confronting his father. "You can't hurt him, not after all you've done to him already!"

Jonathan heard raised voices and looked back just in time to see Makram slap his son across the face. The two men stood as if in a serious confrontation but were too far away to catch anything they were saying.

"I owe him nothing," hissed Makram, lowering his voice. "His father's death was the hand of Allah, Praise be unto Him."

"Please don't do this," begged Saied.

"'Not a direct result,' he said, did you hear him? He meant it was, in fact, related. So he accounts me responsible for the death of both his parents. What would you do if you felt as he does?"

"But you don't have to kill him. What can he possibly do that Mossad's and the PLO's best couldn't?"

"They could not find me yet he did!"

"Because I brought him here! He would never have found us otherwise. Once he's dropped off at the airport, we'll never see him again."

Makram stared coldly at his son. "Did he mention his years in the Japanese military school or being a part of an elite antiterrorist unit?"

Saied shook his head.

"And what of this?" Makram said, opening the folder in his hand and holding out a photo of Jonathan and Gutfreund shaking hands at the Paris café.

"Who am I looking at?" asked Saied.

"Mossad's Counterinsurgency Chief. We asked Umberto to remove him while he was in Paris but he failed and everyone except for Jonathan was hunted down and murdered."

Saied was struck speechless.

"He is turning into his father," hissed Makram, "and I know Lusk self-righteousness and resolve all too well. If we do not remove him now, while we have him within our sights, he will surely come back to kill me. Maybe today. Maybe tomorrow. Maybe next year or in ten. But he will most surely come for me. I do not fear death. I do, however, fear a cessation of the struggle. No one can be allowed to jeopardize its completion."

Loose red stones littered their path, making it difficult to walk. Jonathan and the two HFFP fighters had been forced to spread out a couple of arms' lengths as each picked his own line down the uneven trail.

From what Jonathan knew about his father, he was sure he would not have wanted him to hurt, and especially not kill, his former friend. But his father had always tried obsessively to be fair, even if it meant not being fair to himself or his family. An old Chinese saying fit his father perfectly, "Benevolence, carried to extreme, creates weakness."

Something *Kancho* had once told Jonathan came to mind. "You know to be vigilant among those who hate you or wish you ill. But you should never forget to also guard against those who do not care enough for your safety to give it due consideration."

Makram had known they were at the Levys' party. If he had cared so much about his father, the man he claimed to have idolized, he would have made sure he and his family were nowhere near a bomb.

Then there was the matter of the horn. No one had honked. He would have heard it. And even if he had honked and it had drawn his father outside to safety, the bomb would still have been inside with Jonathan and his mother.

It was disappointing. He had come hoping Dr. Makram would offer a plausible explanation, something he hadn't thought of. This clearly was not the man he had known, or thought he had known – or whom his father considered a good friend. His visit had only confirmed his worst suspicions. And now Makram apparently wanted to finish what his "accident" had failed to achieve in Boston – to take his life too.

Jonathan wasn't sure when the ambush would occur. He assumed it would begin when they were out of earshot of those in the camp. Arabs, as Saied had pointed out and he had experienced in the camps, had a thing about rights of hospitality, something based on the Koran. But he wasn't sure how far those rights extended, distancewise.

They had hiked a mile or so through a narrow *wadi* and then up and around a peaked hillock when the Arab who had taken point glanced around as if looking back toward the camp. But Jonathan caught a quick, almost imperceptible nod to the Arab bringing up the rear. The second man responded by causally shifting his weapon into firing position.

Jonathan stumbled as if he had tripped. "Damn," he said, leaning over, his hands going down toward his ankle. In a blur, he snatched up a rock, spun, and smashed the face of the man behind him. Then he launched a powerful roundhouse kick aimed at the back of the leader's head. The man, however, turned just as the kick arrived and the blow ricocheted off his forehead. Dazed, he staggered back, lifting the muzzle of his Kalashnikov, wisely or reflexively positioning it between himself and Jonathan.

The Arab's head was clearing rapidly. Jonathan's first thought was to snatch up the other man's assault rifle. But if he fired, the sound would bring others. So instead, he threw the rock, striking the terrorist in the face. The blow snapped the man's head back. As it did, he squeezed the trigger of his AK-47, peppering the ground with a short, loud burst.

Jonathan was on him before he could recover. Using *taiho jutsu*, the feudal police arresting art he had learned at the Kami Kan, he quickly bound, gagged, and blindfolded the two men. Snatching up their weapons, he sprinted down the trail. As soon as he had rounded the first bend, however, he climbed up among the rocks and sparse shrubbery. Staying low, he doubled-back toward the camp entrance and Makram.

Chapter Twenty-Seven

A milky-gray Pharaoh's vulture caught a thermal and rode it high over the rocky, deserted lands, climbing until it was little more than a speck against the sky. The bird hovered for a few seconds, then looped downward in easy, ever-enlarging circles before leveling off and crossing directly over where Jonathan hid among the rocks near the entrance to Makram's camp. As it passed, the bird fixed its red eyes on the American. "Check back later," Jonathan muttered. "You're welcome to whatever of me remains."

Sharp voices and the pounding of hoofs drew Jonathan's attention to the cleft. Eleven men on horseback galloped hard through the opening and down the trail toward where he had left his two escorts. He had known someone would be sent to check things out. How long it took to occur would either support his belief that Makram intended to kill him or prove his innocence, at least in this matter. Responding immediately to the sound of shots would have meant they hadn't expected to hear them. Waiting as long as they did, however, meant they were not surprised and only came looking when their men didn't return soon enough.

A rifle shot from inside the enclosure launched a line of Jeeps that raced through the entrance, almost bumper to bumper. Jonathan studied the occupants of each, searching for Makram but seeing only women, children, goats, ducks, geese, tents, every material thing they possessed. Dust boiled up behind them as the uneven line snaked its way east, toward Syria.

A lone Jeep flanked by eight armed men on horseback passed through the cleft. Instead of turning left and following the others across the desert, this group headed straight toward where Jonathan lay on his stomach beside a putrid pool of stagnant water, hidden from easy view only by a scattering of thigh-high boulders and a handful of scraggly shrubs. The Jeep stopped a hundred feet or so away, Makram in the passenger's seat, Saied behind the wheel.

When they come, don't let yourself be distracted, he told himself as he kept his head down. *Focus only on taking out Makram. Then take as many with you as you can.* He slid one of the AK-47s forward, to where he could raise and fire it quickly.

The horses' hooves pounded the earth. The Jeep's engine gunned. Jonathan snatched up the rifle and readied himself for the assault. But it never came. When he lifted his head, the horsemen were galloping down the same trail the other mounted *fedayeen* had taken, and the Jeep had spun around and was racing to catch up with the caravan.

Jonathan swung the rifle up and steadied it on top of the boulder in front of him. He tried to fix a bead on the back of Makram's head but with little luck. The Jeep bucked and jerked across the uneven ground, throwing the men's heads from side to side.

They reached a stretch of flat land and Jonathan quickly aligned the front and rear sights onto his target. *Squeeze. Don't jerk*, he cautioned himself. As he eased the trigger back, the Jeep's right wheel hit a rock and pitched hard to the left, forcing Jonathan to re-aim. But before he could get his shot off, its engine sputtered, backfired, then restarted, shooting forward, kicking up a cloud of red dust so thick Jonathan wasn't able to get another clear shot. All he could do was watch as both the Jeep and his target grew tiny in the distance.

His anger with himself for waiting too long was short-circuited as a pair of mounted *fedayeen* returned, followed by others in groups of two and three. The last to ride up was a bearded old man with bandoliers crisscrossing the front of his black outer garment. He dug out a pair of battered binoculars from his saddlebags and meticulously scanned the surrounding countryside, at one point sweeping directly across where Jonathan crouched low.

"Contact Fahad," he said after several minutes. "He is to assign men to watch the roads, towns, airports and bus stations. Fawzi, you and your men go to the van and wait there. The rest, come with me."

Fearing the old warrior might have left a sniper behind, Jonathan waited until after the sun had set before leaving his hiding place. Knowing it was pointless to attempt to follow Makram, they were traveling too fast and had too much of a head start, Jonathan headed south.

He walked through much of the night before coming to a river bounded on both sides by rows of barbed and razor wire. A loud pop high overhead sent Jonathan onto his stomach as a parachute flare lit up the sky and everything below it. Automatic weapons opened fire in rattling bursts. From the fiery streams of tracer bullets flashing across the river, he could see that they were aiming at someone farther to the south. Another parachute flare went off, this one over that more southerly region.

In the flare's brief blue light, Jonathan could see a footbridge spanning the river a few hundred yards south of him. It was clearly the point of contention. He would have to wait until the battle ended and the dust settled before making his attempt. He hoped it would take days for the hostilities to end.

Fortunately and a bit oddly, he only had to wait a couple of hours. Just before dawn, the firing stopped. Half an hour later, as the sun cleared the eastern horizon, he was surprised to see people walking across the bridge as if nothing had happened. But not one to pass up a gift, Jonathan joined the stream of Palestinian laborers making what was their daily trek to work inside Israel. When the day's work was done, they crossed the bridge again and the nightly battle began.

At the gate, Jonathan explained his situation and the sergeant made a call. Within minutes, an army helicopter transported Jonathan to Jerusalem, where he was debriefed by men who introduced themselves only as associates of Ariel Gutfreund.

Jonathan sat in an ancient olive grove, looking down on the city of Jerusalem. He was not happy with himself. His conversations with Israeli Intelligence hadn't been handled well. He had told them what he knew and they had told him nothing that could help him find Makram again. He should never have assumed their agendas were complementary, especially after Gutfreund's warning in Paris. The only thing he would walk away with was the truth.

His eyes swept the dry gnarled lands surrounding him, where thousand-year-old battles still raged and had even reached across the Atlantic Ocean to strike down his father. But in spite of its long history of turmoil, he felt an affinity for the place. Like Israel, the weight of the past still sat very firmly and heavily on his shoulders too.

He had also been a fool when dealing with Makram. "Rectitude, carried to extreme, creates rigidity," he mumbled out loud, reciting another old Chinese saying, this one applying to him. Rigid he had been. He had had to investigate every detail, finding proof beyond question before finally attempting to do what he should have done in the first place.

"*Do desu ka?*"

Jonathan's head snapped around to see Ojima making his way up the hillside, accompanied by an Israeli IDF sergeant. Jumping to his feet, Jonathan bowed to his *sensei*.

"So I assume you two know each other?" said the sergeant in New York-accented English.

Jonathan nodded. "But surprised to see him here."

"As were we. We had to burn an operative to save his ass in Lebanon. He was trying to find you and ended up with some very bad people."

"I save own ass!" interjected Ojima.

The Israeli laughed. "Well, true enough... for that one battle. He beat two of the bastards to death, literally to death. Then he used their weapons to kill a third, a man we called *The Widow Maker*, and the name well earned. But there was no way he was going to make it out of the country alive. So we made a call and another friend of yours ordered his extraction."

"What are you doing here?" asked Jonathan after the sergeant had left.

"We *tomodachi*. I must help."

"But I asked you to stay at Stanford. This was not something that I could have done with you here. I had to do it alone."

"You gone too long. I wait, wait, then come. *Giri, neh?*"

Jonathan nodded. He did understand. It was *giri*, indebtedness or obligation, that had brought both of them to the Middle East. "*Domo*, thank you," he told Ojima. "You are a true friend. I've only had one other and even though he'd have wanted to come with me too, I would have spent all my time trying to keep him alive."

"I keep self alive… and you also if you allow."

Jonathan nodded tiredly. He couldn't, or more accurately wouldn't, tell Ojima the truth, that he would never allow him to accompany him. With Makram now aware of his existence, aware of his skills, and aware that he possessed new and indisputable reasons to track him down and kill him, he would be on a suicide mission. If all went well, no one would walk away.

Chapter Twenty-Eight

After getting his *sensei* back to Stanford and hopefully convinced to remain there, Jonathan cut his hair short, dyed it auburn, and flew to Paris.

Using a new passport supplied by Mochizuki in the name of Michael Young, he took a suite at the posh Royal-Monceau Hotel. Makram, he figured, would be less apt to look for him there. And, according to both Mochizuki and Gutfreund, he was looking.

His first task was to transfer seventy-five thousand dollars of his inheritance into the Paris branch of Bank of America. There was a lot more if he needed it, almost two million dollars. He was all-in, prepared to spend every penny he had received from his parents and both sets of grandparents clearing the slate on Makram. Besides, it was highly likely that he would have no use for money when the dust cleared.

Next, he answered a small ad for a singing telegram service and hired the owner and sole employee, a college drama student named Raynard. He sent Raynard to Guy's bakery – not to sing, but to make contact.

"I would like to speak with Guy," he told the clerk, as Jonathan had instructed him.

"Guy who?"

"We have business for him but will only be here between four-thirty and five tomorrow afternoon," his messenger said, writing a name and phone number on the bakery receipt pad. "This is where we can be reached. Four-thirty until five tomorrow only."

Jonathan waited in a local wine bar, a pretty Parisian art student in the chair beside him. He had met her that morning at a record shop. She was Eurasian and her dark-hair and olive skin reminded him a little of Nanami. Although she didn't realize it, she was there solely to help him blend in with the other couples enjoying a glass of wine after work. If Guy were as resourceful as Umberto had believed him to be, he could easily match a telephone number with an address. With that information, the Frenchman, if he suspected who Jonathan was and wished him ill (perhaps to avenge Umberto's death or the loss of his business) or sought to collect Makram's bounty, could locate and kill him. Umberto had assured Jonathan that the man was completely without any political agenda, a capitalist pure and simple, and Jonathan was somewhat betting his life that the Italian had been right.

The phone behind the bar rang several times during the hour he waited, making Jonathan tense up every time it did. The large clock over the bar read four-forty-seven when the door opened and a couple of tough-looking workmen ambled in, their eyes making a quick sweep of the place. After speaking briefly with the bartender, the two took a back table, where they were delivered two glasses of red wine and two steaming bowls of onion soup.

At exactly four-fifty-five, the phone rang. The workmen's eyes snapped up from their bowls, sending Jonathan's hand to the Beretta 9mm in his ankle holster.

"Christopher Miller," called the bartender.

Raynard, the singing actor, slid off his barstool and ambled toward the telephone, the workmen's eyes glued to his every move. As the young Parisian pressed the receiver to his ear, one of the workmen pulled something out of his pocket and raised it. Jonathan's pistol flashed up, startling the young woman beside him. But the object in the workman's hand was not a pistol; it was a small camera.

Jonathan slipped out the back door while the workmen were focused on the young actor. He had to hurry. He had only allowed himself – and anyone who might want to ambush him – fifteen minutes to get to his car, drive a little over a mile through traffic, park, and reach the telephone booth. Although he had practiced it many times, he seldom made it with more than a minute or two to spare.

The phone rang at exactly five-fifteen.

"To whom am I speaking?" came the voice on the other end.

"That is not important. Who are you?"

"I am he you asked to call. You have business with me?"

"I could have a great deal of business, if our initial transaction goes well."

"I have a select clientele. I only do business with those I know, or with those recommended by someone I know. If you do not fit either of these descriptions, there is nothing further to discuss."

"Are you calling from a secure phone?" Jonathan asked, having no choice but to be honest.

"It is a pay telephone, chosen at random."

"Good. We never met, not directly. I was working with an Italian acquaintance of yours."

"I thought all associates of that acquaintance died prematurely."

"Your information is almost correct. I survived, thanks to our friend."

"Can you name the contact person for this group?"

"Evelyn."

"I will have my driver pick you up in, say, thirty minutes at...where? The Royal-Monceau, where you are staying?"

Shocked into silence, it was a couple of seconds before Jonathan could respond. "I am impressed," he finally managed to get out, and meant it. "But why would you be interested in tailing me?" The line went dead.

Jonathan waited behind a kiosk, just down the street from his hotel's entrance. He was nervous. Except for his 9mm and a letter he had written and mailed to *Kancho* Kubo, he was completely at Guy's mercy. The letter, of course, could not save him, only bring retribution.

A Citroën pulled up in front of the hotel and flashed its lights. Jonathan grabbed the handle of his Beretta, made a final visual sweep of the street and sidewalks, then approached the Citroën's side window. Everything looked clear inside so Jonathan crossed his fingers and climbed into the back seat.

The driver said nothing as they headed toward the center of town, away from where Jonathan had expected them to go – the countryside, where the meeting had been held with Umberto. They turned onto the Champs Elysees and continued on, their trip ending at the base of the Eiffel Tower.

"He awaits there," the driver said, nodding towards Paris's most famous landmark.

Jonathan took the elevator to the top, where he easily spotted Guy's massive body silhouetted against the Paris skyline. "As you see, you arrived very much alive as promised," said the Frenchman, a twinkle in his eye. "Now, what is it you desire of me?"

"A weapon."

"Type?"

"Hi-Standard .22 automatic."

"How many?"

"Two," he said, not wanting the man to know he was working alone, if he didn't already. "And two boxes of minimum-load shorts."

"Five hundred U.S. each. Bullets? One hundred dollars additional."

Jonathan handed him a fat envelope. It contained ten thousand dollars.

"This is far too much," said Guy, thumbing through the stack of hundred dollar bills.

"It's an advance for information."

"Information?" the fat man said, massaging his layered chin. "About what or whom?"

"Yusuf Makram."

"You are making a joke," said Guy, trying to hand the envelope back.

"I thought you had ears everywhere?"

"I did not say I could not gain information on the man. It is merely that this is not enough for such information."

"And I said this was only an advance. How much?"

"Fifty thousand dollars," the fat man said, looking him straight in the eye.

"Half tomorrow and half after the information checks out."

"All by tomorrow. Afterwards?" he said, shrugging his massive shoulders. "A dead man cannot settle his debts with the living, only with his Maker. Also, our information may not prove correct. Such happens in this business – informants lie or are given erroneous information, sometimes intentionally, sometimes unintentionally. Plans also change. But if what we supply proves incorrect, my people will keep searching at no additional cost."

"I'll get the rest of the money to you tomorrow. How soon will you have the information?"

"Perhaps soon. Perhaps weeks. I can make no promises, only that we will look until we find what you desire."

Jonathan immediately moved out of the Royal-Monceau and into what became the first of a series of hotels. He called Guy's number daily, always from a different pay phone, keeping his conversations short to better ensure they couldn't be traced.

"Nothing today, sorry," the cheerful woman who answered Guy's telephone said every day. But on the seventeenth day, her message changed; they might have something for him later. He was to call back that evening at ten o'clock, which he did. "A driver will pick you up in one hour," said the man on the other end.

He hadn't asked and Jonathan hadn't told him where he was staying. But at precisely eleven o'clock, the Citroën pulled up in front of his hotel and Jonathan climbed inside. As this was his second time around with Guy, this no longer surprised him. What did surprise him, however, was their destination.

The car dropped him off at the Eiffel Tower, which this time was cloaked in a thick blanket of fog. As one of Guy's men took Jonathan to the top, he could smell the stench of old rusty metal, made even more intense by the dampness.

"This wouldn't seem the best place to meet someone in secret?" Jonathan said as soon as he got out of the lift. "If any number of people knew we were here, we would be like sitting ducks."

"It is open. We are very high. And the weather prevents all but a close shot, which would be impossible, considering my men."

"Ever heard of bombs?" scoffed Jonathan.

"But, you see, I have never before gone to the same place twice for such meetings. This could not be anticipated. So relax, my young friend. I have received word that Makram will be in Cyprus for a meeting."

"When?"

"It is tentatively set for next Wednesday. I will soon know the exact date of his arrival, where he is to stay, and the time and place of the meeting. We will supply surveillance for 24 hours. If you need more, it can be supplied at a cost of three hundred dollars per day."

"I'd like at least five days' coverage, possibly seven, if he's there that long. I also need a good scoped sniper rifle, an Uzi, and either another 9mm semi and Hi-Standard .22 or mine smuggled into the country."

"No problem. I suggest you fly to Cyprus as soon as possible to establish yourself there. I can have papers, tickets, reservations for you by tomorrow night...unless you would rather make your own?"

"Yours will be fine," he said, knowing he could change them later if he didn't like the look of them.

Chapter Twenty-Nine

Andre, Guy's man in Cyprus, picked Jonathan up at the airport. As they drove to Nicosia, the island's capital, the chain-smoking French expat filled him in on what they had learned in the interim.

Although they didn't yet know the exact day or time of Makram's arrival, they knew the who and the where. Makram would meet with Marwan Barghouti, who also headed a group opposed to Arafat. The meeting was reportedly to patch up a rift between the two men so they could work together to remove Arafat as head of the PLO and neutralize Sabri al-Nazari, the organization's second-in-command.

The meeting would be held onboard a Soviet ship scheduled to dock at the port of Kyrenia the following day. The Soviets had indicated to port authorities that they would be berthed there for three days. So Jonathan had four days at most in which to carry out his plan, whatever that plan turned out to be.

As Makram and his people were expected to stay at the Apollo Hotel in the capital, Andre put Jonathan into a small apartment just down the street from its main entrance.

The Apollo was a four-storied, stone-and-plaster structure built a century earlier in the Moorish style. Located at the top of one of the city's highest hills, the hotel offered a magnificent view of the island and the blue-green waters of the Mediterranean Sea.

With but ten small rooms on each of its second, third, and fourth floors, the entire hotel, all thirty rooms, had been reserved by a Middle Eastern trading company that had its headquarters in Beirut. Although the rooms hadn't been designated as to occupant, Jonathan guessed Makram would sleep on the third floor, probably in one of the back rooms.

Based on past operations, Andre assumed that the hotel lobby, gift shops, dining room, bar, guest rooms, elevator, and all points of entrance would be swept for bombs. This meant that a device could not be planted before Makram's arrival, if Jonathan wanted one. At least one guard would likely patrol the hallway on each floor. All entrances would surely be manned. Men would be on the roof while others watched the building and grounds from nearby locations. Jonathan would have to take all this into consideration when formulating his plan.

But as had been driven home repeatedly while being trained to protect the Japanese Imperial Family, a dedicated assassin was almost impossible to stop if he didn't mind dying in the process.

"The Heroic Fighters' advance team arrived late last night," announced Andre the next morning.

"Was Makram with them?"

"No. But his men are staying in the Apollo so it will almost surely be his official residence when he does arrive."

"What is security like?"

"Extremely tight, as always."

"Perhaps you wouldn't mind helping me. I'd be happy to pay for it."

"What is it you need?"

"You and Monsieur Guy are obviously far smarter and more experienced than I am in these matters. If you were me, how would you approach Makram?"

Andre smiled as he wagged his finger playfully at Jonathan. "Ah, you are clearly much wiser than your years. I now understand why Monsieur Guy likes you."

Jonathan snickered at the comment. Guy had seemed anything but friendly and wondered how he would treat someone he didn't like.

Andrew rubbed his stubbled chin as he gave the matter some thought. "As I said, their security is always very tight, very precise. But," said Andre, "unlike what they clearly believe, not without weaknesses, which they also repeat, time after time."

The next morning, Andre supplied the final bit of information they had been waiting for – the day and time of the meeting. It would take place that afternoon, meaning Makram was either already in the country or would arrive soon.

"Do you know if he will come here before the meeting or go directly to the ship?"

Andre shrugged.

"So we don't even know if he will ever actually show up at the hotel?"

"We know nothing for sure," said Andre. "However, an order for a freshly killed goat dinner has been placed with the chef. One of Makram's men is in the kitchen, inspecting ingredients and watching every move the chef makes."

"What time's this dinner?"

"Nine-thirty."

"Is his son, Saied, with him?"

"Apparently no. He was seen by one of our people in Istanbul this morning."

That was good news. It meant all options were open. "If I decide to act at close range, do you still think you can get me inside?"

Andre smiled. "Of course. Although he does not yet know it, one of the waiters may soon find himself ill and require a replacement. I would recommend slipping you inside at six-thirty, when the dining room will be at its busiest. This will allow you sufficient time to learn your new duties and for their people to get used to your presence."

"I'll think about it and let you know in plenty of time."

"You realize that if we do take you inside, we may not be able to assist you in exiting?"

Jonathan nodded. "I do."

After Andre left, Jonathan donned a t-shirt, pair of shorts, and sandals he had picked up at the airport. He slipped on his dark glasses, pulled a floppy hat low over his face, and looped the strap of his camera around his neck. When he checked his reflection in the bathroom mirror, he saw just another tourist.

Kill Makram wasn't a plan, he chided himself as he stepped outside. It was a goal. He needed a real plan, a defined series of steps he could take to bring about Makram's death.

Jonathan didn't get far, physically or mentally, before he realized that he had to first decide just how committed he was to killing Makram there, in Cyprus. Sun Tzu had said that the victor would be the general who chose the time and place for a battle. Should he wait until conditions were better, more under his control? No, he decided. There may never be another opportunity. And what about his level of commitment? Was he so committed he could go full-in, and let the chips fall where they may? He had often claimed that he was ready to die but did he really mean it?

If he was, in fact, totally committed, he would have to act from close range, where success would be all but assured. If not, he would have to make his attempt from a distance, where his chances of killing Makram would be significantly reduced, as he had discovered in Lebanon, but his chances of escaping alive, perhaps to try again later, were significantly higher.

Taking photos as he went to throw off any of Makram's people who might be watching from nearby windows, Jonathan ambled down the hill, mentally noting good sniper positions for himself along the way. Fortunately, there was only one road up to the hotel, which would make things much easier if he chose that option.

He reached the bottom of the hill and strolled through the crowded shopping district, oblivious to the many stalls and shop windows, his mind was still debating the pros and cons of each alternative. A sticking point, he realized, was Nanami. A part of him still held out hope that she was not lost, that she would – as she had promised – would never let anyone keep them apart.

In his wanderings, he passed a small library and gravitated inside, the newspaper and magazine racks his destination. On the cover of a two-day old issue of *Japan Today* was a photo of Nanami and her fiancé, standing in formal Japanese attire beside the Emperor and

Empress. He studied Nanami's eyes in each of the eight accompanying photos, searching for any sign of sadness or remorse. He saw the exact opposite, extreme happiness.

"Are you okay, sir?" asked a young librarian, snapping him out of his reverie.

"Yes, sorry. Jet lagged," he offered, returning the magazine to the rack.

"I must look like a real dork," said Jonathan, approaching his bathroom mirror. Surprisingly, he looked a lot better than he had expected. The black riding pants, knee-high leather boots, and white silk shirt made him look like an old Hollywood swashbuckler. Nanami would love it, he thought before catching himself. He had to get her out of his mind. She was gone, out of his life. Makram and his obligation to avenge his father's death was all that remained.

After donning the rest of the traditional Cyprian dancer's costume worn by the Apollo's waitstaff, however, Jonathan lowered his assessment. The open black vest, with its half-dollar sized bronze buttons, red cummerbund, and ornately embroidered gold headwrap made him look stupid. "I can't believe I might actually die dressed like this," he muttered, slipping on a pair of fake horn-rimmed glasses.

He was met by Kader, the restaurant's headwaiter, at the employees' entrance where they faced their first obstacle, Makram's rear-door guard. As Kader yelled at the man to hurry up, that he had angry diners who had waited an hour for service, the man took his time, carefully frisking Jonathan and closely scrutinizing his paper.

"Okay," he finally said, handing back Jonathan's papers.

Jonathan and Kader started inside.

"Wait!" commanded the guard.

The two men stopped.

"I am told all waiters must dance upon request. Let me see you dance."

Oh, god, thought Jonathan, a jolt of fear coursing through him. He should have listened to Dr. Shimizu. As the professor had warned, he had been a fool not to learn how to dance, for many reasons.

Without a choice, Jonathan began moving, dancing as closely as he could to the Cyprian music filtering out from the bar, mimicking the way Dr. Shimizu had rhythmically bobbed and weaved in White Plaza the day they had officially met.

"Enough!" said the guard disgustedly. "You dance like a man who has never known joy." With a flick of his wrist, he waved the men inside.

Kader led Jonathan into the supply room, where he gave him the two pistols he had smuggled in earlier. With Jonathan's weapons hidden securely under his costume, he was assigned to service the back tables, where the lighting was dim and where lovers or insignificant guests were seated.

Nine-thirty came and went and Makram had yet to show, leading Jonathan to believe that either Makram wasn't coming or that something had gone wrong. A few minutes later, he knew which. "Follow me," whispered the headwaiter.

Kader hurried Jonathan through the kitchen and into the stockroom. "Grab something!" he said, picking up a box of tomatoes. Jonathan grabbed a large box of squash. The two men carried their boxes outside and into the back of a produce truck.

"Come, sit," said Andre, who was perched atop a sack of rice. As soon as Jonathan was seated, he slapped the back of the cab and the truck lurched forward.

"An attempt was made on Makram's life," said Andre. "He escaped uninjured but will most assuredly not come here. His people are searching everywhere for those responsible so we must get you out of the country while that is still possible."

"Any idea where he will go?" Jonathan asked.

"Not yet, not for sure. We suspect we know where he will resurface, unless the attempt will cause him to change his plans."

"Where?"

"London. We received a report that he plans to meet there with al-Nazari within the next two weeks. We will attempt to confirm the report and determine if it is still scheduled."

"Where are we heading?"

"To the coast. His men patrol the streets and watch the airport. Guy wants you aboard a boat quickly, before they turn their attention to the sea."

A while later, the truck slowed. Andre glanced through the cab's rear window. "Ah, the boat."

Its captain stood at the bottom of the gangplank. He flicked his fingers and angled his eyes. Andre slapped the back of the cab twice. The truck continued on.

"What's up?" asked Jonathan.

"I do not know."

Chapter Thirty

During the two days since the attempt on Makram's life, Andre's assistant, François, had monitored an unusually high amount of Palestinian radio traffic pouring out of the Middle East. Nothing, however, had come out of their bug inside Makram's headquarters until that morning.

"You must hear this!" François yelled, frantically waving his boss over.

Andre slipped a pair of headphones over his ears and scooted his chair up close to the table. He nodded to François, who stabbed the Play button on a large reel-to-reel tape recorder.

"The first voice is that of Yusuf Makram," said François. "The second is Amin, the nineteen-year-old son of Jibril Antar, who was a former high ranking...."

Andre shushed him. "I know of Antar."

"Have I treated you so poorly that you wish me dead?" came Makram's voice through the headset.

"I do not know what you are talking about?" came a younger man's voice. "I have dedicated my life to you."

"I am talking about taking money from a fat Frenchman? I am talking about selling out your own people in return for a blonde Italian whore with big breasts, a thousand English pounds, and a red Alfa Romeo convertible."

There was a pause. "He assured me they meant you no harm," pleaded Amin. "He said he was a friend of yours. Was that not true?"

"Oh, I know the Frenchman but he is no one's friend."

"You have been as much a father to me as he who gave me life," said the young man, terror now thick in his voice. "I would have said nothing had I thought there was even the slightest chance of danger to you. They told me it was for a rich American boy. I mean…what could a boy do? If he wanted to throw his money away….”

“This 'boy' is the same age as yourself, possibly older.” There was silence, then Makram spoke again. “Would you be interested in helping us gain revenge against these *infidels*?”

“Yes! Just tell me what to do!”

“I want you to inform them through your usual channels of our trip to London, our meeting with Sabri al-Nazari,” said Makram calmly, almost fatherly. “Give them every detail. Hold nothing back.”

“You are too good to me,” Amin gushed.

“We will, of course, be holding your wife and son until we return from England,” said Makram, “just as a precaution.”

“I understand.”

There was a long pause as a chair slid back, footsteps headed away and a door opened. “The next voice is probably Makram’s son, Saied,” shouted François to be heard through Andre’s headphones. After the sound of the door closing, the voices on the tape began again.

“Make sure he dies as soon as Lusk has been removed.”

“How do you know it was Jonathan?” asked Saied.

“A boy? An American? Did I not warn you?”

“Then why tell him where to find us? We will have enough to worry about without having to look over our shoulders for him too.”

“It is a blessing. Not only will he come to us but, more importantly, he will also supply us with the perfect patsy, as the Americans call them. Before we do anything, however, we must first have a discussion with the Frenchman.”

Andre grabbed the phone beside him and dialed a well-known number. “This is Andre, I must speak immediately with Monsieur Guy.” As he waited, his fingers nervously drummed the table top.

A knock on the door. The two men’s eyes fixed on the source of the sound as they quietly rose to their feet. Another knock, harder and more insistent this time.

Both slid out their pistols. Andre took aim, then nodded to François. His assistant crept over to the door. "Who is it?" he said. Bullets ripped through the door, wall, and François's body. A boot sent the door flying inward. Andre managed to get off a shot before he too was dropped.

Within minutes, the well-practiced team of masked Arabs had loaded up every file and audio tape into a box, gathered up the tape recorder, stuffed Andre's and François' bodies into large garbage bags, and were gone.

Chapter Thirty-One

It had taken two full days for Jonathan to reach London, requiring five flights and two channel crossings – the first between Cyprus and Antalya, Turkey, and the second between France and England. But he had arrived safely and was staying in great comfort at the Dorchester Hotel.

Standing on the damp veranda of his 5th-floor suite, Jonathan looked out at the hazy green patch across the street. According to his map, it was Hyde Park. He hoped the sky would clear by sunrise, when his morning run would take him through the park and give him a better grasp of the layout of the city.

After the heat of Cyprus, Turkey, and southern Europe, Jonathan welcomed the cold, allowing it to sink deep into his bare arms, his chest, and his back, drawing his skin taut, uniting his mind, body, and spirit onto a single point of focus, Makram's death.

There was a knock at his door. "Who's there?" Jonathan called, heading inside and snatching up his pistol.

"Guy."

He hesitated. It couldn't be Guy. He had said he never left France. "Where did we meet last time?" Jonathan yelled through the door.

"The Eiffel Tower, as we did before it."

Cautiously, Jonathan opened the door a crack and saw it was the Frenchman, his foot impatiently tapping the floor. After quickly scanning the hallway and spotting one of Guy's men near the elevator and another at the opposite end, Jonathan stepped back so the large man could enter.

"What happened to your ear?" Jonathan asked as the Frenchman angled his rotund frame through the doorway. The top third of Guy's left ear was covered in a straight line of gauze and white tape. Clearly a portion was missing.

"A traffic accident," he grunted dismissively. "The meeting is set," said Guy, shaking a cigarette from a fresh pack and lighting it.

"Do you know when and where?" asked Jonathan.

"This coming Sunday," he said, smoke engulfing his words. "We will not know the exact location until perhaps hours prior."

"That would make it difficult to plant a device."

"Is that what you desire?"

"Maybe. I have to assume that this will be my last chance so I don't want to miss him again. But would there be enough time to plant a device?"

Guy shrugged. "Such is often our profession. I would recommend we place it for you. The time of the detonation would, of course, remain in your hands alone."

"Why don't you prepare a device and I'll let you know if it's a go or no-go once we know the time and place."

"What additional will you need from me?"

"Since we don't know what will be required, let's go with my usual Hi-Standard, plus another Uzi and a good sniper rifle."

"All will be delivered in sufficient time for you to test, as you must do always. Never fail to test every weapon before its use… every weapon." The fat man dropped his chin and stared Jonathan full in the eye until he nodded his agreement.

"I wasn't expecting you so I don't have much cash with me."

The big man smiled – at least the corners of his mouth curled upward while his dark hooded eyes remained cold and hard. "As this will complete a most Herculean task, my young friend, there will be no charge." Guy took Jonathan's hand and clasped it in both of his immense ones, then kissed him on both cheeks. "Do not fail. These are evil men," he said before waddling out the door.

What was that? Jonathan asked himself after closing and locking the door. The man who never left Paris had come to London. The man who Umberto had jokingly claimed would sell his own daughter into white slavery for enough money had offered to give away very expensive weapons free of charge. To top it off, the man who had said he cared nothing for a person's sanity, morality, nationality, religion, or goals as long as he could pay his price, had made a moral judgment on a person he had previously embraced, calling him evil.

There was also his sudden obsession with testing his products. That was new as well. And what about his ear? What type of automobile accident would only lob off the top portion? Something had to be very wrong and it had to have something to do with Makram.

By six the next morning, Jonathan was already up and halfway through a brisk five-mile run that took him past the lake and down Hyde Park's winding paths. He had hoped to wake up with a clearer idea about how to interpret Guy's mixed messages but that hadn't happened. Even as his run ended at the entrance to the Dorchester's exercise room, he was still no closer to an answer than when he began.

Jonathan stretched, did some weight work, and went through his kicks, punches, and *tai sabaki*, or body shifting. But although he could increase his flexibility and fitness levels as well as make his techniques faster and stronger on his own, he needed to train with others to sharpen his reflexes to where they needed to be for what might await him.

He had heard that Great Britain had a strong contingency of traditional Japanese *dojos*. In fact, there was reportedly one almost within walking distance of the hotel. But as he had learned when searching for a school in California to buy a *gi*, he needed to watch a bit before committing to train anywhere.

Almost to a man or woman, the students at the local Shotokan *dojo* looked technically strong. According to photos on the walls, the large collection of medals and trophies scattered about, and the number of championship pennants hanging from the ceiling, many students held British, European, and even world Shotokan titles.

The instructor was not only Japanese but one of the sadistic ones. So Jonathan knew the workout would be demanding, just what he was looking for.

Wearing his black belt into a new *dojo* had gotten Jonathan the exact reaction he had expected. As he was being interrogated about his martial arts background by the *uchi deshi*, the most senior student, the man rolled his eyes, grabbed hold of Jonathan's belt, and pulled him disrespectfully to the farthest end of the line.

The instructor never deigned to speak with or even approach him during most of the class. A cruel smirk tightened his face whenever he looked his way. *That's not good,* Jonathan told himself. It meant he would never be paired with anyone sufficiently skilled to challenge and help him sharpen his timing. If he couldn't face someone good, he was wasting his time.

To guarantee he would be allowed to work with the more skilled *karateka* up the line, he would have to humiliate those at his end, creating an embarrassment to the *dojo*. This would force them to pair him off with their stronger students for honor's sake.

As the class progressed, Jonathan saw that all of the students trained with *tamashii*, a strong fighting spirit, and understandably so. Any mistakes were painfully corrected as they often were in Japan, with a bamboo sword called a *shinai*. Make a mistake and the offending limb received a hard whack. After correction, a student had no trouble remembering which leg to take back or hand to use, it was the painful one with the large, red welt.

Even though he had studied the same style of Japanese *karate* under Ojima *Sensei*, the instructor didn't seem to think his techniques of sufficient quality to even warrant his consideration, never giving him one of the many corrective *shinai* strikes he delivered as he worked his way up and down the line. To their credit, none of the students cried out or complained when hit. They took their lumps, bowed, and thanked him, as students did in Japan.

All were very proficient at the standardized paired drills – *ippon ku-mite* and its variants. But except for those at the upper end of the long line, he knew most would likely be less proficient at *jiyu kumite*, the spontaneous application of their techniques. And it was *jiyu kumite*, free sparring, that Jonathan needed most.

So when everyone was paired off for sparring near the end of class, he went through his middle-aged partner as if he weren't there. This earned him a quick move up the line, where a cocky dockworker eagerly took him on. But he proved little better. And it earned him a much closer look from the Japanese *sensei*.

"You!" he said, pointing at Jonathan. "Here!" He stabbed his finger at a spot near him. "Crouch!" he yelled and Jonathan started down, thinking he meant for him to kneel. But it was the name of one of the higher-ranking students.

Crouch was a tall, V-shaped man. His clenched fists looked like shot-puts and the muscles in his neck stood out in taut cords. Every *dojo* had a defender, whose job it was to prove his school's superiority to visiting black belts and, on occasion, to correct any existing students who stepped out of line. Crouch surely held that position there. *Dojo* defenders were always men who either didn't mind thumping people or enjoyed it. As big and intimidating as Crouch was, he was just what Jonathan needed. But he had to be careful, he warned himself. If he sustained an injury in the process, it could affect his mission.

The massive hulk of a man confidently closed on his smaller oppo-nent. Jonathan knew he had a ferocious front kick. He had seen him use it throughout the night. In addition to being powerful, it was a flat kick that traveled horizontally, making it more difficult to block or evade.

Crouch, as Jonathan expected, immediately pressed forward, try-ing to work his way into kicking range. Staying continually just outside the man's critical distance, the distance in which he could reach him in one action, Jonathan sought to force Crouch to either overextend his technique or to take a step before launching one, giving him time to evade it. But the man knew the *dojo* far better than he did and soon had Jonathan pinned against the wall. The instant his target appeared trapped, Crouch's kick lashed out. Jonathan's lead arm hooked over his leg as he shifted hard to the right, pivoting the big man ninety degrees and throwing his upper body back, far out of alignment. Without missing a beat, Jonathan hooked his right leg behind Crouch's supporting one and swept it out from under him. The floor shook when he landed.

The *sensei* moved quickly in to separate the two as Crouch jumped to his feet, clearly wanting to retaliate against the interloper.

"*Yame!*" ordered the *sensei*.

For a few tense moments, Crouch seemed to have gone deaf and tried to press another attack to gain revenge.

"*Yame!*" the instructor screamed. "Line up!"

Fortunately, everyone did as they were told. After performing the traditional three bows, the class was dismissed.

"You return tomorrow," said the instructor.

Jonathan bowed but said nothing. All eyes were on him as he gathered up his things, slipped on his flip-flops, snatched up his bag, and left, not waiting around to change. There would be too many questions.

After completing his run and gym workout the next morning, Jonathan stuffed a fistful of arrows and his Sasaki bow into his backpack, then drove to an indoor archery range that the concierge had found for him.

The bow was easy to take and use anywhere, which would have been far from the case with a traditional Japanese bow. When disassembled, it was little bigger than the collapsible walking sticks used by the blind and fit easily into his luggage.

The more he used the bow, the more Jonathan came to admire both it and Dr. Sasaki, its designer. In addition to its smaller size and greater maneuverability, it was extremely light, more powerful than even the largest traditional yew bow he had shot in Japan, and more consistently accurate. He could now put every shot in the bull's-eye.

A funny thought occurred to Jonathan as he drew back his last arrow. At the Dai Kan, he had been the arrow catcher; now he was the arrow shooter.

His next few days varied little, always beginning with a run and a workout at the gym, followed by *kyudo*. What did change, and changed daily, was the *karate dojo* he visited. Each night he trained at a different one, not wanting anyone to get too familiar, to ask too many questions.

Plus, the more people he could spar, the more rounded and quick he became. Going up against someone he had never seen before, and who had never seen him, created the perfect challenge, where everything occurred spontaneously as in a real fight. Each combatant was forced to rely solely on pure reflex, both trained and natural. Takuan, the Zen *roshi* who had advised *samurai* during the Golden Age, said the time between an opening presenting itself and a successful counter-attack landing had to be the same interval of time as that between a flint striking steel and a spark being emitted, meaning almost simultaneous.

To react with such extreme speed required a great deal of practice and the right mental state, *kyoshin no kokoro*, which Jonathan had been trained at the Dai Kan to enter whenever he fought. Derived from a quote by the famous Chinese Taoist philosopher, Chuang Tzu, the Dai Kan's samurai founders considered *kyoshin no kokoro*, a mirrorlike-mind, to be the ultimate mental state. "The perfect warrior uses his mind like a mirror," they paraphrased what Chuang Tzu had written. "It grasps at nothing. It refuses nothing. It perceives but it does not keep." It was a mind constantly alert, constantly in the present, and constantly ready to react.

Two days before Makram's supposed meeting, two of Guy's men paid Jonathan a visit. And they didn't come empty-handed. Both carried heavy equipment bags.

"I didn't order all this," objected Jonathan.

"Our employer said we are to deliver it without cost. That is all we know."

Jonathan eyed the bags suspiciously. If Guy was now working with Makram, whether for money or because of coercion (as his ear might indicate), he could be allowing his men to deliver a bomb into his hotel room.

"Would you mind opening the bags before you go… and set everything on the coffee table?" Jonathan asked. The men shrugged, then unzipped each bag and removed its contents.

"Our employer asked we pass on his *démenti*… disclaimer. He purchases from the very best suppliers. But nothing has been tested by us personally and Monsieur Guy recommends you check each item yourself, personally, before attempting to use it in combat." The men tipped their hats and left.

Agreeing to open and empty the bags was a promising sign. It meant the bags weren't rigged. The men also didn't seem in any hurry to leave. So if there was a device, it wasn't set to go off before he had a chance to look things over – unless, of course, Guy thought these men expendable or been paid enough to cover their deaths. But why another warning to test everything? If he was complicit in an attempt to take his life, he would have surely known that it would put him on an even sharper edge.

Jonathan inspected each item carefully. Nothing appeared out of order. The scoped sniper rifle and Uzi he had requested, along with boxes of ammo were all there, as was a radio transmitter for the explosive device Guy's men would attempt to plant. But what surprised him was a suppressed Hi-Standard .22 LR pistol. He hadn't asked for the silencer, didn't even know they were available except to the CIA. What Guy had supplied was a very rare and special model and at no cost. In addition, the Frenchman had included the latest bulletproof vest, along with a pair of high-powered mini binoculars that could fit in his pocket. It all made Jonathan even more nervous.

He field-stripped the Uzi, checking to make sure the barrel wasn't blocked, that the pieces moved freely as designed, that the trigger and firing pin were solid, and that the spring had sufficient tension. He couldn't find anything wrong with it. And he found the same with the pistol and the scoped XM21 sniper rifle.

Although the silenced pistol had dominated his initial attention, the XM21 was equally impressive. Guy had sent him the U.S. Army's latest version, with selective fire and a larger 20-round box clip. He had no idea how Guy had managed to get his hands on one but was glad to have it.

The next morning, after what had become his regular conditioning, body-sharpening routine, Jonathan gathered everything up, loaded it into the trunk of the Ford Cortina that Guy had supplied, and drove to an abandoned excavation pit several miles outside of town.

Although each weapon fired properly, none was sufficiently accurate for reasons that weren't visible. He guessed that either the barrels were not completely straight or the sights were off. With the Uzi, that wasn't a problem. Accuracy wasn't its forte; speed of fire was. But a lack of accuracy was an issue with the Hi-Standard and a critical one with the sniper rifle, whose scope wasn't even close. With but a single box of ammo for all but the Uzi, he had to give up attempting to zero in either the rifle or the pistol, settling instead for the ability to "wind-adjust" his shots slightly to the left for the rifle and to the right for the pistol.

As he drove back to his hotel, Jonathan's mind struggled to piece it all together: Guy's trip to London, the injury to his ear, free weapons, his odd comment about Makram being evil, his repeated warnings to test everything out, and, when he finally did, finding them flawed. If Guy was working with Makram, for whatever reason, why had he given him so many warnings and why hadn't they already killed him, or at least tried?

Normally, with so many questions, so many unknowns, the smart thing to do would have been to simply walk away from the operation. But he might never get another shot at Makram. If his weapons would fire and he could compensate for their inaccuracies, the mission was still on.

Chapter Thirty-Two

It was just after one-forty-five on Saturday afternoon, the day before Makram was scheduled to arrive, when one of Guy's men finally contacted Jonathan. The meeting would be held at eleven o'clock Sunday morning inside the rectory at the Lutheran Church in Kensington.

During Sunday service, Jonathan thought. Lots of cars and parishioners to offer cover but also a high possibility for collateral damage.

Needing to check out the location but not wanting to be spotted by one of Makram's advance teams, which would surely be keeping an eye on the church, Jonathan opted to jog there, as if he were just a local out for an afternoon exercise session.

Being on foot also enabled him to evaluate each of the many side streets located between the hotel and the church. This information could possibly become useful later, should he need an alternative escape route.

When he reached the church's entrance, Jonathan stopped, took a long swig from his water bottle, then knelt down and retied his shoes, buying sufficient time to draw a mental map of the grounds. The ancient sharp-spired Gothic church was encircled by a tall privet hedge. Other than a couple of thin spots, the only gap was the twenty-foot opening that allowed cars and pedestrians to enter the parking lot.

The attached stone rectory, where the meeting was supposed to be held, was situated around the far side of the chapel. Just beyond it was a well-manicured rose garden, which offered the clearest shot at anyone attempting to enter or leave but little cover. Diagonally across the graveled parking lot sat the church cemetery, with a mixture of gravesites ranging from massive family mausoleums to modest and more recent headstones. That would be his preferred setup location. If all went well, the church might donate a plot there for Makram – or him – when all was done.

As soon as he was back in his room, Jonathan drew a map of the church grounds and surrounding streets, noting every detail that could conceivably be of help or hindrance. Then he studied the sheet, plotting the best points of entrance and exit followed by potential setup points, rated from one through five based on their line of sight and risk of detection.

He laid his pencil down and glanced at the dial on his battered Mickey Mouse watch, his father's last gift. It had been repaired after the explosion that took his father's life and again after his accident in the Land Rover while trying to flee Murakami's estate. Scratches and abrasions marred the crystal, nicks and dints the frame, every major event in his life seemed to have left a mark on it.

"Twelve o'twelve," he said, smiling at the look his father would have given him and his mother's corrective *tsk*.

"Prepare well, execute flawlessly," *Kancho* had taught him. But he wasn't well prepared. And he felt far from confident in his ability to execute his plan. Damaged weapons. Possibly questionable intel. But everything he had any control over was as ready as he could make it. His weapons were cleaned and oiled. Magazines fully loaded. A fresh battery in the transmitter.

As for the bomb itself, it was reportedly concealed behind a length of walnut baseboard in the rectory office. Even a thorough room search, Guy's man claimed, should not be sufficient to find it.

Jonathan climbed into bed. But his mind continued to race. Should he buy a backup battery in case the new one failed? Would he need an anti-fogging agent to keep the scope from clouding if it rains? If he didn't get a clear shot as Makram went inside, would he wait until he came back out? Or would he detonate the bomb, taking everyone else, guilty or innocent, with him? That would be the sure approach. But could he live with it?

He considered every detail, every step in his plan, searching for any possible problems that could arise, no matter how remote. If he thought of something he had forgotten, he got up and wrote it down on a growing list that included known unknowns and their possible solutions as well as best guesses for dealing with any unknown unknowns that might conceivably arise.

The faint dial on his watch read a little after two o'clock. *Enough*, he told himself. He had to sleep. With that, Jonathan filled his consciousness with the feel and image of the inside of his throat, of the passage of air in and out past moist membrane. Within minutes, he drifted off, allowing his body the rest it would soon need.

At five-thirty, the sun struggled to penetrate the shroud that enveloped London. Jonathan put on his sweats and set out into it, his running shoes slapping the glistening sidewalks, where no others ventured at that hour. He ran until the exertion and the bone-chilling cold had cleared the drowsiness from his mind.

Tucking his legs beneath him, Jonathan sat for almost an hour in meditation on his damp, frigid veranda, calming his nerves and putting his mind in order. After that was complete, there was but one last thing to do, his death gift.

Using his neatest handwriting, Jonathan jotted his death poem down on a sheet of embossed hotel stationery. He folded it into a small square, then placed it in the middle of a white handkerchief, where he also added the traditional fingernail clippings and lock of hair. Drawing up the cloth's four corners, he tied them in a neat square knot, as he had used so many times to tie his *karate* belt. Jonathan had no idea who would find or ultimately receive his death-gift if he did not return, but tradition dictated one be left.

No, he thought, snatching the bundle back up. If he failed, the past should be sucked up behind him, as if he never existed. He tossed the poem, the hair, the nail clippings into the trash can and burned them.

To improve his chances of surviving long enough to make sure Makram was dead, Jonathan used an old warrior's trick he had learned at the Kami Kan; he ripped a pillowcase into narrow strips and wrapped lengths around his arms and legs, just above the major joints. These would slow bleeding should he be hit.

Jonathan crammed everything – weapons and personal belongings – into the trunk of his small Ford Cortina, climbed behind the wheel, fired up its tiny engine, and headed off towards his destiny.

Chapter Thirty-Three

The Ford's small tires hissed down the wet streets towards Kensington. Being Sunday, traffic was sparse and he arrived earlier than he wanted. His goal had been to pull into the parking lot along with church parishioners, so he would be less noticeable. But when he arrived, there were only two cars in the lot, a Jensen parked beside the rectory and a Morris Minor in the spot reserved for the organist.

Thinking that he must have gotten the time wrong, that the Sunday morning service started at 11:30 instead of 11:00, Jonathan pulled in just far enough to double-check the church sign. But he had read it right.

He drove slowly around the block, even stopping to buy a bouquet of wilted carnations from a street-corner vendor, all the while struggling to formulate an alternative plan should one soon become necessary.

Fortunately, when he got back, a handful of cars were queuing up at the church entrance with many more converging on the narrow entrance. The Cortina tucked in at the end of the line and accompanied the others into the lot, where he parked at the back, next to the cemetery. Before leaving the Dorchester, Jonathan had attached S-hooks to the inside of his raincoat and hung the Uzi and XM21 from them. He crawled out of the car, snatched up the yellow carnations, and lumbered between the mausoleums and tombstones as if he knew where he was going.

At random, he picked one of the more recent gravesites near the back and knelt down beside it. According to its headstone, it was the final resting place of Edith Esther Eddington, who had died three years earlier at the age of fifty-three. It was far enough into the cemetery that he would be blocked from easy view by solid, intervening memorials and statuary while offering him a clear enough line of sight.

Cars and black taxis now poured into the parking lot. Parishioners clustered in uneven knots, tipping their hats and nodding to each other along the approaches and on the church steps and landing. Using the binoculars Guy had given him, Jonathan studied each face. None were Arabs.

The deep-throated rumble of *Amazing Grace* arose from inside the church and those having a final word or smoke finished what they were doing and drifted inside. Jonathan's binoculars fixed on the only person who remained, a dark-complected man in a hat and dark suit. This had to be one of Makram's point men. But as Jonathan watched, the man took a final drag of his cigarette, extinguished it on his heel, then hurried inside the chapel.

The congregation joined in as the organist played a list of hymns that Jonathan hadn't heard since he was a boy in Boston. For some reason, the songs and the sounds of the congregation's voices rising and falling like ocean waves caused his eyes to mist. A slideshow of images flashed through his mind – his confirmation, his father's memorial service (they hadn't found enough of him after the bomb to bury), and his mother's funeral. Although the songs for his father and mother had been different, more somber than those he was hearing now, there had also been a similarity. Maybe it was the organ, an instrument he hadn't heard since leaving the United States fourteen years earlier. But whatever it was, it dug deep into the recesses of his mind to release memories long forgotten.

Soon the organ tapered off and the voices stilled. The sermon had begun. Jonathan glanced at his wristwatch. It was fifteen minutes after eleven. He would remain there another five minutes or so, then accept the fact that Guy had gotten this one wrong.

His thoughts were on his next move when he heard a vehicle door creak open and then slam shut on the street to his left. Over the top of the hedge, he could just make out the flat roof of a white van or delivery truck. Creeping over to a thin spot in the foliage, he saw a city sanitation van parked in the middle of the street. Three brown-uniformed workmen removed a manhole cover and placed a canvas partition around the hole.

While the driver and one assistant stayed with the van, the third workman strode toward the church. Jonathan hurried back and watched as the man searched the grounds.

A sound snapped the workman's head around. A black Bentley had pulled up and stopped just inside the entrance. After several seconds, the big car crept up and parked in front of the rectory. Four Arabs bolted from the car and rushed toward the front door, their heads turning nervously like deer at a watering hole. Keeping low, Jonathan focused his rifle's scope on the head of the squat figure in the center of the group. But it was not Makram. It was Sabri al-Nazari.

The roving workman sped up his search, moving rapidly through the rose garden, then across the graveled parking lot to the front of the cemetery. As his eyes swept the gravesites, they settled on Jonathan, who was tenderly laying the carnations onto the woman's grave. Solemnly, Jonathan removed his cap and dark glasses and closed his eyes. A few seconds later, he said "amen" and reopened them. When he looked back around, the man was gone.

A black Cadillac limousine raced into the lot, made a U-turn, and parked almost nose-to-nose with the Bentley. Six men dressed in traditional Arab *thobe* and headdresses climbed out.

All Jonathan could see were their backs. "*Kuso,*" he hissed under his breath. But as he watched, one of the Arabs stumbled on a step. The man quickly caught himself, then turned his head to say something laughingly to the man next to him. It was Makram.

The butt of Jonathan's sniper rifle started up. A searing pain tore through him. Something smashed into the side of his chest with bone-crushing force, knocking him to the ground. As consciousness slipped away, Jonathan turned his head to see the hazy image of a man peering through a hole in the hedge. He squinted, bringing his eyes into brief focus onto Saied's joyless face, smoke curling from the barrel of the silenced rifle in his hands. Then the world grew dark.

Chapter Thirty-Four

A sharp pain drilled deep inside Jonathan's chest, feeling as if a knife had been plunged up to its hilt. The pain jerked him back to consciousness and let him know that he wasn't dead, at least not yet. His hand went to the spot where the bullet had hit, expecting it to be moist and slick. But there was nothing, only a hole through his raincoat and shirt. Thank karma, thank luck, but mostly thank a fat Frenchman that he had a vest and that it had held.

After checking the hedge to make sure Saied was no longer there, Jonathan gritted his teeth and rolled onto his side. He assumed everyone was gone. But when he looked, the limo still sat in front of the rectory. Opposing groups of Arabs still stood on the walkway, glaring suspiciously at each other. The only thing that had changed was Makram and his aides; they were obviously now safely inside.

Jonathan plunged his hand into his pocket and pulled out the transmitter. A quick flick of his thumb armed the device, illuminating its green light. He aimed the remote at the rectory. The charge was supposedly shaped to take out only the murderers now meeting inside the minister's office. But what if something went wrong? What if the charge was larger than intended or not shaped as promised or the walls less dense than expected? Did he have the right to make innocent people suffer as he and his parents had been made to suffer? No was his immediate answer.

Just push the damn button! Kill him like he killed Dad, he told himself, hoping the words, the images of his father being blown to bits, his mother's disfigurement would give movement to his thumb. But it didn't. It only made him more aware of what could happen to those inside the chapel.

Jonathan powered off the transmitter, and watched with mixed emotions as its green light went dim. His hand was creeping painfully out to gasp the butt of the sniper rifle when an explosion shook the ground and sent a flock of pigeons to flight. Flames and chunks of stone flew from the side of the rectory, peppering the rose garden, followed by a mass of dust and smoke roiling out its side windows. Jonathan stared in disbelief at the transmitter beside him, its arming light still dark.

He snatched up the rifle, intending to shoot Makram if he survived. But the scope was missing, likely knocked off when the rifle fell. Fortunately the Uzi was okay. But it was a close-range weapon. To use it, he would have to work his way closer to the rectory, where both Makram's and al-Nazari's men were on sharp alert.

As Jonathan moved from tombstone to tombstone, an odd series of actions was taking place on the rectory landing, things that Jonathan couldn't explain. Al-Nazari's men had immediately rushed into the building without concern for their own safety, while Makram's had held back. In fact, a couple of them casually opened the limo's doors as the rest waited almost nonchalantly on the steps.

The answer to the riddle came quickly. Makram and the men who had accompanied him inside scurried out the rectory door. Before Jonathan could move to within the Uzi's range, the Palestinians had scrambled into the waiting limo and were racing across the parking lot, scattering the stunned parishioners who had been drawn outside by the explosion. To his left, he heard the van's engine start, doors slam, and tires squeal.

Holding his chest against the pain, Jonathan ran to the Cortina. By the time he had climbed inside and fired up its small engine, the Cadillac was already out of sight and the van soon would be.

As Jonathan hit the street, an orange Datsun pulled away from the curb thirty yards or so behind him and began honking its horn. Three cars fleeing the church lot squeezed in behind the Cortina, preventing Jonathan from getting a look at the Datsun's driver. An orange car of some type had appeared in his rearview mirror on several occasions over the last few days, its color making it stand out. But it had never stayed behind him for long so he hadn't given it much thought.

Up ahead, the van was approaching an intersection. Jonathan floored it, not wanting to miss the light. Luck smiled on him a second time and the signal turned red just as the Cortina passed, cutting off everyone behind him.

As trained to do at the Kami Kan, Jonathan stayed just out of visual range, following the phony workmen from a distance. The van wound its way along a series of London streets before turning abruptly into a shopping center parking lot where Saied and the two other Arabs were picked up by a woman in a dinted Rolls Royce.

Jonathan had no idea where the Rolls was heading until they came to a sign advising travelers that Gatwick Airport was just another kilometer away. They were leaving the country. "If there's a god," Jonathan prayed, "let Makram be there too."

The three Arabs were dropped off in front of the main terminal and quickly disappeared inside. Jonathan parked at the curb and jumped out, taking with him his backpack and pistol, which he hid under his coat. Ignoring the traffic officer's warnings that his car would be towed, he ran toward the entrance. As the double-doors hissed open, he caught a flash of orange out of the corner of his eye. The Datsun was pulling up to the curb.

"You can't leave that there, mate!" the officer yelled at its driver.

Jonathan rushed into the terminal. He spotted Saied and his two partners heading up the escalator and joined the mass of people going up too.

Laughing and joking like three teenagers at the mall, the Arabs strolled along the landing above before disappearing inside an airport restaurant. Creeping up to the glass door, Jonathan peeked inside. The men were being seated at a large empty table in the corner. Saied turned to check the door, forcing Jonathan to spin back out of sight. If Saied was expecting someone, it could only be one person and he didn't want to be standing there when he and his bodyguards arrived.

Hurrying up the long hallway, Jonathan passed a packed bar and continued on another twenty feet to where a mob of unhappy men ringed the entrance to the men's restroom. Three British policemen and an Arab stood shoulder to shoulder, blocking access. The Arab's presence meant that Makram was probably inside. But if so, how did he rate police protection?

Having so many people around Makram when he came out would make it easier to get close enough for the Hi-Standard .22, the CIA's preferred close range ballistic weapon, to do its job. But it also increased the chances that his efforts would be thwarted or that he would hit a by-stander. After considering the potential risks and benefits, it seemed best to wait. They were in a large airport. He would surely get a better shot… at least he hoped he would. He had waited while in the desert and lost his chance. But with the risk of killing innocents so high, he had no choice.

Jonathan retraced his steps back to the bar, where he could disappear among the milling throng but still keep an eye on the bathroom doors in the mirror behind the bar. He didn't have to wait long. Yusuf Makram soon emerged, straightened the front of his long black *thobe*, then pushed out his chin and strode arrogantly up the hallway as his protectors shoved people aside.

Although Makram and his people thought him dead, they weren't blind. He needed a disguise. Searching for inspiration, Jonathan had returned to the main concourse, where thousands of travelers hurried toward and away from the arrival and departure gates.

There were the usual shaved-head followers of Hare Krishna. He had seen them begging occasionally at Stanford, often in San Francisco, and always at airports. They sang "Hare, Hare" and danced barefoot in their flowing saffron robes while accosting everyone they passed for donations. His head was already nearly shaved. He could "borrow" a robe and tambourine from one of them, smear himself with patchouli oil, and dance his way up to where Makram awaited his flight. But it was highly unlikely that Makram's handlers would allow one of the unruly, perhaps drug-induced Hare Krishna anywhere near their leader.

A Buddhist monk worked his way politely along Jonathan's row of plastic seats, bobbing his head and offering his begging bowl to each person he encountered. His flowing black robes and the big-brimmed straw hat that covered his head and face would offer great concealment, Jonathan thought, but was far too obvious. The monk reached him and Jonathan placed a British pound note in his bowl. The Japanese bowed in thanks and moved on.

As he was considering his options, a young Protestant minister settled into a seat across the way. Jonathan ambled over and sat down beside him. After chatting for a few minutes, the man asked Jonathan if he would watch his suitcase while he went to the restroom. "Of course," Jonathan said, feeling guilty already.

The young minister quickly disappeared into the moving mass of travelers. As Jonathan reached out to grab the handle to the man's satchel, an odd sight caught his attention. A Japanese, who looked vaguely familiar, strolled past, dressed in a *karate gi*. He obviously didn't know how to wear it. The black belt was too high, around his stomach, and tied in a regular knot, as a person would tie his shoes. Martial-art belts were always tied in a square knot.

With his eyes focused on the strange *karateka*, Jonathan failed to notice the approach of another man, this one dressed in black, until the last instant. His head snapped around, thinking it was the minister, that he had waited too long. But it was the Buddhist monk, bowing his head and holding out his begging bowl.

"I already made a donation," Jonathan told him.

Ojima looked him directly in the eye. "How…" was all Jonathan got out before his *sensei* pressed a finger to his lips. The Japanese jerked his eyes hard to the left. Two of Makram's men were heading their way. "I remain close," whispered Ojima, before moving to the next person and extending his bowl.

There was no time to respond or argue or even give it any thought. He had to make his move. It was now or never. Jonathan snatched up the minister's suitcase and headed quickly away. Near the end of the concourse, he ducked down a narrow side hallway that led to a janitor's closet. After picking the suitcase's cheap lock, he stuffed everything he needed – white shirt, black pants, black coat, black hat, Bible, and a pair of wire-rimmed glasses – into his backpack. He put a British hundred pound note into the suitcase, closed it, then found a Redcap to return it to the minister with his apology.

As he strolled down the main concourse towards the international gates, Jonathan noticed people ahead of him queuing up. "What's going on?" he asked a janitor.

"Security check, just added last week," the woman answered.

Under the protection of British police, Makram and his people would be allowed to pass through the checkpoint and move on with their weapons in their possession. He would not. If they found the Hi-Standard .22 on him, he would be arrested and Makram would fly away, never to be seen again.

Chapter Thirty-Five

With his pistol now disassembled and lying in pieces at the bottom of three different garbage cans, Jonathan's only weapons were his hands and his Sasaki bow, which had easily passed through security. In fact, the agent had pushed it out of the way in order to reach the bottom of his bag.

Jonathan left the checkpoint and merged with the mob of travelers moving toward the international terminal. At the first bathroom he spotted, he ducked inside. Within minutes, he ambled back out, visually a different man. Dressed in the minister's attire, someone (hopefully even Saied) would have to look hard to recognize him.

The high level of security surrounding Makram, especially his unanticipated British assistance, was making an assassination attempt with nothing but a bow look less and less promising. Jonathan didn't mind dying if he took out Makram in the process. But he couldn't risk throwing his life away on an extreme long-shot, leaving no one alive to collect on Makram's debt. If it was possible to get onto the flight, he would have to make his attempt inside the plane.

Jonathan ducked inside a phone booth and made a call to Guy's London contact. Although the Frenchman had helped him find Makram, made sure he discovered the weapons were flawed, and gave him the vest that saved his life, he had also done things that had not only caused him to fail but almost cost him his life – the explosive device self-detonating and Saied knowing where to find him. So their relationship was anything but clear.

He told the man that he had been shot, which was true, but also that he was in the hospital, which was not. If Guy was part of the plot to kill him, he didn't want to make it easier for the Frenchman to finish the job. In addition to reassuring Jonathan that they were still there to assist him, the man also cleared up his major questions.

After uncovering one of Guy's informants inside the HFFP, one of Makram's lieutenants set up a meeting with the Frenchman, reportedly to hire his organization for a coming operation. But when the lieutenant arrived, he accused Guy of betrayal for assisting Jonathan. The lieutenant forced him down onto his knees and held a knife to his throat. But instead of killing him, he sliced off the top of one ear. Then he offered Guy a choice, either help them or die. Guy, of course, chose the former. But what they requested caught the Frenchman completely by surprise. They didn't want him to lead them to Jonathan, as he expected. Instead, they wanted Guy to protect Jonathan and facilitate his efforts to assassinate Makram, under their direction, of course.

"That doesn't make sense," Jonathan responded.

"Monsieur Guy was also baffled until it became clear. Your presence would assist in the removal of al-Nazari, the PLO's Vice Chairman. With him out of the way, especially if it appeared that you had attempted to kill both of these important men but Allah had chosen to spare only Makram, he would surely acquire the votes needed to replace Arafat as head of the PLO, which should now be all but assured. If so, he will become the leader and Arafat the hunted."

"But they took a big risk. I would have killed him had Saied not shot me."

"They would never have allowed you to get a shot off. Two of Makram's men were assigned to ensure that could not occur."

That was news to Jonathan. He hadn't just missed spotting Saied, he had missed the other hitman too. He would have to be more careful.

"They also altered your weapons to render them inaccurate."

"They didn't know Guy had warned me?"

"*Non.* Their plan was to kill both you and their competitor at the church and lay the blame at your feet. But they do not know the French," said his contact bitterly. "We have long refused to truly bow to any man or fail to make our enemies pay."

"If I were able to proceed," asked Jonathan, "do you know where he is now?"

"At Gatwick Airport, where I am advised you are as well."

Jonathan chuckled at his own foolishness, thinking they would know where Makram was but not him.

"Although their ultimate destination is being kept very top secret, we have learned he is flying to Lebanon, where he will demand a vote."

"Do you know what time and which airline?"

"Jamahiriya, which tends to leave at their leisure."

"Would it be possible to get onboard the flight?"

"*Qui*. In that regard, I am sure you will find this of interest; we have been monitoring chatter between the airline and Colonel Khadafy, its owner. The airline was recently given final notice to either enforce the new international law banning weapons onboard its flights or lose their landing rights at all international airports. The Colonel has ordered his people to deny Makram and his party access with weapons in their possession."

Jonathan scoffed. "But what is the likelihood they will actually follow through?"

"I cannot reveal how airport officials learned to watch this flight more closely," said Guy's contact with a slight chuckle, "but the HFFP will not board with weapons."

After requesting Guy arrange for tickets for him on the flight, just in case he decided to accompany Makram, Jonathan hung up.

The possibility that Makram and his gang of murderers would be unarmed closed the deal in Jonathan's mind and he began running over the obstacles he would face and how he would deal with each of them.

The major obstacle would be the lopsided numbers. If they attacked en masse, he could be overwhelmed before removing Makram. But the layout of a 707 jetliner would be an asset. To attack all at once, they would have to either make their approach down the plane's single aisle or climb over rows of high-back seats. Both would allow him to pick them off one after the other until he ran out of arrows.

He would need something, perhaps some improvised weapon, that could help reduce what *Kancho* Kubo referred to as the *Rate of Closure*. This was the frequency at which an enemy attacked or the number of enemies who attacked at any given time.

Like all Tamashii Kami, Jonathan had been trained in the use of makeshift weapons constructed from commonly available materials, things that he could use to defend himself should he be caught un-armed or his weapon lost or damaged.

As Jonathan considered what materials he might be able to utilize, a chilling thought occurred to him. After he had killed Makram, Saied and his father's henchmen would be hell-bent on avenging his death. If he couldn't stop them, what kind of a death would await him?

Although he fully intended to take as many of Makram's killers with him as he possibly could, he could only kill so many before he ran out of arrows. So he had to assume his death would be slow and painful. These men were experts at torture after all and as cold and heartless as vipers. He could be raped. He could be burned alive, castrated, blinded, beheaded, anything a warped mind could imagine. Knowing this, he had to find a way to make sure they didn't get that chance, at least not while he was still alive. After he was dead, they could do with him as they wished.

Old samurai would fall on their swords or use them to commit *seppuku*, disembowelment, to prevent themselves from being captured and dying dishonorably. But he had no sword or even a knife.

An image flashed in his mind. He saw the student he had found in the bathroom, the one who had used a shard of broken mirror to cut his wrists, and had his solution – *jigaki*. Whereas *seppuku* was a slow, painful process, *jigaki* was quick. Traditionally used by the wives and daughters of *samurai*, this form of ritual suicide involved driving a *tanto* or dagger – or sharp piece of glass – through the carotid arteries in the neck. It was fast and it was sure.

Jonathan strode into the Duty-Free Store. He knew what he want-ed to do and quickly gathered the things he could repurpose to create it.

He snatched up a portable radio, a bottle of 151-proof rum, a cigarette lighter, and a box of bandages.

As he carried his armful of items to the checkout counter, he noticed a copy of *Japan Today* in the magazine rack. The headline read "One More Day!" The cover photo was of Nanami and her fiancé, taken at their rehearsal banquet at the Imperial Palace, the image pouring more salt into the raw, hemorrhaging wound inside his head.

"That's yesterday's issue," said the clerk. "We just got in today's."

"That's okay," Jonathan said, returning the copy in his hand to the rack. He definitely didn't want to see wedding photos. "What do I owe you?"

After paying the clerk, Jonathan knelt down to stuff his purchases into his backpack. Nanami's beautiful face smiled at him from the magazine cover, creating conflicting emotions. The image of her in the arms of another man strengthened his resolve to enter battle as a dead man and efficiently complete his task. But he also realized that there still remained a deep and pervasive love for her, a love that defied reason, defied all his efforts to eradicate. She hadn't just been a woman, she had also been his best and oldest friend. Beneath all the anger, beneath all the jealousy, beneath all the hurt, he realized he could die easier if he left knowing she was happy.

Jonathan snatched up a copy and handed it to the clerk. "Why don't you give me both issues?" The clerk reached behind the counter and shimmied a magazine out of the bound bundle at his feet. As he slipped the two magazines into a thin paper bag, one of Makram's point men strode into view outside the shop's windows. Jonathan turned abruptly away as if he had forgotten something.

"Anything else?"

Jonathan sneaked a quick peek back around and saw the *fedai* had moved on. "No, that's it," he said, paying the man.

Keeping to the edge of the wide walkway, Jonathan tailed Makram's man for fifty yards or so before the concourse forked in two directions. The man took the right and Jonathan followed. Soon, they passed the ticket counters, boarding/arrival gates and waiting areas for EgyptAir, then Turkish Airways. With only one airline left, Jonathan found a seat in a dark corner near the Turkish boarding gate and watched as the *fedai* entered the Jamahiriya waiting area, across and another twenty yards down the corridor.

The man stalked the rows of chairs, searching for bombs and scrutinizing the handful of passengers waiting to board Makram's flight. When he fixed his hard eyes on two small children, a boy and a girl happily chasing each other, their young father snatched them up and sat them down beside him and his wife.

"Restrain them or I will," ordered the point man, before focusing his attention on those seated along the outside wall. "Sit elsewhere!" he ordered.

Everyone except for an old man and his middle-aged son immediately did as they were told. "My father is not well," the son begged, pressing the palms of his hands together in prayer. "His legs are too weak to…" The fighter grasped the senior's collar and launched him out of his chair. The old man flew forward and fell, banging his head on one of the opposing seats.

"You cannot be Muslim!" his son screamed.

The fighter reached into his coat as he closed threateningly on the man.

"Leave him be," said Yusuf Makram, swaggering up. The *fedai* backed away but kept his eyes locked on the man.

Jonathan had been forced to helplessly watch as Makram strolled past him, surrounded by his son and entourage of sour-faced Arabs and British police. It made him even more convinced that confronting him on the plane was the right thing to do. But where should he sit? In his book, *The Pure Fedai*, Makram had said that he always sat over the wing, where there was less turbulence. So Jonathan would have to sit either in the front or the back.

From the back, he could keep a closer eye on everyone onboard. But he would be far from the cockpit. Plus to get to the back without being seen by Makam, Saied, or their men, he would have to board first, which would require him to pass within easy view of the waiting area to pick up his Will-Call ticket and enter the boarding tunnel. So that was out. He would have to board with the last group and hopefully find a seat near the entrance.

A darkly dressed figure slid up beside Jonathan, snapping his head around. It was the monk. "You shouldn't be here," Jonathan whispered as Ojima sat down beside him.

"Old Japanese proverb. Friends no allow friends fly into danger alone."

Jonathan smiled. "I never heard that saying before."

"Okay, new saying. This friend no allow only friend face danger alone."

"How did you find me?"

"You train *karate* at old teammate *dojo*. He think maybe he remember you from WUKO team trials and call. But he say you never return. So I fly London and visit all *dojo*. I find you but think best to only follow so no hurt plans, *neh*? Today, I cannot reach before man shoot." He bowed. "I fail my *giri*. I most happy but why no dead?"

"*Vest desu yo*," Jonathan said, patting his chest.

Ojima nodded.

Although Jonathan had no idea how much time he had left before boarding began, the clock was ticking loudly in his head. And now he had the added burden of getting rid of Ojima. There was no way he could allow his *sensei* to accompany him on what would almost surely be a suicide mission.

"I have to board soon," said Jonathan, nodding towards the boarding gate for Turkish Airways, where passengers were already filing onto the plane.

"I come too."

"Why don't you board first and find a seat at the back. I'll board last and sit in front, near the cockpit. Then we will play it by ear."

Ojima stood up, pressed his palms together, and bowed as if thanking Jonathan for a donation. He ambled casually to the Turkish Airlines ticket counter, bought a ticket, strolled through the metal detector, and disappeared down the boarding ramp.

Across the concourse, the Jamahiriya agent picked up the microphone to make her announcement. As Jonathan watched, Makram's *fedayeen* rushed over, shoving everyone else aside, creating a human corridor through which their leader strolled directly to the boarding gate. When he reached the metal detector, Makram started around it.

"I am sorry, sir," said the female boarding agent, blocking his access to the plane, "but the new law requires everyone must first pass through the metal detector."

"Do you know who he is?" snapped Saied, the British policemen right beside him.

"Yes, sir," she said, lowering her eyes. "But it is the law. No weapons may be carried on board."

"I am not bound by your laws! I answer only to those of Allah, Praise be unto Him!" declared Makram.

A British man in a three-piece suit stood up. He flipped open his wallet and showed his identification to Makram. The British policemen backed away, clearly impressed.

"In this country, you WILL abide by our laws or you will have your weapons confiscated and find yourself imprisoned."

Makram's face reddened. "Is Colonel Khadafy prepared to guarantee my safety?" he demanded.

"Yes, sir. He is aware of your journey."

"Then I will surrender the fate of the Palestinian people into his hopefully worthy hands."

"Thank you, sir."

Makram, his mouth twisted into a scowl, strode through the detector, triggering a loud beep.

"Are you wearing anything metallic, sir – a belt buckle or keys in your pockets?"

Makram removed the chain from around his neck, kissed the key, then dropped it into the agent's hand. She inspected the key and tubular pendant, fashioned somewhat like a cross, before gesturing for him to try again. This time, Makram passed through in silence.

Jonathan couldn't help but smile as Makram's group of murders was forced to grudgingly surrender their pistols, knives, and compact automatic rifles. Every weapon handed to the agent was one less he would have to face.

"The pig, Khadafy," Makram muttered to his son as they strode into the boarding tunnel. "He is afraid we will hijack his precious plane and make him look like the buffoon he is."

"Is there any chance he might move against us?" asked Saied.

"He is not that foolish. No, Khadafy is forced to see us safely into Beirut. If I do not arrive, he must continue to endure Arafat, who has long been a thorn in his side."

Saied nodded.

"Our only thing to fear is the flight itself," added Makram. "Each time I enter the belly of one, I feel I am tempting Allah's grace, Praise be unto Him."

The two men laughed as Makram told his son about horrible flights he had taken while leading eight skyjackings in his younger days. When they reached the center of the jetliner's long fuselage, Makram slid in and sat against the window. Two *fedayeen* continued on another couple of rows and waited as the rest of their entourage filed down the aisle and took seats at the back of the plane.

Next came the eight regular travelers, who scattered themselves around the plane, all staying well clear of Makram and his people. Jonathan had tucked in among the last of this group and, finding the first few rows completely unoccupied, took the first seat, just inside the door.

Jonathan waited until the hatch had been closed and the two stewardesses were into their required preflight safety demonstrations before ducking into the front restroom. He opened the small portable radio and removed its 9-volt battery, which he taped to the bottle's side. After unwinding a section of copper wire from the radio's coil, he poked a small hole in the metal cap of the bottle of 151-proof rum and inserted one end of the wire deep into the dark amber liquid. He connected the free end to one of the battery's two posts. To enable the circuit to be closed and the wire to glow red hot, Jonathan twisted one end of a short second piece of wire around the first, slipped a section of his ballpoint pen over it to protect his finger, then bent the wire so he could press it down with his thumb to make contact with the second post.

When it was done, Jonathan inspected his makeshift bomb. Would it explode? Maybe. But it would likely burn. After all, it was just a fancier version of a Molotov Cocktail, only ignited by a battery-heated wire instead of a gasoline soaked rag. Plus, he had a cigarette lighter and handkerchief as backup. But none of that really mattered. All it had to do was create enough doubt to buy him sufficient time to take out Makram or complete *jigaki*.

"Please be seated for pullback," came the stewardess's voice over the intercom.

With the sound of the jetliner's engines rising, Jonathan put everything back into the Duty-Free bag and returned to his seat. He had barely buckled his seatbelt and settled back when the engines shut down again.

"You finish preparations," said the older stewardess to her younger coworker. "I will let them in."

Jonathan snatched up a newspaper from a nearby seat, opened it wide, and began reading. "Welcome," the woman said. The first man entered to whistles and catcalls from Saied and the rest of the *fedayeen* already on board. Out of the corner of his eye, Jonathan checked the late arrivals as they passed and headed down the aisle. Five more Arab fighters. That was not good. He only had twelve arrows and there were now fourteen potential targets, counting the Makrams.

"Please, hurry, sir," said the stewardess.

A final passenger stopped just inside the door and scanned the cabin. Jonathan could feel his eyes sweep over him before the man moved on, following the *fedayeen* toward the back of the plane.

"Please take your seats quickly, gentlemen, and prepare for departure," announced the younger stewardess in a sweet voice. Her words were drowned out by the fighters at the rear of the plane, who congregated in a loud knot, laughing and joking until a sharp command from an old warrior put an end to it.

The 707 pulled away from the gate. As the big plane began its bumpy ride up the long taxiway, Jonathan dug out his copy of *Japan Today* and studied the ten photos. As always, he searched for any sign of sorrow or even a tinge of regret in her eyes. But she looked happy, almost giddy.

His destiny was now locked and loaded and he was about to click the safety off.

Chapter Thirty-Six

The big jet roared upward, breaking free of the earth and shivering its way through fog and gray clouds to emerge in the pristine blue sky above. As it reached its cruising altitude and leveled off, Jonathan reached into his backpack and grabbed the latest issue of *Japan Today*. He had time to kill, having decided it best to wait until halfway through the flight when people would be lounging in their seats or sleeping and less vigilant before making his move.

He didn't get further than the headline – "Wedding Day Bombshell!" – before catching movement out of the corner of his eye. He turned his head away and, through the reflection in the Plexiglas side window, watched Saied stop at the restroom door and look his way. The young Arab studied him for several seconds before going inside. A minute later, he stepped back out, again looked his way for a few seconds, then strode back down the aisle toward his seat.

Jonathan's timeline now had to be moved up. Saied may not have recognized him, but he had clearly been curious, which meant he might return with men to check him out. He could not afford to have that happen.

Except for the two stewardesses, who were filling the beverage cart with hot and cold drinks, only the elderly gentleman and his middle-aged son were between Jonathan and his target. As soon as the ladies began their beverage service and were approaching Makram's row, their cart blocking the aisle, he would make his move.

Hopefully, his makeshift incendiary device would keep people in their seats long enough for him to get a clear shot at Makram. But what if it didn't? He couldn't take the plane down, killing everyone, just to get Makram... or could he? There were innocent people onboard.

But what about the hundreds or thousands of innocent future lives he would save if he killed this mass murderer now? The Japanese called it The Two-edged Sword – kill a small number of people to save many hundreds.

"Are you okay, sir?"

Jonathan looked up to see the young stewardess. "Sorry. I was praying, perhaps a bit too fervently."

"Would you like something to drink, sir?" the woman asked shyly, her eyes flicking downward when his met hers.

"No thank you," Jonathan said.

As the battered aluminum cart squeaked down the aisle, Jonathan unpacked his bow, snapped the pieces together, and strung it. Holding back one arrow, he loaded the rest into his small quiver, then slipped the strap over his head.

"He said he's hungry, not thirsty!" yelled Saied. "Does Muslim hospitality not extend to your country?"

"You know nothing of Muslims or hospitality!" interjected the son of the old man who had been thrown from his chair in the terminal. "You are little better than vicious dogs!"

Saied and the *fedayeen* sprang to their feet as did Jonathan, his bow in his hands. With every terrorist standing – unfortunately with the sole exception of Makram – and every eye focused on the father and son, Jonathan took a quick inventory of the number of HFFP fighters onboard, where they were seated, and who had sneaked weapons on with them. He counted twelve men, besides Saied and his father. No guns were visible but he saw two knives.

One of the armed men, a leather-faced old *fedai*, strode up the aisle like a rattlesnake closing in on an injected pray. He was the same old man who had led the search for him outside Makram's camp.

When the old warrior reached the serving cart, he gave it a hard shove with his foot. Drinks and ice went flying. Hot coffee splashed onto Saied's chest and he sprang back with a yelp. The older stewardess had jumped out of the cart's way but the younger one absorbed the full brunt of the man's fury, the heavy metal smashing hard into her hip and side of her chest.

The old fighter hoisted his curved knife as he angled his body and maneuvered the narrow row. Grabbing the son by the hair, he yanked him forward, his knife poised to slit his throat. "Please," offered his father in a feeble voice. "He is a good son."

"Leave him, Saleh!" came Makram's voice from his seat beside the window. "We do not want to offend Brother Khadafy, do we? We can teach this one proper manners once we are on the ground."

Saleh? Jonathan thought, lowering his bow. Was this the Palestinian organizer who Makram claimed had made the bomb that killed his father and convinced him to plant it? Saied had said that the man now worked for them. But even if he wasn't the same Saleh, his desire to kill the father and son had moved him into the second spot on Jonathan's hit list.

With the tension quickly settling down, Jonathan retook his seat before Saied could notice him again. As he waited for things to return to normal, he heard the two flight attendants' high heels tapping hurriedly up the aisle and hid his bow and quiver between his body and the fuselage.

The older woman retrieved a handful of towels and headed back to dry Saied's shirt and seat cushion. The younger one began preparing a hot meal for Dr. Makram, tears sliding down her cheeks as she worked.

"Still waiting!" came Saied's irritated voice.

The older stewardess rushed back to the kitchenette to speed things up. Seeing her partner's tears, she snapped something in Arabic that stiffened the young woman.

To calm his growing nerves, Jonathan opened his backpack and pulled out the second copy of *Japan Today*, the special wedding edition. He glanced down at the cover and scoffed. "Wedding Day Bombshell." More bait and switch, he thought. A much earlier edition had sported the headline "Royal Breakup!" His heart had quickened, thinking there might be a chance for him and Nanami after all. But there was no breakup; they just couldn't be together for a few days because he had the flu.

When Jonathan looked at the cover more closely, however, he noticed the subheading – "Princess Pregnant with Gaijin Baby!" It felt as if every drop of his blood had just drained out onto the dirty carpet. Could it possibly be true? And if it was, what on earth would he do now? He was there. He was committed.

Jonathan's mind scrambled for an answer. Was there a way to avenge his parents and still walk off the plane alive? Not likely. Even if he opted to do nothing, lie low and continue on to Beirut as if just a traveling minister, he had two passports – his own and one in the name of Michael Young. Neither, when checked, would come back as a minister. Lebanese customs agents would likely turn him over to Makram, who would finish what Saied had tried to do earlier in the day. If that happened, he would fail on all accounts and lose his life to boot. So he had no option; he had to go through with it.

Jonathan approached the young stewardess, who was still crying softly as she transferred plastic food containers into and out of the warming oven.

"Sorry to bother you but do you have a pen and some paper?" he asked.

She blew her nose, then dug a ballpoint pen and notepad out of her purse. Jonathan returned to his seat and began writing.

"My dearest child. Even though you are receiving this because we will never meet and I will never kiss you or hold you in my arms, I want you to know that I loved you and your mother with all my heart. Had I known you were coming, I would never have allowed myself to be where I am now, without a way out. Even as I write, I would walk away in an instant if given the chance, for your and your mother's sake.

Love beyond measure. Your father, Jonathan Lusk"

Wrapping the paper around his battered Mickey Mouse watch, he slipped the resulting bundle into an inside pocket in his backpack.

Che, he hissed, under his breath. Just when things had gotten simple and death ready to welcome him and he it, he was given reason to live, making things complicated all over again.

Was there a way that he could use his bow and makeshift bomb to keep Makram and his followers at bay long enough to divert the flight to Israel? If so, that would allow him to walk away, while doing to Makram and his thugs what they had done to thousands of innocent people during their skyjackings. But if what Gutfreund had told him was true, that his government now saw Makram as a political figure, they might just set him free.

Jonathan had a thought. There was no statute of limitation on warrants in murder cases. What if he contacted the American Embassy and notified them that he had placed a wanted felon, one who had murdered Americans, under Citizen's Arrest? They would have to send a security team to escort Makram off the plane and ship him back to Boston, where the warrant had been issued. The Israelis would only need to play a supportive role, eliminating that question mark.

"Are you coming or not!" yelled Saied.

The young stewardess rushed Dr. Makram's hot food onto a tray and hurried it down the aisle. Jonathan casually stood up, the bow and arrow in one hand, the bottle in the other. All Arab eyes were fixed on the young woman, who slipped around the beverage cart, then stopped beside where Saied sat. In unison, their eyes dropped as she leaned far over to place Makram's dinner onto his fold-down tray, her stretch hiking the hem of her dress half way up the back of her thighs.

"No one move!" Jonathan yelled, striding down the aisle toward the beverage cart, his bottle-bomb hoisted into the air. The young flight attendant snapped upright. "Leave the cart," Jonathan told her and her partner, "and move to the back of the plane!" The women eagerly did as instructed.

"He murdered my father," Jonathan announced to Makram's followers, his voice quaking slightly. "He has an outstanding warrant and I'm placing him under Citizen's Arrest. He will be taken back to the United States to stand trial. If he's found innocent, he will be acquitted and released. No one needs to get hurt."

Jonathan pointed at Saied. "I want you to move to the back of the plane too!"

Saied didn't budge, Jonathan set the bottle beside him on the end of the cart and raised his bow. "Move to the back or I'll shoot him where he sits!" he said, drawing a bead on Makram's face.

Saied slid quickly over, positioning himself between Jonathan and his father. As he did, Makram leaned forward and away, hiding himself behind the high seatbacks. Almost nonchalantly, the senior Makram unscrewed the odd tubular piece of artwork that had, along with the key to his old family home, hung for many years from a gold chain around his neck.

Saied pointed at Jonathan's makeshift bomb and laughed. "That thing won't explode. Look at these guys," he said, sweeping his arm back toward where their fighters stood watching. "Each one of them knows more about making real bombs than you could possibly learn in your entire lifetime, even if you didn't die in the next few minutes."

As the young men argued, Makram reassembled two of the interlocking pieces of finely machined steel, creating a straight hollow tube. He slid another section, slightly larger in diameter, over it. Lastly, he slipped the final piece, a solid cylinder of metal with a spike at one end and tiny hooks on either side of the other, inside the smaller tube and attached it to the larger with an elastic band. Then Makram studied his tiny zip gun, clearly happy with what he saw.

"You think I won't kill you?" said Jonathan, his eyes and voice dead flat, dead serious. "After what you did in London and tried to do in Lebanon, I have no qualms whatsoever returning the favor."

Makram slipped off his left shoe and sock and removed four .22 short bullets from between his toes. Keeping one in his hand, he placed the rest in his pocket. As the two continued yelling at each other, Makram slid the bullet into the tiny chamber, then pulled back on the firing pin, testing its tension.

"If you don't think it'll ignite, call me on it," challenged Jonathan. "If not, get to the back with the rest of the murderers, and get there now!"

"You're going to kill everyone?" said Saied, pointing toward a family a couple of rows back, "that little boy and girl, who did nothing...."

Makram calmly stood up. "How cute," he sneered, "a little Tinker Toy bow and arrow. I think Saied made one of those once... when he was four or five." He raised his zip gun and took aim. "Say hello to your father for me."

Jonathan released the bow string the same instant Makram did his firing pin. Unlike when he was shot leaving Murakami's estate, Jonathan felt this bullet enter his body. Although he had twisted violently, the round was fired from so close a range that it couldn't be evaded and hit him in the lower left side of his abdomen, just above his hip.

Saied screamed. Clutching the arrow shaft protruding from his throat, his father fell sideways against the fuselage, then slid down, his eyes bulging and filled with fear.

"I'd tell you to say hello to my father for me," said Jonathan, "but where you're going is far from where he's at."

Saied yanked the arrow from his father's throat. Blood erupted out of the hole, squirting in rapid pulses. Desperate, the younger Makram clamped his hand over the opening but all he managed to do was divert the flow down into his father's lungs, causing Makram to gurgle and flail.

Men rushed up the aisle, the first in line brandishing a knife.

"Stop or die!" Jonathan warned.

No one slowed. Even after he put an arrow between the first man's eyes, dropping him in the middle of the aisle, they kept coming, rushing over the body, obviously thinking they could reach Jonathan before he could ready another arrow. They were wrong. When they saw his next shot ready to go, the group stopped in unison.

Wedging the cart between two opposing rows, Jonathan snatched up the fire-bomb and retraced his steps backwards, never taking his eyes off the terrorists who inched up to where their leader now lay dead. Even with the cart blocking the aisle, he knew he was far from home-free. If they all came at once, climbing over the cart and chairbacks, he would run out of arrows before he ran out of attackers.

Keeping an especially close eye on Saied, who would surely now be in possession of the zip gun, Jonathan rapped his knuckles on the cockpit door. "Get the pilot out here!" he yelled.

The door opened a crack. An eye peered through the opening. Jonathan held the bottle up for the pilot to see. The door opened wider and a narrow-faced Arab stuck his head out.

"I want you to change course," said Jonathan. "We're going to Tel Aviv. Do you understand?"

"Yes, sir."

"I have been there before. I will recognize the airport. If we land anywhere else, I blow the plane. Tell them to have either Ariel Gutfreund or his aide, Sherm Osterman, waiting when we arrive."

"We will do whatever you request. Please do not hurt any of our passengers."

"You're a dead man!" screamed Saied as he jumped on top of the cart and launched himself off it. He landed and broke into a sprint. Jonathan readied an arrow and waited patiently.

"Don't make me kill you too!" Jonathan warned, to no avail.

When Saied was a couple of rows away, he raised his father's zip gun. Jonathan snapped his body sideways and the small bore bullet crackled past him, imbedding itself in the cockpit door. Jonathan's right foot thrust out and buried itself deep into his former best friend's stomach, doubling him over. Without missing a beat, his left foot caught Saied on the point of his chin. The young Makram's body went rigid and he fell straight backwards, hitting his head on an armrest, then the floor.

Jonathan retrieved the zip gun and two remaining bullets and slipped them into his pocket. Then, while the terrorists huddled up, apparently to formulate a plan of attack, Jonathan used an extra bow string to secure Saied's wrists and ankles behind his back, preventing him from going anywhere when he woke back up.

A slender young Arab emerged from the group of terrorists and took point. Jonathan drew a bead on his thin chest. In one motion, the agile young fighter sprang completely over the cart. The arrow struck him in mid-jump, puncturing one of his lungs. He fell like a shot duck, landing in the middle of the aisle, where he let out a high-pitched scream that grew in volume with each red frothy breath.

"Act a man!" came the gravelly voice of the old *fedai*, the one Makram had called Saleh.

Saleh climbed awkwardly onto the beverage cart, likely the burn of arthritis and old injuries fighting his movements, preventing joints from bending as they once did. He defiantly sprang from the top but his legs gave way and he fell onto one knee. When he rose, his face was pinched in a fearful, pained scowl.

"If I am hit," growled Saleh to the men behind him, "do not hesitate. Attack as one. He cannot kill us all."

Just as Jonathan released his arrow, the plane hit a patch of rough air and the arrow went low, catching the old man in the gut. He hunched over, gripping the shaft. "Attack!" he said through gritted teeth.

"Do and you die!" Jonathan yelled, nocking another arrow.

Clutching the shaft with one hand and his knife in the other, Saleh started forward. "What are you wai...," the old man managed to get out before Jonathan's second arrow buried its tip deep just left of his breastbone, over where his heart would be if he had one.

Every dark eye fixed on Jonathan, who stood waiting, another arrow nocked and ready. "He cannot have sufficient arrows left to kill all of us!" someone shouted from the group.

"I have more than enough," Jonathan responded as nonchalantly as he could. He held up the makeshift Molotov cocktail. "And I still have this." He hadn't kept track but estimated he only had around five arrows left, counting the one now in the bow. It wouldn't be enough.

Why hadn't he at least read the magazine's cover in the Duty-Free Shop? He could have walked away and settled the score with Makram later, after he had had time to plan better. Sun Tzu had said the victor would be the one who chose the time and place for a battle to occur. He hadn't chosen either and now appeared about to pay the price.

A barrel-chested Arab pushed through his cohorts. He grabbed the cart, hoisted it above his head, and tossed it, aiming for the elderly father and son. Fortunately, its heavy metal frame was so wide that it landed atop the seatbacks, leaving the two men scared but unharmed beneath it.

After he had dropped as many as he could, his plan was to fall back to his seat near the hatch. The zip gun could possibly allow him to hit another two. But they would have to be close and it lacked stopping force, as evidenced by the round that had hit him.

There was also his makeshift Molotov cocktail. But Jonathan had no intention of detonating it and possibly hurting innocent people. He had already achieved far more than he had hoped. He had killed Makram, with Saleh thrown in as a bonus. When it became clear his time was about up, he would break the bottle and drive a shard of glass through the carotid arteries in his neck, committing *jigaki*. Death would be sure and swift.

Jonathan filled his lungs, then exhaled and centered himself. He took careful aim at the center of the big *fedai's* barrel chest. The man broke into a waddling run, trying to reach him before he could shoot but his body was not built for speed.

The arrow struck exactly where Jonathan had willed it, just left of the center of his chest. But the result was not what he had envisioned. The bull of a man kept coming, forcing him to rush another arrow onto the string. He drew it back as far as it would go, wanting to drive it so deep into the man's heart it couldn't help but stop his charge. As he was about to let it fly, the *fedai's* massive knees buckled. He went down face-first, driving the tip of his first arrow through his body and out the back.

The men following were now bunched up in a knot, slowed by the huge body blocking the narrow walkway. They jockeyed nervously around, wanting to continue their attack but not wanting to disrespectfully walk across their dead comrade. As they hesitated, Jonathan sent an arrow into the chest of the next in line. That man went down too, making it even harder for those behind to get through.

Two men leapt over their downed cohorts. Another three were close behind. Jonathan raised his bow to shoot but the men ducked into nearby rows. On someone's command, they sprinted out and continued their charge. He downed one of them. The others slowed but kept coming, although more cautiously now. Jonathan shot one more, then moved toward the bulkhead and his seat. Once they rounded the corner, they would be on him in seconds. Time had come to prepare for *jigaki*.

Jonathan grabbed the neck of his makeshift fire bomb and hammered the tall bottle of 151-proof rum against the metal front of a nearby armrest. Nothing. As he drew it back to try again, the three men reached row's end.

Jonathan thrust the bottle into the air as if to detonate it, bringing them to a quick halt. The leader's eyes narrowed as he studied the bottle. Then he snickered and muttered something to his four followers. Catching a quick glimpse, Jonathan saw what was so funny; the copper arming wire had come loose, making it impossible to close the circuit.

Plan B – threaten to ignite it by hand. Jonathan unscrewed the bottle's cap. But before he could finish extracting his cigarette lighter, the men charged. He swung the open mouth of the bottle around, dousing the first man's face and eyes with alcohol. On his backswing, he also drenched the two behind him.

He flicked the lighter. The lead man saw its flame and froze. The others, however, didn't and continued on, pushing him forward. The man's face flashed, engulfed in blue fire, filling the air with the odor of burning hair and flesh. As the man spun and slapped at the flames, he ignited those behind him. The three screamed, sprinting back down the aisle, their hair, beards, and clothes aflame.

Knowing he only had at most a minute of respite before the fires would be snuffed and another charge launched, Jonathan struck the bottle hard against the more solid metal bracing beneath the seat. This time it shattered.

Selecting a dagger-shaped shard, he scanned the cabin once more to make sure he had enough time. As he expected, another group, this one made up of three men, were heading up the aisle, their resolve etched into their faces.

Jonathan pressed his finger against the spot on his neck where one of his two carotid arteries pulsed rapidly. He touched the shard's tip against it. He would drive the razor-sharp piece of glass straight through his throat, severing both blood vessels. Death would come within seconds.

Jonathan Lusk took his final breath and steeled himself. "Goodbye, my Nanami Sama. Kiyoshi was right. Love was not enough."

As he started the point inward, releasing the first trickle of blood, he noticed that the men had stopped and were looking toward the back of the plane. Jonathan stopped too. A fight had erupted near the rear hatch. A flailing knot of men grunted and cursed. Bones crunched. Noses splattered. People cried out. Whoever was locked in the ferocious battle with Makram's men appeared to be holding his own, relentlessly kicking, punching, and striking in rapid succession. A ridge-hand struck one of the Arabs full in the throat. The man clutched his neck and stumbled away.

As Jonathan's three intended attackers were briefly distracted, he snatched up his bow and rushed to the center aisle. The instant the three turned back around, he sent his next-to-last arrow deep into the leader's eye socket. Before the other two could recover, he nocked his final arrow and strode confidently down the aisle toward them as if he had more arrows left. Clearly not wanting to be the recipient of his next shot, both fighters turned and ran. Jonathan reached the bodies of the big man and the other who had followed him. He recovered two arrows there and continued on, picking up another three along the way.

Every *fedai* at the back of the plane had converged on the solitary warrior, who seemed to be gamely giving more than he received. If he hadn't watched his *sensei* board the Turkish Airways flight and heard the plane leave, he might have thought it could be Ojima.

Although Jonathan didn't know who was helping him or why, he was an ally, at least for the time being. Enemies of my enemies are sometimes, but not always, my friends, he reminded himself, stifling the urge to run down the aisle and give the man a hand or to loose all of his arrows in his defense. *Be careful,* a voice whispered inside him, *He could be with Arafat and no friend of yours.*

From amidst the mob of *fedayeen* now encircling the man, Jonathan caught the flash of a blade. One of the fighters had slid up behind his prey, knife poised above his head. Before he could bring it down, an arrow buried its tip deep into his temple.

Keeping one of his five arrows nocked and at the ready, Jonathan approached where he had dropped Saleh. With a fair amount of pleasure, he pressed the sole of his shoe against the man's face, frozen for eternity in a hateful scowl, and yanked out both arrows. Another was recovered from the agile young Arab before reaching where Makram lay on the floor. Jonathan studied his face for a second. He looked almost peaceful, like the man he had known in Boston. The arrow that had downed him was added to the growing collection in his quiver. The first man he shot gave up yet another.

Now almost completely rearmed, Jonathan turned his full attention to those still fighting along the rear exit row. The remaining four *fedayeen* were circling the lone defender, striking and being struck as they moved. Although he couldn't get a clear view of the man, it was evident from the glimpses he was able to catch that he was injured, perhaps badly.

Although he didn't know which side the defender was on, there was no doubt about the man's attackers. So Jonathan sent an arrow into the back of a *fedai's* head. The Arab shrieked and stumbled sideways before going down. Another arrow dropped a second. When the remaining two saw Jonathan about to shoot again, they ran to the back of the plane, where they ducked down behind the back seats.

Jonathan cautiously approached the wide rear-exit aisle and found his black cloaked ally on one knee, his head slumped against his heaving chest. His fears grew as he crept nearer. The man looked up. Ojima. He must have realized he had been fooled and doubled back, coming in with the late arrivals.

As hurt as he appeared to be, the Japanese was true to his nature, refusing Jonathan's help as they moved toward the front of the plane. "I okay," he insisted. "You follow, make cover."

Jonathan turned and shuffled slowly backward, staying just behind Ojima. His eyes immediately fixed on the remaining two *fedayeen*, who were peeking over the top of the last row of seats, obviously waiting for an opportunity to attack.

"Can you make it okay? I need to take care of something," Jonathan said.

"*Hai.*"

The two terrorists ducked down when they saw Jonathan striding their way. "Stand up!" he ordered as he got closer. Both did as they were told. "Hands!" he yelled. The nearest man's hands shot into the air. Before the second followed suit, however, Jonathan heard something solid hit the floor near the man's feet.

"Into the restroom!" Jonathan ordered the first man, who hurried inside and closed the door behind him. Keeping his bow trained on the second terrorist's face, he slid over and looked down the row. A knife lay on the floor. "Kick it under the seats!" The man complied. "Now get into the empty restroom!" Jonathan said, backing away. The man went inside, then closed and locked the door. "Stay there and you'll live."

Even though the two adjoining doors could only be locked from the inside, Jonathan would be able to observe both from the front of the plane, which was where he headed next.

"You're in shit deeper than you can possibly imagine," Jonathan heard Saied yell, followed by a quick thump. As he got nearer, he saw Saied lying unconscious on the floor, blood oozing from his nose.

"He no more make kick to legs," said Ojima, his voice feeble, his step uneven.

The Japanese reached the front row, rounded the corner, and suddenly staggered. Jonathan rushed forward, flipped up the armrests, and helped his *sensei* to lie down. The fact that Ojima had offered no resistance told Jonathan that he was bad off. "Have you contacted the Israelis?" he yelled, banging on the cockpit door.

"Yes, sir. They said everything would be made ready as you requested."

"Call them back. Tell them to bring a doctor. We have someone who needs help quick!"

"*Iie!* I okay. No doctor! Hate doctor!" said the Japanese. "Just need rest."

Jonathan's attempts to check out Ojima's injuries were rebuffed by the Japanese, leaving him nothing to do but wait, worry, and keep watch.

He settled down onto the stewardess's jump seat. From its location beside the front hatch, he had a clear view of everything critical – Ojima, Saied, the cockpit door, and the rear bathrooms. Plus, when the time came, the porthole beside him would allow him to make sure they were landing at the right airport.

Jonathan hadn't been sure how he would feel after killing Makram. He probably should have felt ecstatic. He had, after all, removed the man who had murdered his father, maimed his mother, snuffed out the lives of Dwayne Ackerman and the Levys, and killed or injured eighteen of their guests while robbing many more of their hearing, sight, or mobility. But there had been no joy in taking his life, as there hadn't been in taking Murakami's. What he did feel, however, was a tremendous sense of relief. It was as if the planet had filled with helium and floated off his chest to travel somewhere else and lay its crushing burden down on some other poor bastard.

For the first time, Jonathan felt that he could breathe deeply and freely. His muscles slackened. His mind calmed. The voices inside his head had grown suddenly silent. Those who had watched, judged, and evaluated his every thought, his every action throughout his entire life had switched off the light and moved on, leaving him free to get on with his life. And it appeared he had a life to get on with.

Things quieted down inside the cabin and time began to drag, as it always seemed to do whenever awaiting help. In the void, the dull burning ache in Jonathan's side became more prominent, demanding his attention. He hadn't found an exit wound, which meant the bullet was still somewhere inside him.

Considering its location, the lower left side of his midsection, and its small caliber, he didn't think it life-threatening. But it was always hard to predict such things. The bullet didn't have to be very big to do serious, even fatal damage.

As a precaution, Jonathan did as he had after being shot in Japan; he slowed his breathing, calmed his mind, and imagined masses of microscopic cells rushing in to repair the injured site, again using the mental healing technique taught to him by Kenji the Healer. Although he still wasn't sure if it held any benefit, he knew it surely wouldn't hurt.

With fatigue setting in, his mind emptied in meditation, and lulled by the plane's droning engines, his eyelids grew heavy.

"Sir!"

Jonathan's eyes sprang open. He wasn't sure if he had drifted off or not, or if he had, how long he had been sleeping. But something had alerted him.

"Sir!" the voice came again from back a few rows.

Just as Jonathan started up to identify the caller, the plane's engines suddenly slowed. "What's going on?" he yelled.

"We are approaching Israeli airspace," answered the pilot. "They sent a fighter escort."

Jonathan leaned over and looked through the small round hatch-window. An Israeli F-4 Phantom jet flew just beyond their wingtip. Or was it an F-4 painted to look like an Israeli fighter? Be careful, he warned himself, you're too eager to believe it's finally ending.

A fist smashed into the base of Jonathan's skull. His legs buckled and he fought to remain conscious. As he slid down the curved fuselage, he turned to see Saied standing over him. His former best friend reached back and handed his bow to one of his men, who had obviously managed to sneak out of the restroom. The man took it and laid his knife into Saied's upturned palm.

Saied's eyes were hate-filled, his lips curled into a sadistic smile as he drove the knife's sharp edge downward. Jonathan ducked reflexively, his hands rising feebly in an attempt to intercept Saied's arm.

A bloodcurdling scream. Saied spun, his face pinched in pain as Ojima clinched his testicles from behind and was squeezing with all his might. The Arab stabbed at the Japanese but Ojima parried it away with his free hand.

"Help me, Jamal!" Saied yelled to his friend. But instead of offering aid, the young Arab dropped the bow and fled. Gritting his teeth against the pain, Saied rotated back around, intending to quickly finish off Jonathan so he could turn his full attention to the Japanese.

The tiny zip gun popped little louder than a child's cap pistol. The knife fell to the floor as Saied's hands went to the dark hole in the center of his forehead. Jonathan shoved the Arab away, then rushed the final bullet into the small tube in case he needed to fire again. His former best friend stumbled backward and fell in front of the cockpit door, where he lay motionless, his eyes fixed and open.

"Are you okay?" Jonathan asked Ojima.

"I okay. Tomorrow we train. I kick ass for you no tell."

"*Oos, sensei*! I deserve it."

After dragging Saied away from the door, Jonathan slid the knife into his belt, nocked an arrow, and made his way cautiously down the aisle, knowing there could be two terrorists on the loose.

"Sir!" came the same male voice that had awakened him. Jonathan looked over to see the middle-aged son pointing toward the rear restrooms. He nodded and continued on. As he neared the first door, he reached out with his foot and kicked it lightly. "Open up!" he ordered.

"I did not leave! It was not me!" came a frightened voice from inside.

"Okay. Stay there. Do not come out!"

Jonathan slid over. He kicked the second door. "I stay! I stay!" came Jamal's voice from inside.

"You'd better," Jonathan spat. "If you hadn't freed Saied, I wouldn't have had to kill him. So I'd love an excuse to kill you too."

Using his newly acquired knife, Jonathan cut off a set of seatbelts from an aisle seat. He wrapped the loose ends around the two door handles, then tied them together, preventing the doors from opening more than a crack.

"There's still two on their feet but we should be okay until we set down," said Jonathan as he returned to the front row. "You okay?" he asked, seeing Ojima lying face down on the floor. Getting no response, he rolled his *sensei* onto his back.

Pressing two fingers against Ojima's carotid artery, he felt for a pulse. There was none. Jonathan pounded on the cockpit door. "Get us on the ground, quick! And tell them to have an ambulance waiting." He moved over a couple of feet and knocked on the front restroom door, knowing the two stewardesses were inside. "Please, I need help."

Heated voices arose from inside. Bodies banged into walls for a few seconds before the door opened. The older woman glared at the young stewardess as she rushed over to where Jonathan knelt beside Ojima.

"Do you know how to do CPR?" he asked.

She shook her head. "What is it?"

Jonathan's face sagged. "Something new," he sighed. He had heard that firemen, ambulance crews, and flight attendants were being trained in the procedure, but that must have only been in Japan and America. The responsibility for saving his friend's life rested solely in his hands.

One of the other things that Kenji the Healer had taught him was the *kappo* technique for treating someone whose heart had stopped. But *kappo* was an ancient healing system, developed hundreds of years earlier to treat injured *samurai*. Plus it had been at least four years since he learned this particular technique. He wasn't even sure if he remembered the steps correctly.

Given no other option, Jonathan rolled his *sensei* onto his stomach. He felt around until he had located the ridge running through the middle of Ojima's left shoulder blade. Sliding his finger spineward, he stopped over a heart meridian whose name he couldn't remember and gave it a solid rap with the heel of his hand. Rolling the Japanese onto his back, he placed the palms of both hands over Ojima's chest and pressed downward, three strokes.

He rechecked his *sensei's* pulse. Still nothing. Had he forgotten a step, hit the wrong point, or struck it at the wrong angle? He didn't think so. Not knowing what else to do, Jonathan flipped his *sensei* onto his stomach again, and again struck the heart point before performing more compressions, these more frantic than the last. "Why didn't you stay on the other plane?" he yelled in frustration.

"Maybe I go doctor," mumbled Ojima, his voice little more than a whisper.

A wet, slobbery laugh escaped Jonathan's lips and he fought the *gaijin* urge to hug his friend. Before he could say anything, he heard the grinding whine of the wing-flaps extending into landing position, the second best sound he had heard in a long time.

Jonathan glanced out the side window and saw the gentle curve of Israel's tan coastline. In less than a minute, they were circling Tel Aviv. Although he still had a faint pulse, Ojima hadn't moved since speaking and Jonathan couldn't wait to get on the ground. A half-minute later, the plane straightened itself and began its approach, dropping rapidly, skimming palm trees and flat-topped houses.

Tires chirped as they kissed the baked concrete runway. The engines reversed thrust and roared as if in pain. Soon the grating screech of brakes joined the cacophony, all working together to slow the big plane to a crawl, then a stop.

Because of the terrorists onboard, the pilot had been ordered to park on a side apron, well away from the terminal and other planes. After what seemed an eternity, the ground crew finally managed to wrestle the portable ramp the extra distance and into position.

The young stewardess swung the hatch open. Four Israeli IDF soldiers rushed inside, guns at the ready, with Ariel Gutfreund and two medics fast on their heels.

While the soldiers relayed their way down the aisle, the barrels of their Uzis sweeping side to side, the first medic checked Ojima's pupils, then pressed a stethoscope against his chest. "Gurney!" he called out as his partner immediately began CPR.

Two aides rushed a portable gurney through the hatch, loaded up Ojima's limp body, and quickly carried him down the steps and into a waiting ambulance. Before they could close the doors, Jonathan jumped into the back and took a seat across from his friend.

Throughout their race down the busy Tel Aviv streets, the medic never missed a beat, continuing his chest compressions and mouth-to-mouth as if he were a machine. Jonathan watched him closely, memorizing the procedure in case he ever had to perform it himself. Surprisingly CPR was not all that different from the *kappo* he had been taught.

A group of doctors and nurses met them at the hospital's emergency entrance and hurried Ojima inside. Jonathan tried to follow them into the operating room but a nurse spotted the oval of blood on his borrowed white shirt and, against his best efforts to remain with his friend, diverted him into a treatment room. A young doctor, who had obviously treated many gunshot wounds before, dexterously extracted the tiny bullet and presented it to him. After a shot of antibiotics and the application of some gauze and tape, the doctor moved on to his next gunshot victim and Jonathan hurried to the surgical nurses' station, where Gutfreund was waiting for him.

"Doc says you're okay," said Gutfreund.

Jonathan nodded, then fixed his eyes on the operating-room door.

"They said it's too early to tell," said Gutfreund, gesturing toward the small waiting area. The men walked over and sat down. "Would you like to go clean up, get something to eat or drink? I can find you if we hear anything," offered the Israeli.

"Thanks but I want to be here when he wakes up… or…" Jonathan said, his voice trailing off. "What happened to the other people on the plane?" he asked, needing to change the subject. "There were some nice people there too."

"Except for the pair you left in the crappers and the two who had had the living shit beat out of them but were miraculously still alive, we sent the rest on their way."

"Two were still moving?" asked Jonathan, angry with himself for missing them.

"Not very quickly but, yeah. Hard to kill cockroaches. They're getting medical treatment... from their mortal enemy no less. But then, they would have done the same for ours, right?" Gutfreund said sarcastically, then remembered something. "That pretty young flight attendant was worried about you," he said, smiling slyly, "and your friend, of course. She asked me to apologize for how some of her faith behaved and hoped you wouldn't judge Islam by their actions."

"Without her and the gentleman traveling with his father, I may not have walked away. So I'll always think of them as representative of their religion."

The Israeli stood up. "Yeah, we can't let five million bad apples spoil it for the rest, can we?" He handed Jonathan his business card and told him to call if he needed anything or help cutting red tape.

It was almost midnight before the doctor finally walked through the double doors. The look on his face was so somber that Jonathan's heart sank.

"Had you asked me when Mr. Ojima arrived what were his chances, I would have told you 'zero.' But..." the doctor said, shrugging.

Jonathan laughed a little too loudly. "He's a very tough guy," he said, relieved beyond words.

"The first thing he said was 'Where clothes?'" said the doctor, in imitative Japanese. "He tried to get up and leave! That was a first."

"So he'll be okay?"

"I don't know if 'okay' would ever be an apt description for Mr. Ojima. But if he allows himself sufficient time to heal properly, he will eventually return to whatever condition he was in before paying us a visit."

"What about his heart?"

The doctor shrugged. "We ran a complete screen. The only thing we could find was a bruise, probably from a strong blow to the chest. He has some lacerations and damaged ribs but it should all heal in time."

"How long before he's well enough to travel back to the States?"

"Seven days would be a safe estimate, unless his condition deteriorates."

The phone rang at the reception counter and the receptionist answered it.

"I can't thank you enough, doctor. Can I see him?"

"If you go in now, he will attempt to recruit you as an accomplice in his quest to leave early. It would be best if he had no visitors for a couple of days."

"Mr. Lusk?" called the receptionist, holding up the telephone receiver. The doctor shook Jonathan's hand and headed back into surgery.

Figuring it had to be Gutfreund or someone from the American Embassy, Jonathan pressed the receiver to his ear. "This is Jonathan Lusk." There was silence on the other end. "Hello?"

"Jonason?" came a small voice, almost like a child's. It could only belong to one person.

"Is that really you?" he asked, tears flooding his eyes.

"Yes, yes. It is me, Jonason. I love you. I love saying your name. I was forbidden to say it, even to think it. Now, I can shout it. Jonason!"

"I love you too!"

"Soon we have baby, Jonason! You. Me. Auntie. Uncle Eli. All together in one tiny new person. I am so excited! I cannot wait to see you!"

"Where are you?"

"Still in Japan. I cannot yet leave." She hesitated. "A small amount, a very small amount, they are concerned for my health."

"Are you okay?"

"Yes. But because of my small size, they worry for the baby. I must insure he is okay so we are being most careful."

"You scared me. Everyone I've ever known has…"

"That luck is no more. You and I and this baby and more babies will live 100 years!"

"I'm a little confused," he said, needing to pose the question that had been nagging him since reading the news. "You told me you were taking birth control pills."

"After we moved in together, I stopped, wanting this outcome so my parents would be forced to allow us to marry."

"You are so brilliant," said Jonathan, laughing through his tears. "So brilliant and so beautiful. But you said HE has to be okay. Do you know it will be a boy?"

"Not know but insist. I order it to be a boy! And his name shall be Eli."

Jonathan laughed so hard that soon she was laughing too. "Oh, Jonason. You must come to Japan as soon as I am released from the hospital. We will have…"

"Hospital!"

"Special Imperial Hospital… but not serious. So do not think on it. When you come, we will have the most beautiful wedding, never to be surpassed! It will be a true wedding of love, not like with the horrible person they plotted for me to marry. But what are you doing in Israel? *Kancho* Kubo would tell me nothing."

He was tempted to tell her at least that his father and mother could now rest in peace but she would never let it go at that. She would want to know all of the details and this was not the best time or place to have that conversation. "Boring stuff. Research for a class."

"I am sorry, Jonason Sama. Doctor has come to chide me. He had forbidden me to call, claiming concern for my health. But it is fear of my father that truly worries him. Someone very close, I will not divulge his name, brought me a phone on which to call. Let me give you my number so you can call me often."

Jonathan wrote down her telephone number, even though he was all but certain that her father would either order the phone removed or the line disconnected.

After they said their goodbyes, Jonathan shuffled back to his seat. He couldn't remember ever feeling so drained. But he also couldn't remember ever feeling so happy. He struggled to keep his joy from showing on his face, afraid it might cause it to be taken from him.

"No!" Jonathan scolded himself. Nanami was right. No more negative thinking. He had been allowed to avenge his father. He and Ojima would both walk away. Soon he would rejoin the only woman he would ever love. And he would have a son... not a daughter but a son, he thought, chuckling. If Nanami wanted them to live for a hundred years, they would live for a hundred years. If she wanted a boy, it would be a boy. And his name would be Eli.

The phone rang in a luxurious penthouse, its massive picture windows offering a panoramic view of the busy port of Yokohama. Kazio Zuma snatched up the receiver, light sparkling off the diamond and gold rings lining his fingers.

"It has been confirmed," came the voice on the other end. "The baby is that of Jonason Lusk."

"Will her family allow her to deliver it? Or will they make it disappear?"

"According to our informant, she gives them no choice. She is determined to bring it into this world, although all are against it."

"I want that baby dead! Kill it inside her belly if necessary!"

www.ingramcontent.com/pod-product-compliance
Lightning Source LLC
Chambersburg PA
CBHW071145260626
47162CB00003B/926